Susan Ferrier

Marriage - A Novel

Volume I

Susan Ferrier

Marriage - A Novel
Volume I

ISBN/EAN: 9783337031459

Printed in Europe, USA, Canada, Australia, Japan

Cover: Foto ©Andreas Hilbeck / pixelio.de

More available books at **www.hansebooks.com**

MARRIAGE

A Novel

"Life consists not of a series of illustrious actions; the greater part
of our time passes in compliance with necessities—in the performance
of daily duties—in the removal of small inconveniences—in the pro-
curement of petty pleasures; and we are well or ill at ease, as the
main stream of life glides on smoothly, or is ruffled by small and
frequent interruption."—JOHNSON.

Edinburgh Edition

IN TWO VOLUMES

VOLUME I.

LONDON

RICHARD BENTLEY & SON

Publishers in Ordinary to Her Majesty the Queen

1881

PREFATORY NOTE.

Miss Ferrier's Novels have, since their first appearance, suffered curtailment in all subsequent Editions. The present Edition is the first reprint from the original Editions, and contains the whole of the omissions in other reprints. It is, therefore, the only perfect Edition of these Novels.

Works which have received the praise of Sir Walter Scott and Sir James Mackintosh, and been thought worthy of discussion in the *Noctes Ambrosianæ*, require no further introduction to the reader. The almost exceptional position which they occupy as satirizing the foibles rather than the more serious faults of human nature, and the caustic character of that satire, mingled with such bright wit and genial humour, give Miss Ferrier a place to herself in English fiction; and it is felt that a

time has come to recognize this by producing her
works in a form which fits them for the library,
and in a type which enables them to be read with
enjoyment.

G. B.

New Burlington Street,
     December 1881.

MISS FERRIER'S NOVELS.[1]

IN November 1854 there died in Edinburgh one who might, with truth, be called almost the last, if not *the* last, of that literary galaxy that adorned Edinburgh society in the days of Scott, Jeffrey, Wilson, and others. Distinguished by the friendship and confidence of Sir Walter Scott, the name of Susan Edmonstone Ferrier is one that has become famous from her three clever, satirical, and most amusing novels of *Marriage*, *The Inheritance*, and *Destiny*. They exhibit, besides, a keen sense of the ludicrous almost unequalled. She may be said to have done for Scotland what Jane Austen and Maria Edgeworth have respectively done for England and Ireland—left portraits, painted in undying colours, of men and women that will live for ever in the hearts and minds of her readers. In the present redundant age of novel-writers and novel-readers, and when one would suppose the supply must far exceed the demand from the amount of puerile and often at the same time prurient literature in the department of fiction that

---

[1] Reprinted from the *Temple Bar* Magazine for November 1878.

daily flows from the press, it is refreshing to turn to
the vigorous and, above all, healthy moral tone of
this lady's works.   To the present generation they
are as if they had never been, and to the question,
"Did you ever read *Marriage?*" it is not uncommon
in these times to get such an answer as, "No, never.
Who wrote it?"   "Miss Ferrier."   "I never heard of
her or her novels."   It is with the view, therefore,
of enlightening such benighted ones that I pen the
following pages.

Miss Ferrier was the fourth and youngest daughter
of James Ferrier, Writer to the Signet, and was born
at Edinburgh, 7th of September 1782.   Her father
was bred to that profession in the office of a distant
relative, Mr. Archibald Campbell of Succoth (great-
grandfather of the present Archbishop of Canterbury).
To his valuable and extensive business, which included
the management of all the Argyll estates, he ultimately
succeeded.   He was admitted as a member of the
Society of Writers to the Signet in the year 1770.
He was also appointed a Principal Clerk of Session
through the influence (most strenuously exerted) of
his friend and patron, John, fifth Duke of Argyll,[1]
and was a colleague in that office with Scott.   He

---

[1] To this nobleman, in his later years, Mr. Ferrier devoted
much of his time, both at Inveraray and Roseneath.   He died
in 1806.   His Duchess was the lovely Elizabeth Gunning.   Mr.
Ferrier died at 25 George Street, Edinburgh, January 1829,
aged eighty-six.   Sir Walter Scott attended his funeral.   After
his death Miss Ferrier removed to a smaller house, in Nelson
Street.

also numbered among his friends Henry Mackenzie, the "Man of Feeling," Dr. Hugh Blair, and last, though not least, Burns the poet. His father, John Ferrier, had been in the same office till his marriage with Grizzel, only daughter and heiress of Sir Walter Sandilands Hamilton, Bart., of Westport, county Linlithgow.[1] John Ferrier was the last Laird of Kirklands, county Renfrew, subsequently sold to Lord Blantyre. Mr. James Ferrier was the third son of his parents, and was born 1744.[2] Miss Ferrier was in the habit of frequently visiting at Inveraray Castle in company with her father, and while there had ample opportunity afforded her of studying fashionable life in all its varied and capricious moods, and which have been preserved to posterity in her admirable delineations of character. Her reason for becoming an authoress is from her own pen, as follows, and is entitled a preface to *The Inheritance :*—

[1] Sir Walter's father, Walter Sandilands of Hilderston, a cadet of the Torphichen family (his father was commonly styled Tutor of Calder), assumed the name of Hamilton on his marriage with the heiress of Westport.

[2] His brothers were : William, who assumed the name of Hamilton on succeeding his grandfather in the Westport estate. He was in the navy, and at the capture of Quebec, where he assisted the sailors to drag the cannon up the heights of Abraham ; m. Miss Johnstone of Straiton, co. Linlithgow ; died 1814. Walter ; m. Miss Wallace of Cairnhill, co. Ayr, father of the late Colonel Ferrier Hamilton of Cairnhill and Westport. Ilay, major-general in the army ; m. first Miss Macqueen, niece of Lord Braxfield, second, Mrs. Cutlar of Orroland, co. Kirkcudbright. He was Governor of Dumbarton Castle, and died there 1824.

"An introduction had been requested for the first of
these three works, *Marriage;* but while the author was
considering what could be said for an already thrice-told
tale, it had passed through the press with such rapidity
as to outstrip all consideration. Indeed, what can be said
for any of them amounts to so little, it is scarcely worth
saying at all. The first was begun at the urgent desire
of a friend, and with the promise of assistance, which, however, failed long before the end of the first volume ; the
work was then thrown aside, and resumed some years
after.[1] It afforded occupation and amusement for idle
and solitary hours, and was published in the belief that
the author's name never would be guessed at, or the work
heard of beyond a very limited sphere. ' Ce n'est que le
premier pas qu'il coute' in novel-writing, as in carrying
one's head in their hand ; *The Inheritance* and *Destiny*
followed as matters of course. It has been so often and
confidently asserted that almost all the characters are
individual portraits, that the author has little hope of
being believed when she asserts the contrary. That some
of them were sketched from life is not denied ; but the
circumstances in which they are placed, their birth, habits,
language, and a thousand minute particulars, differ so
widely from the originals as ought to refute the charge of
personality. With regard to the introduction of religious
sentiment into works of fiction, there exists a difference
of opinion, which, in the absence of any authoritative
command, leaves each free to act according to their own
feelings and opinions. Viewing this life merely as the
prelude to another state of existence, it does seem strange
that the future should ever be *wholly* excluded from
any representation of it, even in its motley occurrences,
scarcely less motley, perhaps, than the human mind itself.
The author can only wish it had been her province to
have raised plants of nobler growth in the wide field of

---

[1] It underwent several changes before its final publication in
1818.

Christian literature ; but as such has not been her high calling, she hopes her 'small herbs of grace' may, without offence, be allowed to put forth their blossoms amongst the briars, weeds, and wild flowers of life's common path.

"Edinburgh, *April* 1840."

The friend on whose assistance she relied was Miss Clavering, daughter of Lady Augusta Clavering, and niece of the late Duke of Argyll. Between this lady and our author an early friendship existed, which was severed only by death. It commenced in 1797, when Miss Ferrier lost her mother,[1] and when she

---

[1] Mrs. Ferrier (*née* Coutts) was the daughter of a farmer at Gourdon, near Montrose. She was very amiable, and possessed of great personal beauty, as is attested by her portrait by Sir George Chalmers, Bart., in a fancy dress, and painted 1765. At the time of her marriage (1767) she resided at the Abbey of Holyrood Palace with an aunt, the Honourable Mrs. Maitland, widow of a younger son of Lord Lauderdale's, who had been left in poor circumstances, and had charge of the apartments there belonging to the Argyll family. After their marriage Mr. and Mrs. Ferrier occupied a flat in Lady Stair's Close (Old Town of Edinburgh), and which had just been vacated by Sir James Pulteney and his wife Lady Bath. Ten children were the fruit of this union (six sons and four daughters), viz.—

1. John, W.S., of 12 York Place, Edinburgh, d. 1851 ; m. Miss Wilson, sister of Professor Wilson, and father of the late Professor Ferrier of St. Andrews, N.B.

2. Archibald Campbell, W.S., d. 1814 ; m. Miss Garden.

3. Lorn, d. 1801, at Demerara.

4. James, d. in India, 1804.

5. William Hamilton, d. 1804, in India. } Both officers.

6. Walter, W.S., d. 1856 ; m. Miss Gordon.

7. Jane (Mrs. Graham), d. 1846.

8. Janet (Mrs. Connell), d. 1848.

9. Helen (Mrs. Kinloch), d. 1866, at Torquay, aged 90.

10. Susan Edmonstone.

went with her father to Inveraray Castle she was then
fifteen, and her friend only eight. Miss Clavering
became the wife of Mr. Miles Fletcher, advocate, but
was better known in later years as Mrs. Christison.
She inherited all the natural elegance and beauty of
face and form for which her mother, and aunt Lady
Charlotte Campbell, were so distinguished, and died
at Edinburgh, 1869, at an advanced age. While con-
cocting the story of her first novel, Miss Ferrier
writes to her friend in a lively and sprightly vein :—

"Your proposals flatter and delight me, but how in
the name of Postage are we to transport our brains to
and fro ? I suppose we'd be pawning our flannel petticoats to bring about our heroine's marriage, and lying on
straw to give her Christian burial. Part of your plot I
like much, some not quite so well—for example, it wants
a *moral*—your principal characters are good and interesting, and they are tormented and persecuted and punished
from no fault of their own, and for no possible purpose.
Now I don't think, like all penny-book manufacturers,
that 'tis absolutely necessary that the good boys and girls
should be rewarded and the naughty ones punished. Yet
I think, where there is much tribulation, 'tis fitter it
should be the *consequence* rather than the *cause* of miscon-
duct or frailty. You'll say that rule is absurd, inasmuch
as it is not observed in human life : that I allow, but we
know the inflictions of Providence are for wise purposes,
therefore our reason willingly submits to them. But as
the only good purpose of a book is to inculcate morality
and convey some lesson of instruction as well as delight,
I do not see that what is called a *good moral* can be dispensed with in a work of fiction. Another fault is your
making your hero attempt suicide, which is greatly too
shocking, and destroys all the interest his misfortunes

would otherwise excite—that, however, could be easily altered, and in other respects I think your plot has great merit. You'll perhaps be displeased at the freedom of my remarks ; but in the first place freedom is absolutely necessary in the cause in which we are about to embark, and it must be understood to be one if not the chief article of our creed. In the second (though it should have been the first), know that I always say what I think, or say nothing. Now as to my own deeds—I shall make no apologies (since they must be banished from our code of laws) for sending you a hasty and imperfect sketch of what I think might be wrought up to a tolerable form. I do not recollect ever to have seen the sudden transition of a high-bred English beauty,[1] who thinks she can sacrifice all for love, to an uncomfortable solitary Highland dwelling[2] among tall red-haired sisters and grim-faced aunts. Don't you think this would make a good opening of the piece ? Suppose each of us try our hands on it ; the moral to be deduced from that is to warn all young ladies against runaway matches, and the character and fate of the two sisters would be *unexceptionable*. I expect it will be the first book every wise matron will put into the hand of her daughter, and even the reviewers will relax of their severity in favour of the morality of this little work. Enchanting sight ! already do I behold myself arrayed in an old mouldy covering, thumbed and creased and filled with dogs'-ears. I hear the enchanting sound of some sentimental miss, the shrill pipe of some antiquated spinster, or the hoarse grumbling of some incensed dowager as they severally inquire for me at the circulating library, and are assured by the master that 'tis in such demand that though he has thirteen copies

---

[1] Lady Juliana.
[2] Glenfern. Dunderawe Castle, on Loch Fyne, was in Miss Ferrier's mind when she drew this sketch of a "solitary Highland dwelling."

they are insufficient to answer the calls upon it, but that
each of them may depend upon having the very first that
comes in ! ! !   Child, child, you had need be sensible of
the value of my correspondence.   At this moment I'm
squandering mines of wealth upon you when I might be
drawing treasures from the bags of time !   But I shall
not repine if you'll only repay me in kind—speedy and
long is all that I require ; for all things else I shall take
my chance.   Though I have been so impertinent to your
book, I nevertheless hope and expect you'll send it to me.
Combie[1] and his daughter (or Marc, as you call her) are
coming to town about this time, as I'm informed, and you
may easily contrive to catch them (wild as they are) and
send it by them, for there's no judging what a picture
will be like from a mere pen-and-ink outline—if that
won't do, is there not a coach or a carrier ?   One thing
let me entreat of you : if we engage in this undertaking,
let it be kept a profound secret from every human being.
If I was suspected of being accessory to such foul deeds,
my brothers and sisters would murder me, and my father
bury me alive—and I have always observed that if a
secret ever goes beyond those immediately concerned in its
concealment it very soon ceases to be a secret."

Again she writes to her friend and copartner in
her literary work :—

"I am boiling to hear from you, but I've taken a
remorse of conscience about Lady Maclaughlan and her
friends: if I was ever to be detected, or even suspected, I
would have nothing for it but to drown myself.   I mean,
therefore, to let her alone till I hear from you, as I think
we might compound some other kind of character for her
that might do as well and not be so dangerous.   As to
the misses, if ever it was to be published they must be
altered or I must fly my native land."

---

[1] Campbell of Combie.

Miss Clavering writes in answer :—

"ARDENCAPLE CASTLE, *Sunday Morning.*

"First of all I must tell you that I approve in the most signal manner of Lady Maclaughlan. The sort of character was totally unexpected by me, and I was really transported with her. Do I know the person who is the original? The dress was vastly like Mrs. Damer,[1] and the manners like Lady Frederick.[2] Tell me if you did not mean a touch at her. I love poor Sir Sampson vastly, though it is impossible, in the presence of his lady, to have eyes or ears for any one else. Now you must not think of altering her, and it must all go forth in the world ; neither must the misses upon any account be changed. I have a way now of at least offering it to publication by which you never can be discovered. I will tell the person that I wrote it (indeed, quothà, cries Miss Ferrier, and no great favour ; see how she loves to plume herself with borrowed fame !). Well, however, my way is quite sure, and the person would never think of speaking of it again, so never let the idea of detection come across your brain while you are writing to damp your ardour.

"Positively neither Sir Sampson's lady nor the foolish virgins must be displaced."

Again she writes from Inveraray Castle (of date December 1810), eight years before the work was published :—

[1] Daughter of General Seymour Conway, and a distinguished sculptor. She was niece of the fifth Duke of Argyll.

[2] Lady Frederick Campbell is believed to have suggested the character of Lady Maclaughlan to Miss Ferrier, and there is little doubt she was the original. She was the widow of Earl Ferrers, of Tyburn notoriety, and was burnt to death at Coombe Bank, Kent, in 1807.

"And now, my dear Susannah, I must tell you of the success of your first-born. I read it to Lady Charlotte [1] in the carriage when she and I came together from Arden-caple, Bessie [2] having gone with mamma. If you will believe, I never yet in my existence saw Lady C. laugh so much as she did at that from beginning to end; and, seriously, I was two or three times afraid that she would fall into a fit. Her very words were, 'I assure you I think it without the least exception the cleverest thing that ever was written, and in wit far surpassing Fielding.' Then she said as to our other books they would all sink to nothingness before yours, that they were not fit to be mentioned in the same day, and that she felt quite dis-couraged from writing when she thought of yours. The whole conversation of the aunties [3] made her screech with laughing; and, in short, I can neither record nor describe all that she said; far from exaggerating it, I don't say half enough, but I only wish you had seen the effect it produced. I am sure you will be the first author of the age."

In another letter she writes :—

"I had an immense packet from Lady C. the other day, which I confess rather disappointed me, for I expected volumes of new compositions. On opening it, what should it prove but your book returned? so I shall keep it safe till I see you. She was profuse in its praises, and so was mamma, who said she was particularly taken with Lady

---

[1] Lady Charlotte Campbell, her aunt, better known latterly as Lady Charlotte Bury, and celebrated for her beauty and accomplishments.

[2] Miss Mure of Caldwell.

[3] These oddities were the three Misses Edmonstone, of the Duntreath family, and old family friends, after one of whom Miss Ferrier was named.

Juliana's brother,[1] he was so like the duke. Lady C. said she had read it all deliberately and critically, and pro-nounced it *capital*, with a dash under it. Lady C. begs that in your enumeration of Lady Olivia's peccadilloes you will omit waltzes."

That dance had just been introduced in London (1811), and the season of that year Miss Clavering spent with her aunt, Lady Charlotte, in the metro-polis, in a round of gaiety, going to parties at Ken-sington Palace (where the Princess of Wales[2] then lived), Devonshire House, and the witty Duchess of Gordon's, one of the "Empresses of Fashion," as Walpole calls her. *Apropos* of waltzes, she writes to Miss Ferrier :—

"They are all of a sudden become so much the rage here that people meet in the morning at one another's houses to learn them. And they are getting on very much. Lady Charlotte and I get great honour for the accomplishment, and I have improved a few scholars. Clanronald[3] is grown so detestably fine. He waltzes with me because he thinks he thereby shows off his figure, but as to speaking to me or Lady Charlotte he thinks himself much above that. He is in much request at present because of his dancing ; next to him Lord Hartington is, I think, the best dancer ; he is, besides, very fond of it, and is much above being fine ; I never met with a more natural, boyish creature."

To return to the novel. The only portion from

[1] Lord Courtland.
[2] Lady Charlotte was one of the Princess's ladies-in-waiting.
[3] Macdonald of Clanronald, a great beau in the fashionable London world.

Miss Clavering's pen is the history of Mrs. Douglas
in the first volume, and are, as she herself remarked,
"the only few pages that will be skipped." She
further adds :—

"Make haste and print it then, lest one of the Miss
Edmonstones should die, as then I should think you
would scarce venture for fear of being haunted.

. . . . .

"I shall hasten to burn your last letter, as you mention something of looking out for a father for your *bant-
ling,* so I don't think it would be decent to let anybody
get a sight of such a letter !"

At last, in 1818, the novel was published by the
late Mr. Blackwood, and drew forth loud plaudits
from the wondering public, as to who the author of
so original a book could be. "In London it is much
admired, and generally attributed to Walter Scott,"
so writes a friend to Miss Ferrier; and she replies in
her humorous style: "Whoever it is, I have met
with nothing that has interested me since." Sir
Walter must have been flattered at his being supposed
its father, for he says, in the conclusion of the *Tales
of my Landlord :—*

"There remains behind not only a large harvest, but
labourers capable of gathering it in ; more than one writer
has of late displayed talents of this description, and if the
present author, himself a phantom, may be permitted to
distinguish a brother, or perhaps a sister, shadow, he would
mention in particular the author of the very lively work
entitled *Marriage.*"

Mr. Blackwood, whose opinion is of some value,

thought very highly of *Marriage*, and he writes to Miss
Ferrier (1817) :—

" Mr. B. will not allow himself to think for one moment
that there can be any uncertainty as to the work being
completed. Not to mention his own deep disappointment,
Mr. B. would almost consider it a crime if a work possessing so much interest and useful instruction were not given
to the world. The author is the only critic of whom
Mr. B. is afraid, and after what he has said, he anxiously
hopes that this censor of the press will very speedily affix
the *imprimatur*."

In allusion to Sir Walter's eulogium on the novel
above quoted, Mr. Blackwood writes to the author :—

" I have the pleasure of enclosing you this concluding
sentence of the new *Tales of my Landlord*, which are to
be published to-morrow. After this call, surely you will
be no longer silent. If the great magician does not conjure you I shall give up all hopes."

But Miss Ferrier seems to have been proof against
the great magician even. *Marriage* became deservedly
popular, and was translated into French, as appears
from the annexed :—

" We perceive by the French papers that a translation
of Miss Ferrier's clever novel *Marriage* has been very successful in France."—*New Times*, 6 Oct. '25.

For *Marriage* she received the sum of £150. Her
second venture was more successful in a pecuniary
sense. Space, however, prohibits me from dwelling
any longer on *Marriage*, so we come next to *The
Inheritance*. This novel appeared six years after, in

1824, and is a work of very great merit. To her sister
(Mrs. Kinloch, in London) Miss Ferrier writes :—

"John (her brother) has now completed a bargain with
Mr. Blackwood, by which I am to have £1000 for a novel
now in hand, but which is not nearly finished, and possibly never may be. Nevertheless he is desirous of
announcing it in his magazine, and therefore I wish to
prepare you for the *shock*. I can say nothing more than
I have already said on the subject of *silence*, if not of
secrecy. I never will avow myself, and nothing can hurt
and offend me so much as any of my friends doing it for
me ; this is not *façon de parler*, but my real and unalterable feeling ; I could not bear the fuss of authorism !"

Secrecy as to her authorship seems to have been
the great desire of her heart, and much of *The Inheritance* was written in privacy at Morningside House,
old Mr. Ferrier's summer retreat near Edinburgh, and
she says, "This house is so small, it is very ill-calculated
for concealment."

It was not till 1851 that she publicly avowed herself by authorising her name to be prefixed to a
revised and corrected edition of her works.[1] Sir
Walter Scott was delighted with this second novel,
a proof of which was conveyed to Miss Ferrier by
Mr. Blackwood :—

"On Wednesday I dined in company with Sir Walter
Scott, and he spoke of the work in the very highest terms.
I do not always set the highest value on the baronet's

---

[1] Published by the late Mr. Richard Bentley, to whom she
sold her copyrights in 1841. A previous edition was published
by him in 1841.

favourable opinion of a book, because he has so much kindness of feeling towards every one, but in this case he spoke so much *con amore*, and entered so completely, and at such a length, to me, into the spirit of the book and of the characters, that showed me at once the impression it had made on him. Every one I have seen who has seen the book gives the some praise of it. Two or three days ago I had a note from a friend, which I copy : 'I have nearly finished a volume of *The Inheritance*. It is unquestionably the best novel of the class of the present day, in so far as I can yet judge. Lord Rossville, Adam Ramsay, Bell Black and the Major, Miss Pratt and Anthony Whyte, are capital, and a fine contrast to each other. It is, I think, a more elaborate work than *Marriage*, better told, with greater variety, and displaying improved powers. I congratulate you, and have no doubt the book will make a prodigious *sough*.'"[1]

Mr. Blackwood adds : "I do not know a better judge nor a more frank and honest one than the writer of this note."

Again he writes :—

"On Saturday I lent in confidence to a very clever friend, on whose discretion I can rely, the two volumes of *The Inheritance*. This morning I got them back with the following note : 'My dear Sir—I am truly delighted with *The Inheritance*. I do not find as yet any one character quite equal to Dr. Redgill,[2] except, perhaps, the good-natured, old-tumbled (or troubled, I can't make out which) maiden,[3] but as a novel it is a hundred miles

---

[1] Sensation.

[2] In *Marriage* the gourmet physician to Lord Courtland, and "the living portrait of hundreds, though never before hit off so well."

[3] Miss Becky Duguid.

above *Marriage*. It reminds me of Miss Austen's very best things in every page. And if the third volume be like these, no fear of success triumphant.'"

Mr. Blackwood again says :—

"You have only to go on as you are going to sustain the character Sir Walter gave me of *Marriage*, that you had the rare talent of making your conclusion even better than your commencement, for, said this worthy and vera-cious person, 'Mr. Blackwood, if ever I were to write a novel, I would like to write the two first volumes, and leave anybody to write the third that liked.'"

In the following note, Lister, author of *Granby*, also expresses his admiration in graceful terms, and with a copy of his own novel for Miss Ferrier's acceptance :—

T. H. Lister to Miss Ferrier.

"17 HERIOT Row, *Feb.* 3, 1836.

"MY DEAR MADAM—I should feel that, in requesting your acceptance of the book which accompanies this note, I should be presuming too much upon the very short time that I have had the honour of being known to you, if Mrs. Lister had not told me that you had kindly spoken of it in approving terms. I hope, therefore, I may be allowed, without presumption, to present to you a book which you have thus raised in the opinion of its writer, and the composition of which is associated in my mind with the recollection of one of the greatest pleasures I have derived from novel-reading, for which I am indebted to you. I believe the only novel I read, or at any rate can now remember to have read, during the whole time I was writing *Granby*, was your *Inheritance.*—Believe me, my dear Madam, your very faithful, T. H. LISTER."

From Mrs. Lister (afterwards Lady Theresa Cornewall Lewis) Miss Ferrier also received the following complimentary note :—

Mrs. Lister to Miss Ferrier.

"*Thursday Night.*　　　　　17 HERIOT ROW.

"MY DEAR MISS FERRIER—I cannot leave Edinburgh without a grateful acknowledgment of your very kind and flattering gift. Mr. Lister called upon you in hopes of being able to wish you good-bye, and to tell you in person how much we were pleased with the proof you have given us that we are not unworthy of enjoying and appreciating your delightful works—pray accept our very best thanks, and I hope as *an authoress* you will not feel offended if I say that they will now have an added charm in our eyes from the regard which our personal acquaintance with the writer has engendered. I know that, to those who do not mix much in society, the acquaintance with strangers is often irksome : we therefore feel the more obliged to you for having allowed us the pleasure of knowing you, and I hope that if we return in the course of the year that we may find you less suffering in health, but as kindly disposed to receive our visits as you have hitherto been. We feel very grateful for all the kindness we have met with in Edinburgh, and amongst the pleasant reminiscences of the last five months we must always rank high the having received from you as a token of regard so acceptable a gift.—Believe me (or, indeed, I ought to say us), my dear Miss Ferrier, yours most sincerely,　　　　　M. THERESA LISTER."

Lord Murray, the late Scotch Judge, writes to a mutual friend of his and Miss Ferrier's (Miss Walker of Dalry) :—

"I received a copy of *Inheritance* in the name of the author, and as I do not know who the *author* is, and I suspect that you know more than I do, I trust you will find some channel through which you will convey my thanks. I read *Inheritance* with very great pleasure. The characters are very well conceived, and delineated with great success. I may add I have heard it highly commended by much better judges. Jeffrey speaks very favourably. He is particularly pleased with the Nabob (Major) and spouse, the letter from the Lakes, and the *P.S.* to it. Lord Gwydyr, who lives entirely in fashionable circles, said to me much in its praise, in which I concurred.

"From many other symptoms I have no doubt of its complete success."

Miss Hannah Mackenzie, daughter of the "Man of Feeling," writes to her friend Miss Ferrier :—

"Walter Scott dined here the other day, and both he and papa joined heartily in their admiration of uncle Adam, and their wish to know who he is. Sir W. also admires Miss Becky Duguid, and said he thought her quite a new character. I should like much to see you, and talk all over at length, but fear to invite you to my own bower for fear of suspicion ; but I trust you will soon come boldly, and face my whole family. I do not think you need fear them much ; of course, like other people, they have their 'thoughts,' but by no means speak with certainty, and Margaret has this minute assured us that she does *not* think it Miss Ferrier's."

Uncle Adam, with "his seventy thousand pounds," and as "cross as two sticks," in some degree resembled old Mr. Ferrier, who was somewhat brusque and testy in his manner, and alarmed many people who were otherwise unacquainted with the true genuine worth and honesty of his character. Miss Becky is a poor old maid, saddled with commissions from all her friends of a most miscellaneous description.

"She was expected to attend all *accouchements,* christenings, deaths, chestings, and burials, but she was seldom asked to a marriage, and never to any party of pleasure."

She is an admirable pendant to the "Pratt," who is inseparable, however, from her invisible nephew, Mr. Anthony Whyte. Miss Pratt is a sort of female Paul Pry, always turning up at the most unexpected moment at Lord Rossville's, and finally puts the finishing stroke to the pompous old peer by driving up to his castle door in the hearse of Mr. M'Vitie, the Radical distiller, being unable to procure any other mode of conveyance during a heavy snow-storm, and assured every one that she fancied she was the first person who thought herself in luck to have got into a hearse, but considered herself still luckier in having got well out of one.

Caroline, Duchess of Argyll,[1] expresses her appreciation of *The Inheritance* to the author, for whom she entertained a warm friendship :—

"UPPER BROOK STREET, *Monday Evening.*

"What can I say sufficiently to express my thanks either to you, my dear Miss Ferrier, or to the *author of*

---

[1] Daughter of Lord Jersey, and wife of the first Marquis of Anglesea, whom she divorced, when Lord Paget, in 1810 : m. the same year George, sixth Duke of Argyll.

The Inheritance, whoever she may be, for the most perfect
edition of that *most perfect* book that was ever written !
and now that I may be allowed to have my *suspicion*, I
shall read it again with double pleasure.   It was so kind
of you to remember your promise !   When I received
your kind letter and books this morning I was quite
delighted with my beautiful present, and to find I was
not forgotten by one of my best friends."

The Inheritance—a fact not generally known—was
dramatised and produced at Covent Garden, but had
a very short run, and was an utter failure, as might
have been expected.   Mrs. Gore was requested to
adapt it for the stage by the chief comic actors of the
day, and she writes to Miss Ferrier on the subject :—

" Since the management of Covent Garden Theatre fell
into the hands of Laporte, he has favoured me with a
commission to write a comedy for him, and the subject
proposed by him is again the French novel of *L'Héretière*,
which turns out to be a literal translation of *The Inheritance*.   He is quite bent upon having Miss Pratt on the
stage.   I have not chosen to give Monsieur Laporte any
positive answer on the subject without previously applying to yourself to know whether you have any intention
or inclination to apply to the stage those admirable
talents which are so greatly appreciated in London."

Mrs. Gore, meanwhile, had been forestalled in her
attempt, as a play on the subject had been laid before
the reader to Covent Garden, and she writes again to
Miss Ferrier :—

" I have since learned with regret that the play is the
production of a certain Mr. Fitzball, the distinguished
author of the *Flying Dutchman*, and sixty other successful

melodramas, represented with great applause at the Surrey, Coburg, City, and Pavilion Theatres, etc.; in short, a writer of a very low class. The play of *The Inheritance* has been accepted at Covent Garden ; but, from my knowledge of the general engagements of the theatre, I should say that it has not the slightest chance of approaching to representation. For your sake it cannot be better than in the black-box of the manager's room, which secures it at least from performance at the Coburg Theatre."

We must let the curtain, so to speak, drop on *The Inheritance,* and pass on to *Destiny.* This novel also appeared six years after, in 1831, and was dedicated to Sir Walter Scott. And he acknowledges the compliment as follows :—

Sir Walter Scott to Miss Ferrier.

"MY DEAR MISS FERRIER—Ann returned to-day, and part of her Edinburgh news informs me that you meditated honouring your present literary offspring with my name, so I do not let the sun set without saying how much I shall feel myself obliged and honoured by such a compliment. I will not stand bandying compliments on my want of merit, but can swallow so great a compliment as if I really deserved it, and indeed, as whatever I do not owe entirely to your goodness I may safely set down to your friendship, I shall scarce be more flattered one way or the other. I hope you will make good some hopes, which make Ann very proud, of visiting Abbotsford about April next. Nothing can give the proprietor more pleasure, for the birds, which are a prodigious chorus, are making of their nests and singing in blithe chorus. 'Pray come, and do not make this a flattering dream.' I know a little the value of my future godchild, since I had a peep at some of the sheets when I was in town

during the great snowstorm, which, out of compassion
for an author closed up within her gates, may prove an
apology for his breach of confidence. So far I must say
that what I have seen has had the greatest effect in making
me curious for the rest.

"Believe me, dear Miss Ferrier, with the greatest
respect, your most sincere, humble servant,

"WALTER SCOTT.

"Abbotsford, *Tuesday Evening.*"

In the next note he acknowledges a copy of *Destiny*,
sent him by the author :—

Sir Walter Scott to Miss Ferrier.

"DEAR MISS FERRIER—If I had a spark of gratitude
in me I ought to have written you well-nigh a month
ago, to thank you in no common fashion for *Destiny*,
which by the few, and at the same time the probability,
of its incidents, your writings are those of the first person
of genius who has disarmed the little pedantry of the
Court of Cupid and of gods and men, and allowed youths
and maidens to propose other alliances than those an early
choice had pointed out to them.   I have not time to tell
you all the consequences of my revolutionary doctrine.
All these we will talk over when you come here, which
I am rejoiced to hear is likely to be on Saturday next,
when Mr. Cadell[1] will be happy to be your beau in the
Blucher,[2] and we will take care are met with at the toll.
Pray do not make this a flattering dream.   You are of
the initiated, so will not be *de trop* with Cadell.—I am,
always, with the greatest respect and regard, your faithful
and affectionate servant,   WALTER SCOTT.

"Abbotsford, *Wednesday Evening.*"

---

[1] *Destiny* was published by Cadell through Sir Walter's
intervention, and by it the author realised £1700.

[2] Name of the stage-coach.

In 1832, the year after the birth of his godchild *Destiny*, poor Sir Walter began to show signs of that general break-up of mind and body so speedily followed by his death. Of this sad state Miss Ferrier writes to her sister, Mrs. Kinloch (in London):—

"Alas! the night cometh when no man can work, as is the case with that mighty genius which seems now completely quenched. Well might he be styled 'a bright and benignant luminary,' for while all will deplore the loss of that bright intellect which has so long charmed a world, many will still more deeply lament the warm and steady friend, whose kind and genuine influence was ever freely diffused on all whom it could benefit. I trust, however, he may be spared yet awhile; it might be salutary to himself to con over the lessons of a death-bed, and it might be edifying to others to have his record added to the many that have gone before him, that all below is vanity. But till we *feel* that we shall never believe it! I *ought* to feel it more than most people, as I sit in my dark and solitary chamber, shut out, as it seems, from all the 'pride of life'; but, alas! worldly things make their way into the darkest and most solitary recesses, for their dwelling is in the heart, and from thence God only can expel them."

Her first visit to the author of *Waverley* was in the autumn of 1811, when she accompanied her father to Ashestiel. The invitation came from Scott to Mr. Ferrier:—

Walter Scott, Esq., to James Ferrier, Esq.

"MY DEAR SIR—We are delighted to see that your feet are free and disposed to turn themselves our way— a pleasure which we cannot consent to put off till we have a house at Abbotsford, which is but a distant prospect. We are quite disengaged and alone, saving the company of Mr. Terry the comedian, who is assisting me in planning my cottage, having been bred an architect under Wyat. He reads to us after coffee in the evening, which is very pleasant. This letter will reach you to-morrow, so probably *Thursday* may be a convenient day of march, when we shall expect you to dinner about five o'clock, unless the weather should be very stormy, in which case we should be sorry Miss Ferrier should risk getting cold. To-day is clearing up after a week's dismal weather, which may entitle us to expect some pleasant October days, not the worst of our climate. The road is by Middleton and Bankhouse ; we are ten miles from the last stage, and thirty from Edinburgh, hilly road. There is a ford beneath Ashestiel generally very passable, but we will have the boat in readiness in case Miss Ferrier prefers it, or the water should be full. Mrs. Scott joins in kind respects to Miss Ferrier, and I ever am, dear Sir,—yours truly obliged, W. SCOTT.

"Ashestiel, *October* 7."

It was in 1811 that Scott was appointed a clerk of session, and to Mr. Ferrier he was in some measure indebted for that post.

Her last visit to Abbotsford is touchingly alluded to by Lockhart in his *Life of Scott :*—

"To assist them in amusing him in the hours which he spent out of his study, and especially that he might make these hours more frequent, his daughter had invited his friend the authoress of *Marriage* to come out to Abbotsford, and her coming was serviceable. For she knew and loved him well, and she had seen enough of affliction akin to his to be well skilled in dealing with it. She could not be an hour in his company without observ-

ing what filled his children with more sorrow than all
the rest of the case. He would begin a story as gaily as
ever, and go on, in spite of the hesitation in his speech,
to tell it with highly picturesque effect—but before he
reached the point, it would seem as if some internal spring
had given way. He paused and gazed round him with
the blank anxiety of look that a blind man has when he
has dropped his staff. Unthinking friends sometimes
gave him the catch-word abruptly. I noticed the delicacy
of Miss Ferrier on such occasions. Her sight was bad,
and she took care not to use her glasses when he was
speaking, and she affected also to be troubled with deafness,
and would say, 'Well, I am getting as dull as a post, I
have not heard a word since you said so and so,' being
sure to mention a circumstance behind that at which he
had really halted. He then took up the thread with his
habitual smile of courtesy, as if forgetting his case entirely
in the consideration of the lady's infirmity."

A very interesting account of her recollections of
visits to Ashestiel and Abbotsford appeared in the
February (1874) number of this magazine : it is short,
but gives a sad and pathetic picture of the great man
and his little grandson as they sat side by side at
table.

The following letter on *Destiny* is from Mrs.
Fletcher,[1] a distinguished citizen of Edinburgh at
the commencement of this century, and a leader of
the Whig society there. For that reason it is worthy
of insertion here. Her son married Miss Clavering,
as before mentioned : —

---

[1] Her *Memoir*, by her daughter, Lady Richardson, was published not long since.

Mrs. Fletcher to Miss Ferrier.

"TADCASTER, *April* 16, 1831.

"MY DEAR MISS FERRIER—I should not have been so long in thanking you for your kind present, had I not wished to subject *Destiny* to a severer test than that chosen by the French dramatist. *His* old woman probably partook of the vivacity of her nation, but my old aunt, as Mary will tell you, is sick and often very sorrowful, and yet *Destiny* has made her laugh heartily, and cheated her of many wearisome hours of lamentation. My grandson, Archibald Taylor, too, forsook football and cricket for your fascinating book, and told me ' he could sit up all night to see what had become of Ronald.' Mr. Ribley and ' Kitty, my dear,' hit his comic fancy particularly. My two most bookish neighbours, one an Oxford divine, and the other a Cambridge student, declare that ' Glenroy and M'Dow are exquisite originals.' My own favourite, ' Molly Macaulay,' preserves her good-humour to the last, though I thought you rather unmerciful in shutting her up so long in Johnnie's nursery. The fashionable heartlessness of Lady Elizabeth and her daughter is coloured to the life, and the refreshment of returning to nature, truth, affection, and happiness at Inch Orran is admirably managed. Mary tells me you have returned from Fife with fresh materials for future volumes. Go on, dear Miss Ferrier, you are accountable for the talents entrusted to you. Go on to detect selfishness in all its various forms and foldings ; to put pride and vanity to shame ; to prove that vulgarity belongs more to character than condition, and that all who make the world their standard are essentially vulgar and low-minded, however noble their exterior or refined their manners may be, and that true dignity and elevation belong only to those to whom Milton's lines may be applied :

"'Thy care is fixed, and zealously attends
To fill thy odorous lamp with deeds of light,
And hope that reaps not shame.'"

The following letter from Joanna Baillie gives a very just and truthful criticism on *Destiny :*—

Miss Joanna Baillie to Miss Ferrier.

"HAMPSTEAD, *May* 1831.

"MY DEAR MADAM—I received your very kind present of your last work about three weeks ago, and am very grateful for the pleasure I have had in reading it, and for being thus remembered by you. I thank you also for the pleasure and amusement which my sisters and some other friends have drawn from it. The first volume struck me as extremely clever, the description of the different characters, their dialogues, and the writer's own remarks, excellent. There is a spur both with the writer and the reader on the opening of a work which naturally gives the beginning of a story many advantages, but I must confess that your characters never forget their outset, but are well supported to the very end. Your Molly Macaulay[1] is a delightful creature, and the footing she is on with Glenroy very naturally represented, to say nothing of the rising of her character at the end, when the weight of contempt is removed from her, which is very good and true to nature. Your minister, M'Dow,[2] hateful as he is, is very amusing, and a true representative of a few of the Scotch clergy, and with different language and manners of

---

[1] The humble and devoted dependant of the proud chief Glenroy, and governess to his children. She was drawn from life, for Mrs. Kinloch writes to her sister, Miss Ferrier: "Molly Macaulay is charming; her niece, Miss Cumming, is an old acquaintance of mine, and told me the character was drawn to the life. The old lady is still alive, in her ninety-first year, at Inveraray, and Miss C., who is a very clever, pleasing person, seems delighted with the truth and spirit of the whole character of her aunty."

[2] Lord Jeffrey considered M'Dow "an entire and perfect chrysolite, not to be meddled with."

a great many of the English clergy—worldly, mean men, who boldly make their way into every great and wealthy family for the sake of preferment and good cheer. Your Lady Elizabeth, too, with all her selfishness and excess of absurdity, is true to herself throughout, and makes a very characteristic ending of it in her third marriage. But why should I tease you by going through the different characters? Suffice it to say that I thank you very heartily, and congratulate you on again having added a work of so much merit to our stock of national novels. Perhaps before this you have received a very short publication of mine on a very serious subject. I desired my bookseller to send a copy to you, enclosed along with one to your friend, Miss Mackenzie. How far you will agree with my opinions regarding it I cannot say, but of one thing I am sure, that you will judge with candour and charity. I should have sent one to Mr. Alison had I not thought it presumptuous in me to send such a work to any clergyman, and, with only one exception (a Presbyterian clergyman), I have abstained from doing so. I was very much obliged to Mrs. Mackenzie, Lord M.'s lady, for the letter she was so good as to write me in her sister-in-law's stead. If you should meet her soon, may I beg that you will have the goodness to thank her in my name. I was very sorry indeed to learn from her that Miss Mackenzie had been so ill, and was then so weak, and that the favourable account I had received of your eyes had been too favourable. With all good wishes to you, in which my sister begs to join me,—I remain, my dear Madam, gratefully and sincerely yours,

"J. BAILLIE."

Granville Penn, the descendant of the founder of Pennsylvania, records the impression *Destiny* made on him, and which he communicates to Miss Erskine of Cardross, who copied and sent it to the author, as follows :—

"MY DEAR MADAM—I return your book, but I am
unable to return you adequate thanks for being the cause
of my reading it. I have done this (and all with me)
with delight, from the interest and admiration at the
whole composition, the novelty and excitement of its plan,
the exquisite and thrilling manner of its disclosure, the
absence of all flat and heavy intervals, the conception and
support of the characters, the sound and salutary moral
that pervades it all—these make me love and honour its
valuable authoress, and lament that I am not in the
number of her acquaintance. We all *doat* upon Miss
Macaulay, and grieve that she is not living at Richmond
or Petersham; and Mr. M'Dow has supplied me with a
new name for our little young dog, whom I have called,
in memorial of his little nephew (or niece), Little M'Fee.
With all the thanks, however, that I can offer, etc.

" GRANVILLE PENN.

" Devonshire Cottage, 1st *May* 1831."

The next tribute of admiration bestowed on *Destiny*
was from Sir James Mackintosh:—

Sir James Mackintosh to Miss Ferrier.

" LONDON, 10th *June* 1831.

" DEAR MISS FERRIER—Let me tell you a fact, which
I hope you will excuse me from mentioning, as some sub-
sidiary proof of your power. On the day of the dissolu-
tion of Parliament, and in the critical hours between
twelve and three, I was employed in reading part of the
second volume of *Destiny*. My mind was so completely
occupied on your colony in Argyleshire, that I did not
throw away a thought on kings or parliaments, and was
not moved by the general curiosity to stir abroad till I
had finished your volume. It would have been nothing
if you had so agitated a youth of genius and susceptibility,
prone to literary enthusiasm, but such a victory over an

old hack is perhaps worthy of your notice.—I am, my
dear Miss Ferrier, your friend and admirer,

                    "J. MACKINTOSH."

Professor Wilson, "Christopher North," and his
uncle, Mr. Robert Sym, W.S., "Timothy Tickler,"
discuss the merits of *Destiny* in the far-famed *Noctes :*

" *Tickler.*—' I would also except Miss Susan Ferrier.
Her novels, no doubt, have many defects, their plots are
poor, their episodes disproportionate, and the characters
too often caricatures ; but they are all thick-set with such
specimens of sagacity, such happy traits of nature, such
flashes of genuine satire, such easy humour, sterling good
sense, and, above all—God only knows where she picked
it up—mature and perfect knowledge of the world, that
I think we may safely anticipate for them a different fate
from what awaits even the cleverest of juvenile novels.'

" *North.*—' They are the works of a very clever woman,
sir, and they have one feature of true and melancholy
interest quite peculiar to themselves.   It is in them alone
that the ultimate breaking-down and debasement of the
Highland character has been depicted.   Sir Walter Scott
had fixed the enamel of genius over the last fitful gleams
of their half-savage chivalry, but a humbler and sadder
scene—the age of lucre-banished clans—of chieftains
dwindled into imitation squires, and of chiefs content to
barter the recollections of a thousand years for a few
gaudy seasons of Almacks and Crockfords, the euthanasia
of kilted aldermen and steamboat pibrochs was reserved
for Miss Ferrier.'

" *Tickler.*—' She in general fails almost as egregiously
as Hook does in the pathetic,[1] but in her last piece there

---

[1] This is not true, as there are many pathetic passages in
Destiny, particularly between Edith, the heroine, and her faith-
less lover, Sir Reginald.

is one scene of this description worthy of either Sterne or Goldsmith. I mean where the young man[1] supposed to have been lost at sea, revisits, after a lapse of time, the precincts of his own home, watching unseen in the twilight the occupations and bearings of the different members of the family, and resolving, under the influence of a most generous feeling, to keep the secret of his preservation.'

" *North.*—' I remember it well, and you might bestow the same kind of praise on the whole character of Molly Macaulay. It is a picture of humble, kind-hearted, thorough-going devotion and long-suffering, indefatigable gentleness, of which, perhaps, no sinner of our gender could have adequately filled up the outline. Miss Ferrier appears habitually in the light of a hard satirist, but there is always a fund of romance at the bottom of every true woman's heart who has tried to stifle and suppress that element more carefully and pertinaciously, and yet who has drawn, in spite of herself, more genuine tears than the authoress of *Simple Susan.*' "

The story of *Destiny*, like its predecessors, is laid in Miss Ferrier's favourite Highlands, and it contains several picturesque and vivid descriptions of scenery there, — Inveraray, and its surroundings generally, forming the model for her graphic pen. Much of this novel was written at Stirling Castle, when she was there on a visit to her sister, Mrs. Graham,[2] whose

[1] Ronald Malcolm.

[2] Celebrated by Burns, the poet, for her beauty. She inspired his muse when turning the corner of George Street, Edinburgh. The lines addressed to her are to be found in his *Poems.* She was also a highly-gifted artist. The illustrations in the work called the *Stirling Heads* are from her pencil. It was published by Blackwood, 1817.

husband, General Graham, was governor of that
garrison. After the publication of this last work,
and the offer of a thousand pounds from a London
publisher for anything from her pen,[1] she entirely
ceased from her literary labours, being content to rest
upon the solid and enduring reputation her three
"bantlings" (as she called her novels) had won for
her. The following fragment, however, was found
among her papers, and is the portrait of another old
maid, and might serve as a companion to Miss Pratt.
As it is amusing, and in the writer's satirical style, I
lay it before my readers :—

"Miss Betty Landon was a single lady of small fortune, few personal charms, and a most jaundiced imagination. There was no event, not even the most fortunate,
from which Miss Betty could not extract evil ; everything,
even the milk of human kindness, with her turned to gall
and vinegar. Thus, if any of her friends were married,
she sighed over the miseries of the wedded state ; if they
were single, she bewailed their solitary, useless condition ;
if they were parents, she pitied them for having children ;
if they had no children, she pitied them for being child-
less. But one of her own letters will do greater justice
to the turn of her mind than the most elaborate description.

"'MY DEAR MISS——I ought to have written to
you long before now, but I have suffered so much from
the constant changes of the weather that the wonder is
I am able to hold a pen. During the whole summer the
heat was really quite intolerable, not a drop of rain or
a breath of wind, the cattle dying for absolute want, the

---

[1] She says (1837), "I made two attempts to write *something*,
but could not please myself, and would not publish *anything*."

vegetables dear and scarce, and as for fruit—that, you know, in this town, is at all times scarce and bad, and particularly when there is the greatest occasion for it. In the autumn we never had two days alike, either wind or rain, or frost, or something or another ; and as for our winter—you know what that is—either a constant splash of rain, or a frost like to take the skin off you. For these six weeks I may say I have had a constant running at my head, with a return of my old complaint ; but as for doctors, I see no good they do, except to load people's stomachs and pick their pockets : everything now is imposition ; I really think the very pills are not what they were thirty years ago. How people with families continue to live is a mystery to me ; and people still going on marrying, in the face of national debt, taxes, a new war, a starving population, ruined commerce, and no outlet for young men in any quarter—God only knows what is to be the end of all this ! In spite of all this, these thoughtless young creatures, the Truemans, have thought proper to make out their marriage ; he is just five-and-twenty, and she is not yet nineteen ! so you may judge what a prudent, well-managed establishment it will be. He is in a good enough business at present, but in these times who can tell what's to happen ? He may be wallowing in wealth to-day, and bankrupt to-morrow. His sister's marriage with Fairplay is now quite off, and her prospects for life, poor thing, completely wrecked ! Her looks are entirely gone, and her spirits quite broken. She is not like the same creature, and, to be sure, to a girl who had set her heart upon being married, it must be a great and severe disappointment, for this was her only chance, unless she tries India, and the expense of the outfit must be a complete bar to that. You would hear that poor Lady Oldhouse has had a son—it seemed a desirable thing, situated as they are with an entailed property ; and yet when I look around me, and see the way that sons go on, the dissipation and extravagance, and the

heartbreak they are to their parents, I think a son anything but a blessing. No word of anything of that kind
to the poor Richardsons; with all their riches, they are
without any one to come after them. The Prowleys are
up in the air at having got what they call "a fine appointment" for their fourth son, but for my part I'm really
sick of hearing of boys going to India, for after all what
do they do there? I never hear of their sending home
anything but black children, and when they come home
themselves, what do they bring but yellow faces, worn-out
constitutions, and livers like cocked-hats, crawling about
from one watering-place to another, till they are picked
up by some light-hearted, fortune-hunting miss, who does
not care twopence for them.'"

A beautiful and strong feature in Miss Ferrier's
character was her intense devotion to her father, and
when he died the loss to her was irreparable. She
also was much attached to a very handsome brother,
James; he was colonel of the 94th regiment, or Scots
Brigade, and died in India in 1804, at the early age
of twenty-seven. He had been at the siege of Serin-
gapatam in 1799, and was much distinguished by
the notice of Napoleon at Paris in February 1803,
whence he writes to his sister Susan :—

"I think I wrote you I had been introduced to the
Chief Consul. I was on Sunday last presented to his
lady, whom I do not at all admire. The great man spoke
to me then again, which is a very unusual thing, and I am
told by the French I must be in his good graces ; however,
I myself rather think it was my good fortune only : at all
events it has given me much pleasure, for it would have
only been doing the thing half if he had not spoken to
me. I do not think any of the pictures like him much,

although most of them have some resemblance ; they give him a frown in general, which he certainly has not—so far from it, that when he speaks he has one of the finest expressions possible."

Here, unfortunately, this interesting description comes abruptly to an end, the rest of the letter being lost. On account of failing health and increased bodily languor, Miss Ferrier latterly lived a very retired life, seeing few but very intimate friends, and, as she said, "We are more recluse than ever, as our little circle is yearly contracting, and my eyes are more and more averse to light than ever."

Again she writes :—

"I can say nothing good of myself, my cough is very severe, and will probably continue so, at least as long as this weather lasts ; but I have many comforts, for which I am thankful ; amongst those I must reckon silence and darkness, which are my best companions at present."

For years she had suffered from her eyes, being nearly quite blind of one.[1] In 1830 she went to London to consult an oculist, but unfortunately derived little benefit. While there, she visited Isleworth, in order to see a villa belonging to Lord Cassillis, and which subsequently figured in *Destiny* as "Woodlands," Lady Waldegrave's rural retreat near London. A valued friend[2] who saw much of her remarked :—

[1] Lady Morgan, a fellow-sufferer from her eyes, was most anxious she should consult Mr. Alexander, the eminent oculist, as he entirely cured her after four years' expectation of total blindness. [2] Lady Richardson.

"The wonderful vivacity she maintained in the midst of darkness and pain for so many years, the humour, wit, and honesty of her character, as well as the Christian submission with which she bore her great privation and general discomfort when not suffering acute pain, made every one who knew her desirous to alleviate the tediousness of her days, and I used to read a great deal to her at one time, and I never left her darkened chamber without feeling that I had gained something better than the book we might be reading, from her quick perception of its faults and its beauties, and her unmerciful remarks on all that was mean or unworthy in conduct or expression."

But perhaps the most faithful picture of her is conveyed in this brief sentence from Scott's diary, who describes her

"As a gifted personage, having, besides her great talents, conversation the least *exigeante* of any author-female, at least, whom I have ever seen among the long list I have encountered ; simple, full of humour, and exceedingly ready at repartee, and all this without the least affectation of the blue-stocking."

From the natural modesty of her character she had a great dislike to her biography, or memorial of her in any shape, being written, for she destroyed all letters that might have been used for such a purpose, publicity of any kind being most distasteful to her, evidence of which is very clearly shown in the first part of this narrative. The chief secret of her success as a novelist (setting aside her great genius) was the great care and time she bestowed on the formation of each novel—an interval of six years occurring between each, the result being delineations of character that are unique.

Unfortunately there is little to relate regarding her childhood, that most interesting period of human existence in the lives of (and which is generally distinguished by some uncommon traits of character) people of genius—save that she had for a school companion and playfellow the late Lord Brougham, the distinguished statesman; she was remarkable also for her power of mimicry. An amusing anecdote of this rather dangerous gift is the following: Her brothers and sisters returned home from a ball, very hungry, and entered her room, where they supposed she lay asleep, and, while discussing the events of the evening and the repast they had procured by stealth (unknown to their father), they were suddenly put to flight by the sounds and voice, as they thought, of their dreaded parent ascending the stairs, and in their confusion and exit from the room overturned chairs and tables, much to the amusement of little Susan, who, no doubt, enjoyed the fright and commotion she had caused, and who mimicked under the cover of the bedclothes the accents of her redoubtable parent— a fit punishment, as she thought, for their ruthless invasion of her chamber, and their not offering her a share of their supper. An old Miss Peggy Campbell (sister to Sir Islay Campbell, President of the Court of Session) was also taken off by her, and so like that her father actually came into the room, where she was amusing her hearers, thinking that Miss Campbell

was really present.   When she died a blank was left
in her native city that has not been since filled, the
modern Athens having somewhat deteriorated in the
wit, learning, and refinement that so distinguished her
in the days that are gone.

RECOLLECTIONS OF VISITS
TO ASHESTIEL AND ABBOTSFORD.[1]

By SUSAN EDMONSTONE FERRIER,

Author of 'Marriage,' 'Inheritance,' and 'Destiny.'

I HAVE never kept either note-book or journal, and as my memory is not a retentive one I have allowed much to escape which I should now vainly attempt to recall. Some things must, however, have made a vivid and durable impression on my mind, as fragments remain, after the lapse of years, far more distinct than occurrences of much more recent date; such, amongst others, are my recollections of my visits to Ashestiel and Abbotsford.

The first took place in the autumn of 1811, in consequence of repeated and pressing invitations from Mr. Scott to my father, in which I was included. Nothing could be kinder than our welcome, or more gratifying than the attentions we received during our stay; but the weather was too broken and stormy to admit of our enjoying any of the pleasant excursions our more weather-proof host had intended for us.

---

[1] Reprinted from the *Temple Bar* Magazine for February 1874.

My father and I could therefore only take short drives with Mrs. Scott, while the bard (about one o'clock) mounted his pony, and accompanied by Mr. Terry the comedian, his own son Walter, and our young relative George Kinloch, sallied forth for a long morning's ride in spite of wind and rain. In the evening Mr. Terry commonly read some scenes from a play, to which Mr. Scott listened with delight, though every word must have been quite familiar to him, as he occasionally took a part in the dialogue impromptu; at other times he recited old and awesome ballads from memory, the very names of which I have forgot. The night preceding our departure had blown a perfect hurricane; we were to leave immediately after breakfast, and while the carriage was preparing Mr. Scott stepped to a writing-table and wrote a few hurried lines in the course of a very few minutes; these he put into my hand as he led me to the carriage; they were in allusion to the storm, coupled with a friendly adieu, and are to be found in my autograph album.

> " The mountain winds are up, and proud
> O'er heath and hill careering loud ;
> The groaning forest to its power
> Yields all that formed our summer bower.
> The summons wakes the anxious swain,
> Whose tardy shocks still load the plain,
> And bids the sleepless merchant weep,
> Whose richer hazard loads the deep.
> For me the blast, or low or high,
> Blows nought of wealth or poverty ;
> It can but whirl in whimsies vain
> The windmill of a restless brain,

And bid me tell in slipshod verse
What honest prose might best rehearse ;
How much we forest-dwellers grieve
Our valued friends our cot should leave,
Unseen each beauty that we boast,
The little wonders of our coast,
That still the pile of Melrose gray,
For you must rise in minstrel's lay,
And Yarrow's birk immortal long
For you but bloom in rural song.
Yet Hope, who still in present sorrow
Whispers the promise of to-morrow,
Tells us of future days to come,
When you shall glad our rustic home ;
When this wild whirlwind shall be still,
And summer sleep on glen and hill,
And Tweed, unvexed by storm, shall guide
In silvery maze his stately tide,
Doubling in mirror every rank
Of oak and alder on his bank ;
And our kind guests such welcome prove
As most we wish to those we love."[1]

Ashestiel, October 13, 1811.

The invitation had been often repeated, but my dear father's increasing infirmities made him averse to leave home, and when, in compliance with Sir Walter's urgent request, I visited Abbotsford in the autumn of 1829, I went alone. I was met at the outer gate by Sir Walter, who welcomed me in the kindest manner and most flattering terms ; indeed, nothing could surpass the courtesy of his address on such occasions. On our way to the house he stopped and called his two little grandchildren, Walter and Charlotte Lockhart,

[1] Lines written by Walter Scott while the carriage was waiting to convey my father and me from Ashestiel.—S. E. F.

who were chasing each other like butterflies among the
flowers—the boy was quite a Cupid, though not an *al
fresco* one; for he wore a Tartan cloak, whose sundry
extras fluttered in the breeze as he ran to obey the
summons, and gave occasion to his grandfather to present him to me as "Major Waddell;"[1] the pretty little
fairy-looking girl he next introduced as "Whipper-
stowrie," and then (aware of my love for fairy lore)
he related the tale, in his own inimitable manner,
as he walked slowly and stopped frequently in our
approach to the house. As soon as I could look
round I was struck with the singular and picturesque
appearance of the mansion and its *environs*. Yet I
must own there was more of *strangeness* than of admiration in my feelings; too many objects seemed crowded
together in a small space, and there was a "felt want"
of breadth and repose for the eye. On entering the
house I was however charmed with the rich imposing
beauty of the hall, and admired the handsome antique
appearance of the dining-room with its interesting
pictures. After luncheon Sir Walter was at pains to
point them out to my notice, and related the histories
of each and all; he then conducted me through the
apartments, and showed me so much, and told me so
many anecdotes illustrative of the various objects
of interest and curiosity they contained, that I retain
a very confused and imperfect recollection of what I
saw and heard. It was a strong proof of his good-

[1] One of Miss Ferrier's characters in her novel of *The
Inheritance*.

nature that in showing the many works of art and
relics of antiquity he had continued to accumulate and
arrange with so much taste and skill, he should have
been at such pains to point out the merits and relate
the history of most of them to one so incapable of
appreciating their value. But he never allowed one
to feel their own deficiencies, for he never appeared
to be aware of them himself.

It was in the quiet of a small domestic circle I
had again an opportunity of enjoying the society of
Sir Walter Scott, and of witnessing, during the ten
days I remained, the unbroken serenity of his temper,
the unflagging cheerfulness of his spirits, and the un-
ceasing courtesy of his manners. I had been promised
a quiet time, else I should not have gone ; and indeed
the state of the family was a sufficient guarantee
against all festivities. Mrs. Lockhart was confined to
bed by severe indisposition, while Mr. Lockhart was
detained in London by the alarming illness of their
eldest boy, and both Captain Scott and his brother were
absent. The party, therefore, consisted only of Sir
Walter and Miss Scott, Miss Macdonald Buchanan
(who was almost one of the family), and myself.
Being the only stranger, I consequently came in for a
larger share of my amiable host's time and attention
than I should otherwise have been entitled to expect.
Many a pleasant tale and amusing anecdote I might
have had to relate had I written down half of what I
daily heard ; but I had always an invincible repugnance to playing the *reporter* and taking down people's

words under their own roof. Every day Sir Walter
was ready by one o'clock to accompany us either in
driving or walking, often in both, and in either there
was the same inexhaustible flow of legendary lore,
romantic incident, apt quotation, curious or diverting
story; and sometimes old ballads were recited, com-
memorative of some of the localities through which
he passed. Those who had seen him only amidst the
ordinary avocations of life, or even doing the honours
of his own table, could scarcely have conceived the
fire and animation of his countenance at such times,
when his eyes seemed literally to kindle, and even
(as some one has remarked) to change their colour
and become a sort of deep sapphire blue; but, perhaps,
from being close to him and in the open air, I was
more struck with this peculiarity than those whose
better sight enabled them to mark his varying expression at other times. Yet I must confess this was
an enthusiasm I found as little infectious as that of
his antiquarianism. On the contrary, I often wished
his noble faculties had been exercised on loftier themes
than those which seemed to stir his very soul.

The evenings were passed either in Mrs. Lockhart's bedroom or in chatting quietly by the fireside
below, but wherever we were he was always the
same kind, unostentatious, amusing, and *amusable*
companion.

The day before I was to depart Sir David Wilkie
and his sister arrived, and the Fergussons and one or
two friends were invited to meet him. Mrs. Lockhart

was so desirous of meeting this old friend and distinguished person, that, though unable to put her foot
to the ground, she caused herself to be dressed and
carried down to the drawing-room while the company
were at dinner. Great was her father's surprise and
delight on his entrance to find her seated (looking
well and in high spirits) with her harp before her,
ready to sing his favourite ballads. This raised his
spirits above their usual quiet pitch, and towards the
end of the evening he proposed to wind up the whole
by all present standing in a circle with hands joined,
singing,

> " Weel may we a' be !
> Ill may we never see ! "

Mrs. Lockhart was, of course, unable to join the festive
band. Sir David Wilkie was languid and dispirited
from bad health, and my feelings were not such as to
enable me to join in what seemed to me little else
than a mockery of human life; but rather than "dis-
place the mirth," I *tried*, but could not long remain
a passive spectator; the glee seemed forced and unnatural. It touched no sympathetic chord; it only
jarred the feelings; it was the last attempt at gaiety
I witnessed within the walls of Abbotsford.

Although I had intended to confine my slight
reminiscence of Sir Walter Scott to the time I had
passed with him under his own roof in the country,
yet I cannot refrain from noticing the great kindness
I received from him during the following winter in
town.

I had, when at Abbotsford in the autumn, spoken
to him for the *first* time of my authorship and of the
work on which I was then engaged.   He entered into
the subject with much warmth and earnestness, shook
his head at hearing how matters had hitherto been
transacted, and said unless I could make a better bargain in this instance I must leave to him the disposal
of *Destiny.*   I did so, and from the much more liberal
terms he made with Mr. Cadell I felt, when too late,
I had acted unwisely in not having sooner consulted
him or some one versant in these matters.   But *secrecy*
at that time was all I was anxious about, and so I
paid the penalty of trusting entirely to the good faith
of the publishers.

I saw Sir Walter frequently during the winter, and
occasionally dined *en famille* with Miss Scott and him,
or with one or two friends, as I did not go into parties,
neither indeed did he give any, but on account of the
state of his affairs lived as retiredly as he possibly
could.

In the month of February he sustained a paralytic
shock ; as soon as I heard of this I went to Miss Scott,
from whom I learned the particulars.   She had seen
her father in his study a short time before, apparently
in his usual health.   She had returned to the drawing-
room when Sir Walter opened the door, came in, but
stood looking at her with a most peculiar and *dreadful* expression of countenance.   It immediately struck
her he had come to communicate some very distressing intelligence, and she exclaimed, "Oh, papa ! is

Johnnie gone?" He made no reply, but still continued standing still and regarding her with the same fearful expression. She then cried, "Oh, papa! speak! Tell me, is it Sophia herself?" Still he remained immovable. Almost frantic, she then screamed, "It is Walter! it is Walter! I know it is." Upon which Sir Walter fell senseless on the floor. Medical assistance was speedily procured. After being bled he recovered his speech, and his first words were, "It was very strange! very horrible." He afterwards told her he had all at once felt very queer, and as if unable to articulate; he then went upstairs in hopes of getting rid of the sensation by movement; but it would not do, he felt perfectly tongue-tied, or rather *chained*, till overcome by witnessing her distress. This took place, I think, on the 15th, and on the 18th I was invited to dine with him, and found him without any trace of illness, but as cheerful and animated as usual.

Not being very correct as to dates, I should scarcely have ventured to name the day had not a trifling circumstance served to mark it. After dinner he proposed that instead of going to the drawing-room we should remain with him and have tea in the dining-room. In the interval the post letters were brought, and amongst others there was one from a sister of Sir Thomas Lawrence (Mrs. Bloxam), enclosing a letter of her brother's, having heard that Sir Walter had expressed a wish to have some memorial of him, "rather of his pencil than his pen," said he, as he handed the letter to me, who, as a collector of autographs, would probably value them more than he did, and on referring to Mrs. Bloxam's letter I find the Edinburgh post-mark February the 18th.

I received repeated invitations to Abbotsford, and had fixed to go on the 17th of April, when, the day before, Mrs. Skene called upon me with the sad tidings of another paralytic stroke, which not only put a stop to my visit for the present, but rendered it very doubtful whether I should ever see him again. But the worst fears of his friends were not yet to be realised.

Early in May the invitation was renewed in a note from himself, which I availed myself of, too well assured it was a privilege I should enjoy for the last time. On reaching Abbotsford I found some morning visitors (Mr. and Mrs. James, etc.) in the drawing-room, but as soon as they were gone Sir Walter sent for me to his study. I found him seated in his armchair, but with his habitual politeness he insisted upon rising to receive me, though he did so with such extreme difficulty I would gladly have dispensed with this mark of courtesy. His welcome was not less cordial than usual, but he spoke in a slow and somewhat indistinct manner, and as I sat close by him I could perceive but too plainly the change which had taken place since we last met. His figure was unwieldy, not so much from increased bulk as from diminished life and energy; his face was swollen and puffy, his complexion mottled and discoloured, his eyes heavy and dim; his head had been shaved, and he wore a small black silk cap, which was extremely unbecoming. Altogether, the change was no less striking than painful to behold. The impression, however, soon wore off (on finding, as I believed), that his mind was unimpaired and his warm kindly feelings unchanged.

There was no company, and the dinner party consisted of Mr. and Mrs. Lockhart, Miss Scott, and myself. Sir Walter did not join us till the dessert, when he entered, assisted by his servant, and took his place at the foot of the table. His grandchildren were then brought in, and his favourite, Johnnie Lockhart, was seated by his side. I must have forgot most things before I can cease to recall that most striking and impressive spectacle, each day repeated, as it seemed, with deepening gloom. The first transient glow of cheerfulness which had welcomed my arrival had passed away, and been succeeded by an air of languor and dejection which sank to deepest sadness when his eye rested for a moment on his once darling grandson, the child of so much pride and promise, now, alas! how changed. It was most touching to look upon one whose morning of life had been so bright and beautiful and, still in the sunny days of childhood, transformed into an image of decrepitude and decay. The fair blooming cheek and finely chiselled features were now shrunk and stiffened into the wan and rigid inflexibility of old age; while the black bandages which swathed the little pale sad countenance, gave additional gloom and harshness to the profound melancholy which clouded its most in

tellectual expression. Disease and death were stamped
upon the grandsire and the boy as they sat side by side
with averted eyes, each as if in the bitterness of his
own heart refusing to comfort or be comforted. The
two who had been wont to regard each other so fondly
and so proudly, now seemed averse to hold communion
together, while their appearance and style of dress,
the black cap of the one and the black bandages of
the other, denoted a sympathy in suffering if in
nothing else. The picture would have been a most
affecting and impressive one viewed under any circumstances, but was rendered doubly so by the contrast which everywhere presented itself.

The month was May, but the weather had all the
warmth of summer with the freshness and sweetness
of spring. The windows of the dining-room were
open to admit the soft balmy air which "came and
went like the warbling of music," but whose reviving
influence seemed unfelt by the sufferers. The trees,
and shrubs, and flowers were putting forth their tender
leaves and fragrant blossoms as if to charm *his* senses
who used to watch their progress with almost paternal
interest, and the little birds were singing in sweet
chorus as if to cheer *him* who was wont to listen to
their evening song with such placid delight. All
around were the dear familiar objects which had
hitherto ministered to his enjoyment, but now, alas!
miserable comforters were they all! It was impossible
to look upon such a picture without beholding in it
the realisation of those solemn and affecting passages

of Holy Writ which speak to us of the ephemeral
nature of all earthly pleasures and of the mournful
insignificance of human life, even in its most palmy
state, when its views and actions, its hopes and desires,
are confined to this sublunary sphere: "Whence then
cometh any wisdom, and where is the place of understanding?" "Thus saith the Lord, Let not the wise
man glory in his wisdom, neither let the mighty man
glory in his might; let not the rich man glory in his
riches: but let him that glorieth glory in this, that
he understandeth and knoweth me, that I am the
Lord."

MARRIAGE.

CHAPTER I.

"Love!—A word by superstition thought a God; by use turned to an humour; by self-will made a flattering madness."

Alexander and Campaspe.

"COME hither, child," said the old Earl of Courtland to his daughter, as, in obedience to his summons, she entered his study; "come hither, I say; I wish to have some serious conversation with you: so dismiss your dogs, shut the door, and sit down here."

Lady Juliana rang for the footman to take Venus; bade Pluto be quiet, like a darling, under the sofa; and, taking Cupid in her arms, assured his Lordship he need fear no disturbance from the sweet creatures, and that she would be all attention to his commands —kissing her cherished pug as she spoke.

"You are now, I think, seventeen, Juliana," said his Lordship in a solemn important tone.

"And a half, papa."

"It is therefore time you should be thinking of establishing yourself in the world. Have you ever turned your thoughts that way?"

Lady Juliana cast down her beautiful eyes, and was silent.

"As I can give you no fortune," continued the Earl, swelling with ill-suppressed importance, as he proceeded, "you have perhaps no great pretensions to a very brilliant establishment."

"Oh! none in the world, papa," eagerly interrupted Lady Juliana; "a mere competence with the man of my heart."

"The man of a fiddlestick!" exclaimed Lord Courtland in a fury; "what the devil have you to do with a heart, I should like to know? There's no talking to a young woman now about marriage, but she is all in a blaze about hearts, and darts, and—and—But hark ye, child, I'll suffer no daughter of mine to play the fool with her heart, indeed! She shall marry for the purpose for which matrimony was ordained amongst people of birth—that is, for the aggrandisement of her family, the extending of their political influence—for becoming, in short, the depository of their mutual interest. These are the only purposes for which persons of rank ever think of marriage. And pray, what has your heart to say to that?"

"Nothing, papa," replied Lady Juliana in a faint dejected tone of voice. "Have done, Cupid!" addressing her favourite, who was amusing himself in pulling and tearing the beautiful lace veil that partly shaded the head of his fair mistress.

"I thought not," resumed the Earl in a triumphant

tone—"I thought not, indeed." And as this victory over his daughter put him in unusual good humour, he condescended to sport a little with her curiosity.

"And pray, can this wonderful wise heart of yours inform you who it is you are going to obtain for a husband?"

Had Lady Juliana dared to utter the wishes of that heart she would have been at no loss for a reply; but she saw the necessity of dissimulation; and after naming such of her admirers as were most indifferent to her, she declared herself quite at a loss, and begged her father to put an end to her suspense.

"Now, what would you think of the Duke of L——?" asked the Earl in a voice of half-smothered exultation and delight.

"The Duke of L——!" repeated Lady Juliana, with a scream of horror and surprise; "surely, papa, you cannot be serious? Why, he's red-haired and squints, and he's as old as you."

"If he were as old as the devil, and as ugly too," interrupted the enraged Earl, "he should be your husband: and may I perish if you shall have any other!"

The youthful beauty burst into tears, while her father traversed the apartment with an inflamed and wrathful visage.

"If it had been anybody but that odious Duke," sobbed the lovely Juliana.

"If it had been anybody but that odious Duke!" repeated the Earl, mimicking her, "they should not

have had you. It has been my sole study, ever since
I saw your brother settled, to bring about this alliance;
and, when this is accomplished, my utmost ambition
will be satisfied. So no more whining—the affair is
settled; and all that remains for you to do is to study
to make yourself agreeable to his Grace, and to sign
the settlements. No such mighty sacrifice, methinks,
when repaid with a ducal coronet, the most splendid
jewels, the finest equipages, and the largest jointure
of any woman in England."

Lady Juliana raised her head, and wiped her eyes.
Lord Courtland perceived the effect his eloquence had
produced upon the childish fancy of his daughter, and
continued to expatiate upon the splendid joys that
awaited her in a union with a nobleman of the
Duke's rank and fortune; till at length, dazzled, if not
convinced, she declared herself "satisfied that it was
her duty to marry whoever papa pleased; but—" and
a sigh escaped her as she contrasted her noble suitor
with her handsome lover: "but if I should marry him,
papa, I am sure I shall never be able to love him."

The Earl smiled at her childish simplicity as he
assured her that was not at all necessary; that love
was now entirely confined to the *canaille;* that it was
very well for ploughmen and dairymaids to marry
for love; but for a young woman of rank to think of
such a thing was plebeian in the extreme!

Lady Juliana did not entirely subscribe to the
arguments of her father; but the gay and glorious
vision that floated in her brain stifled for a while the

pleadings of her heart; and with a sparkling eye and an elastic step she hastened to prepare for the reception of the Duke.

For a few weeks the delusion lasted. Lady Juliana was flattered with the homage she received as a future Duchess; she was delighted with the éclat that attended her, and charmed with the daily presents showered upon her by her noble suitor.

"Well, really, Favolle," said she to her maid, one day, as she clasped on her beautiful arm a resplendent bracelet, "it must be owned the Duke has a most exquisite taste in trinkets; don't you think so? And, do you know, I don't think him so very—very ugly. When we are married I mean to make him get a Brutus, cork his eyebrows, and have a set of teeth." But just then the smiling eyes, curling hair, and finely formed person of a certain captivating Scotsman rose to view in her mind's eye; and, with a peevish "pshaw!" she threw the bauble aside.

Educated for the sole purpose of forming a brilliant establishment, of catching the eye, and captivating the senses, the cultivation of her mind or the correction of her temper had formed no part of the system by which that aim was to be accomplished. Under the auspices of a fashionable mother and an obsequious governess the froward petulance of childhood, fostered and strengthened by indulgence and submission, had gradually ripened into that selfishness and caprice which now, in youth, formed the prominent features of her character. The Earl was too much engrossed

by affairs of importance to pay much attention to anything so perfectly insignificant as the mind of his
daughter. Her *person* he had predetermined should
be entirely at his disposal, and therefore contemplated
with delight the uncommon beauty which already distinguished it; not with the fond partiality of parental
love, but with the heartless satisfaction of a crafty
politician.

The mind of Lady Juliana was consequently the
sport of every passion that by turns assailed it. Now
swayed by ambition, and now softened by love, the
struggle was violent, but it was short. A few days
before the one which was to seal her fate she granted
an interview to her lover, who, young, thoughtless,
and enamoured as herself, easily succeeded in persuad-
ing her to elope with him to Scotland. There, at the
altar of Vulcan, the beautiful daughter of the Earl of
Courtland gave her hand to her handsome but penni-
less lover; and there vowed to immolate every ambitious desire, every sentiment of vanity and high-born
pride. Yet a sigh arose as she looked on the filthy
hut, sooty priest, and ragged witnesses; and thought
of the special license, splendid saloon, and bridal
pomp that would have attended her union with the
Duke. But the rapturous expressions which burst
from the impassioned Douglas made her forget the
gaudy pleasures of pomp and fashion. Amid the
sylvan scenes of the neighbouring lakes the lovers
sought a shelter; and, mutually charmed with each
other, time flew for a while on downy pinions.

At the end of two months, however, the enamoured husband began to suspect that the lips of his "angel Julia" could utter very silly things; while the fond bride, on her part, discovered that though her "adored Henry's" figure was symmetry itself, yet it certainly was deficient in a certain air—a *je ne sçais quoi*—that marks the man of fashion.

"How I wish I had my pretty Cupid here," said her Ladyship, with a sigh, one day as she lolled on a sofa: "he had so many pretty tricks, he would have helped to amuse us, and make the time pass; for really this place grows very stupid and tiresome; don't you think so, love?"

"Most confoundedly so, my darling," replied her husband, yawning sympathetically as he spoke.

"Then suppose I make one more attempt to soften papa, and be received into favour again?"

"With all my heart."

"Shall I say I'm very sorry for what I have done?" asked her Ladyship, with a sigh. "You know I did not say that in my first letter."

"Ay, do; and, if it will serve any purpose, you may say that I am no less so."

In a few days the letter was returned, in a blank cover; and, by the same post, Douglas saw himself superseded in the Gazette, being absent without leave!

There now remained but one course to pursue; and that was to seek refuge at his father's, in the Highlands of Scotland. At the first mention of it Lady Juliana was transported with joy, and begged that a letter might be instantly despatched, containing the offer of a visit: she had heard the Duchess of M. declare nothing could be so delightful as the style of living in Scotland: the people were so frank and gay, and the manners so easy and engaging—oh! it was delightful! And then Lady Jane G. and Lady Mary L., and a thousand other lords and ladies she knew, were all so charmed with the country, and all so sorry to leave it. Then dear Henry's family must be so charming: an old castle, too, was her delight; she would feel quite at home while wandering through its long galleries; and she quite loved old pictures, and armour, and tapestry; and then her thoughts reverted to her father's magnificent mansion in D——shire.

At length an answer arrived, containing a cordial invitation from the old Laird to spend the winter with them at Glenfern Castle.

All impatience to quit the scenes of their short-lived felicity, they bade a hasty adieu to the now fading beauties of Windermere; and, full of hope and expectation, eagerly turned towards the bleak hills of Scotland. They stopped for a short time at Edinburgh, to provide themselves with a carriage, and some other necessaries. There, too, she fortunately met with an English Abigail and footman, who, for double wages, were prevailed upon to attend her to the Highlands; which, with the addition of two dogs, a tame squirrel, and mackaw, completed the establishment.

CHAPTER II.

" What transport to retrace our early plays,
  Our easy bliss, when each thing joy supplied ;
  The woods, the mountains, and the warbling maze
  Of the wild brooks."   THOMSON.

MANY were the dreary muirs and rugged mountains
her Ladyship had to encounter in her progress to
Glenfern Castle ; and, but for the hope of the new
world that awaited her beyond those formidable
barriers, her delicate frame and still more sensitive
feelings must have sunk beneath the horrors of such
a journey. But she remembered the Duchess had
said the inns and roads were execrable ; and the face
of the country, as well as the lower orders of people,
frightful ; but what signified those things? There
were balls, and sailing parties, and rowing matches,
and shooting parties, and fishing parties, and parties
of every description ; and the certainty of being re-
compensed by the festivities of Glenfern Castle,
reconciled her to the ruggedness of the approach.

Douglas had left his paternal home and native
hills when only eight years of age. A rich relation
of his mother's happening to visit them at that time,

took a fancy to the boy; and, under promise of making
him his heir, had prevailed on his parents to part with
him.   At a proper age he was placed in the Guards,
and had continued to maintain himself in the favour
of his benefactor until his imprudent marriage, which
had irritated this old bachelor so much that he
instantly disinherited him, and refused to listen to
any terms of reconciliation.   The impressions which
the scenes of his infancy had left upon the mind of
the young Scotsman, it may easily be supposed, were
of a pleasing description.   He expatiated to his
Juliana on the wild but august scenery that surrounded his father's castle, and associated with the
idea the boyish exploits, which though faintly remembered, still served to endear them to his heart.
He spoke of the time when he used to make one of
a numerous party on the lake, and, when tired of
sailing on its glassy surface to the sound of soft
music, they would land at some lovely spot; and,
after partaking of their banquet beneath a spreading
tree, conclude the day by a dance on the grass.

Lady Juliana would exclaim, "How delightful! I
doat upon, picnics and dancing!—*àpropos*, Henry,
there will surely be a ball to welcome our arrival?"

The conversation was interrupted; for just at that
moment they had gained the summit of a very high
hill, and the post-boy, stopping to give his horses
breath, turned round to the carriage, pointing at the
same time, with a significant gesture, to a tall thin
gray house, something resembling a tower, that stood

in the vale beneath. A small sullen-looking lake was in front, on whose banks grew neither tree nor shrub. Behind rose a chain of rugged cloud-capped hills, on the declivities of which were some faint attempts at young plantations; and the only level ground consisted of a few dingy turnip fields, enclosed with stone walls, or dykes, as the post-boy called them. It was now November; the day was raw and cold; and a thick drizzling rain was beginning to fall. A dreary stillness reigned all around, broken only at intervals by the screams of the sea-fowl that hovered over the lake, on whose dark and troubled waters was dimly descried a little boat, plied by one solitary being.

"What a scene!" at length Lady Juliana exclaimed, shuddering as she spoke. "Good God, what a scene! How I pity the unhappy wretches who are doomed to dwell in such a place! and yonder hideous grim house—it makes me sick to look at it. For Heaven's sake, bid him drive on." Another significant look from the driver made the colour mount to Douglas's cheek, as he stammered out, "Surely it can't be; yet somehow I don't know. Pray, my lad," letting down one of the glasses, and addressing the post-boy, "what is the name of that house?"

"Hoose!" repeated the driver; "ca' ye thon a hoose? Thon's gude Glenfern Castle."

Lady Juliana, not understanding a word he said, sat silently wondering at her husband's curiosity respecting such a wretched-looking place.

"Impossible! you must be mistaken, my lad:

why, what's become of all the fine wood that used to
surround it?"

"Gin you mean a wheen auld firs, there's some
o' them to the fore yet," pointing to two or three tall,
bare, scathed Scotch firs, that scarcely bent their
stubborn heads to the wind, that now began to howl
around them.

"I insist upon it that you are mistaken; you must
have wandered from the right road," cried the now
alarmed Douglas in a loud voice, which vainly
attempted to conceal his agitation.

"We'll shune see that," replied the phlegmatic
Scot, who, having rested his horses and affixed a
drag to the wheel, was about to proceed, when Lady
Juliana, who now began to have some vague suspicion
of the truth, called to him to stop, and, almost breathless with alarm, inquired of her husband the meaning
of what had passed.

He tried to force a smile, as he said, "It seems
our journey is nearly ended; that fellow persists in
asserting that that is Glenfern, though I can scarcely
think it. If it is, it is strangely altered since I left it
twelve years ago."

For a moment Lady Juliana was too much alarmed
to make a reply; pale and speechless, she sank back
in the carriage; but the motion of it, as it began to
proceed, roused her to a sense of her situation, and
she burst into tears and exclamations.

The driver, who attributed it all to fears at descending the hill, assured her she need na be the least

feared, for there were na twa cannier beasts atween
that and Johnny Groat's hoose; and that they wad
ha'e her at the castle door in a crack, gin they were
ance down the brac."

Douglas's attempts to soothe his high-born bride
were not more successful than those of the driver: in
vain he made use of every endearing epithet and
tender expression, and recalled the time when she
used to declare that she could dwell with him in a
desert; her only replies were bitter reproaches and
upbraidings for his treachery and deceit, mingled with
floods of tears, and interrupted by hysterical sobs.
Provoked at her folly, yet softened by her extreme
distress, Douglas was in the utmost state of perplexity—now ready to give way to a paroxysm of
rage; then yielding to the natural goodness of his
heart, he sought to soothe her into composure; and,
at length, with much difficulty succeeded in changing
her passionate indignation into silent dejection.

That no fresh objects of horror or disgust might
appear to disturb this calm, the blinds were pulled
down, and in this state they reached Glenfern Castle.
But there the friendly veil was necessarily withdrawn,
and the first object that presented itself to the high-
bred Englishwoman was an old man clad in a short
tartan coat and striped woollen night-cap, with blear
eyes and shaking hands, who vainly strove to open
the carriage door.

Douglas soon extricated himself, and assisted his
lady to alight; then accosting the venerable domes-

tic as "Old Donald," asked him if he recollected
him.

"Weel that, weel that, Maister Hairy, and ye're
welcome hame; and ye tu, bonny sir"[1] (addressing
Lady Juliana, who was calling to her footman to
follow her with the mackaw); then, tottering before
them, he led the way, while her Ladyship followed,
leaning on her husband, her squirrel on her other
arm, preceded by her dogs, barking with all their
might, and attended by the mackaw, screaming with
all his strength; and in this state was the Lady Juliana
ushered into the drawing-room of Glenfern Castle!

[1] The Highlanders use this term of respect indifferently to
both sexes.

CHAPTER III.

" What can be worse,
Than to dwell here ?"

Paradise Lost.

It was a long, narrow, low-roofed room, with a number of small windows, that admitted feeble lights in every possible direction. The scanty furniture bore every appearance of having been constructed at the same time as the edifice ; and the friendship thus early formed still seemed to subsist, as the high-backed worked chairs adhered most pertinaciously to the gray walls, on which hung, in narrow black frames, some of the venerable ancestors of the Douglas family. A fire, which appeared to have been newly kindled, was beginning to burn, but, previous to showing itself in flame, had chosen to vent itself in smoke, with which the room was completely filled, and the open windows seemed to produce no other effect than that of admitting the rain and wind.

At the entrance of the strangers a flock of females rushed forward to meet them. Douglas good humouredly submitted to be hugged by three long-chinned spinsters, whom he recognised as his aunts ; and warmly saluted five awkward purple girls he guessed

to be his sisters; while Lady Juliana stood the image
of despair, and, scarcely conscious, admitted in silence
the civilities of her new relations; till, at length, sinking into a chair, she endeavoured to conceal her
agitation by calling to the dogs, and caressing her
mackaw.

The Laird, who had been hastily summoned from
his farming operations, now entered. He was a good-
looking old man, with something the air of a gentleman, in spite of the inelegance of his dress, his rough
manner, and provincial accent. After warmly welcom-
ing his son, he advanced to his beautiful daughter-in-
law, and, taking her in his arms, bestowed a loud and
hearty kiss on each cheek; then, observing the pale-
ness of her complexion, and the tears that swam in
her eyes, "What! not frightened for our Hieland
hills, my leddy? Come, cheer up—trust me, ye'll find
as warm hearts among them as ony ye ha'e left in your
fine English *policies*"—shaking her delicate fingers in
his hard muscular gripe as he spoke.

The tears, which had with difficulty been hitherto
suppressed, now burst in torrents from the eyes of
the high-bred beauty, as she leant her cheek against
the back of a chair, and gave way to the anguish
which mocked control.

To the loud, anxious inquiries, and oppressive
kindness of her homely relatives, she made no reply;
but, stretching out her hands to her husband, sobbed,
"Take, oh, take me from this place!"

Mortified, ashamed, and provoked, at a behaviour

so childish and absurd, Douglas could only stammer out something about Lady Juliana having been frightened and fatigued ; and, requesting to be shown to their apartment, he supported her almost lifeless to it, while his aunts followed, all three prescribing different remedies in a breath.

"For heaven's sake, take them from me !" faintly articulated Lady Juliana, as she shrank from the many hands that were alternately applied to her pulse and forehead.

After repeated entreaties and plausible excuses from Douglas, his aunts at length consented to withdraw, and he then exerted all the rhetoric he was master of to reconcile his bride to the situation love and necessity had thrown her into. But in vain he employed reasoning, caresses, and threats ; the only answers he could extort were tears and entreaties to be taken from a place where she declared she felt it impossible to exist.

"If you wish my death, Harry," said she, in a voice almost inarticulate from excess of weeping, "oh! kill me quickly, and do not leave me to linger out my days, and perish at last with misery here."

"For heaven's sake, tell me what you would have me do," said her husband, softened to pity by her extreme distress, "and I swear that in everything possible I will comply with your wishes."

"Oh, fly then, stop the horses, and let us return immediately. Do run, dearest Harry, or they will be gone; and we shall never get away from this odious place."

"Where would you go?" asked he, with affected calmness.

"Oh, anywhere; no matter where, so as we do but get away from hence : we can be at no loss."

"None in the world," interrupted Douglas, with a bitter smile, "as long as there is a prison to receive us. See," continued he, throwing a few shillings down on the table, "there is every sixpence I possess in the world, so help me heaven !"

Lady Juliana stood aghast.

At that instant the English Abigail burst into the room, and in a voice choking with passion, she requested her discharge, that she might return with the driver who had brought them there.

"A pretty way of travelling, to be sure, it will be," continued she, "to go bumping behind a dirty chaise-driver; but better to be shook to a jelly altogether than stay amongst such a set of *Oaten-touds*." [1]

"What do you mean?" inquired Douglas, as soon as the voluble Abigail allowed him an opportunity of asking.

"Why, my meaning, sir, is to leave this here place immediately; not that I have any objections either to my Lady or you, sir; but, to be sure, it was a sad day for me that I engaged myself to her Ladyship. Little did I think that a lady of distinction would be coming to such a poor pitiful place as this. I am

[1] Hottentots.

sure I thought I should ha' swooned when I was showed the hole where I was to sleep."

At the bare idea of this indignity to her person the fury of the incensed fair one blazed forth with such strength as to choke her utterance.

Amazement had hitherto kept Lady Juliana silent; for to such scenes she was a stranger. Born in an elevated rank, reared in state, accustomed to the most obsequious attention, and never approached but with the respect due rather to a *divinity* than to a mortal, the strain of vulgar insolence that now assailed her was no less new to her ears than shocking to her feelings. With a voice and look that awed the woman into obedience, she commanded her to quit her presence for ever; and then, no longer able to suppress the emotions of insulted pride, wounded vanity, and indignant disappointment, she gave way to a violent fit of hysterics.

In the utmost perplexity the unfortunate husband by turns cursed the hour that had given him such a wife; now tried to soothe her into composure; but at length, seriously alarmed at the increasing attack, he called loudly for assistance.

In a moment the three aunts and the five sisters all rushed together into the room, full of wonder, exclamation, and inquiry. Many were the remedies that were tried and the experiments that were suggested; and at length the violence of passion exhausted itself, and a faint sob or deep sigh succeeded the hysteric scream.

Douglas now attempted to account for the behaviour

of his noble spouse by ascribing it to the fatigue she
had lately undergone, joined to distress of mind at
her father's unrelenting severity towards her.

"Oh, the amiable creature!" interrupted the un-
suspecting spinsters, almost stifling her with their
caresses as they spoke : "Welcome, a thousand times
welcome, to Glenfern Castle," said Miss Jacky, who
was esteemed by much the most sensible woman, as
well as the greatest orator in the whole parish;
"nothing shall be wanting, dearest Lady Juliana, to
compensate for a parent's rigour, and make you happy
and comfortable. Consider this as your future home!
My sisters and myself will be as mothers to you; and
see these charming young creatures," dragging forward two tall frightened girls, with sandy hair and
great purple arms; "thank Providence for having
blest you with such sisters!" "Don't speak too
much, Jacky, to our dear niece at present," said Miss
Grizzy; "I think one of Lady Maclaughlan's composing draughts would be the best thing for her."

"Composing draughts at this time of day!" cried
Miss Nicky; "I should think a little good broth a
much wiser thing. There are some excellent family
broth making below, and I'll desire Tibby to bring
a few."

"Will you take a little soup, love?" asked Douglas.
His lady assented; and Miss Nicky vanished, but
quickly re-entered, followed by Tibby, carrying a huge
bowl of coarse broth, swimming with leeks, greens,
and grease. Lady Juliana attempted to taste it; but

her delicate palate revolted at the homely fare; and she gave up the attempt, in spite of Miss Nicky's earnest entreaties to take a few more of these excellent family broth.

"I should think," said Henry, as he vainly attempted to stir it round, "that a little wine would be more to the purpose than this stuff."

The aunts looked at each other; and, withdrawing to a corner, a whispering consultation took place, in which Lady Maclaughlan's opinion, "birch, balm, currant, heating, cooling, running risks," etc. etc., transpired. At length the question was carried; and some tolerable sherry and a piece of very substantial *shortbread* were produced.

It was now voted by Miss Jacky, and carried *nem. con.* that her Ladyship ought to take a little repose till the hour of dinner.

"And don't trouble to dress," continued the considerate aunt, "for we are not very dressy here; and we are to be quite a charming family party, nobody but ourselves; and," turning to her nephew, "your brother and his wife. She is a most superior woman, though she has rather too many of her English prejudices yet to be all we could wish; but I have no doubt, when she has lived a little longer amongst us, she will just become one of ourselves."

"I forget who she was," said Douglas.

"A grand-daughter of Sir Duncan Malcolm's, a very old family of the ——— blood, and nearly allied to the present Earl. And here they come," exclaimed she, on hearing the sound of a carriage; and all rushed out to receive them.

"Let us have a glimpse of this scion from a noble stock," said Lady Juliana, mimicking the accent of the poor spinsters, as she rose and ran to the window.

"Good heavens, Henry! do come and behold this equipage;" and she laughed with childish glee as she pointed to a plain, old-fashioned whisky, with a large top. A tall handsome young man now alighted, and lifted out a female figure, so enveloped in a cloak that eyes less penetrating than Lady Juliana's could not, at a single glance, have discovered her to be a "frightful quiz."

"Only conceive the effect of this dashing equipage in Bond Street!" continued she, redoubling her mirth at the bright idea; then suddenly stopping, and sighing—"Ah, my pretty *vis-à-vis!* I remember the first time I saw you, Henry, I was in it at a review;" and she sighed still deeper.

"True; I was then aid-de-camp to your handsome lover, the Duke of L——."

"Perhaps I might think him handsome now. People's tastes alter according to circumstances."

"Yours must have undergone a wonderful revolution, if you can find charms in a hunchback of fifty-three."

"He is not a hunchback," returned her Ladyship warmly; "only a little high shouldered; but at any-rate he has the most beautiful place and the finest house in England."

Douglas saw the storm gathering on the brow of his capricious wife, and clasping her in his arms, "Are you indeed so changed, my Julia, that you have forgot the time when you used to declare you would prefer a desert with your Henry to a throne with another."

"No, certainly, not changed; but—I—I did not very well know then what a desert was; or, at least, I had formed rather a different idea of it."

"What was your idea of a desert?" said her husband, laughing. "Do tell me, love."

"Oh! I had fancied it a beautiful place, full of roses and myrtles, and smooth green turf, and murmuring rivulets, and, though very retired, not absolutely out of the world; where one could occasionally see one's friends, and give *dejeunés et fêtes champêtres.*"

"Well, perhaps the time may come, Juliana, when we may realise your Elysian deserts; but at present, you know, I am wholly dependent on my father. I hope to prevail on him to do something for me; and that our stay here will be short; as, you may be sure, the moment I can, I will take you hence. I am sensible it is not a situation for you; but for my sake, dearest Juliana, bear with it for a while, without betraying your disgust. Will you do this, darling?" and he kissed away the sullen tear that hung on her cheek.

"You know, love, there's nothing in the world I wouldn't do for you," replied she, as she played with her squirrel; "and as you promise our stay shall be short, if I don't die of the horrors I shall certainly try to make the agreeable. Oh! my cherub!" flying to her pug, who came barking into the room, "where have you been, and where's my darling Psyche, and sweet mackaw? Do, Harry, go and see after the darlings."

"I must go and see my brother and his wife first. Will you come, love?"

"Oh, not now; I don't feel equal to the encounter; besides, I must dress. But what shall I do? Since that vile woman's gone I can't dress myself. I never did such a thing in my life, and I am sure it's impossible that I can," almost weeping at the hardships she was doomed to experience in making her own toilet.

"Shall I be your Abigail?" asked her husband, smiling at the distress; "methinks it would be no difficult task to deck my Julia."

"Dear Harry, will you really dress me? Oh! that will be delightful! I shall die with laughing at your awkwardness;" and her beautiful eyes sparkled with childish delight at the idea.

"In the meantime," said Douglas, "I'll send some one to unpack your things; and after I have shook hands with Archie, and been introduced to my new sister, I shall enter on my office."

"Now do, pray, make haste; for I die to see your great hands tying strings and sticking pins."

Delighted with her gaiety and good humour, he left her caressing her favourites; and finding rather a scarcity of female attendance, he despatched two of his sisters to assist his helpless beauty in her arrangements.

CHAPTER IV.

" And ever against eating cares,
Lap me in soft Lydian airs."

L'Allegro.

WHEN Douglas returned he found the floor strewed with dresses of every description, his sisters on their knees before a great trunk they were busied in un-packing, and his Lady in her wrapper, with her hair about her ears, still amusing herself with her pets.

"See how good your sisters are," said she, pointing to the poor girls, whose inflamed faces bore testimony to their labours. "I declare I am quite sorry to see them take so much trouble," yawning as she leant back in her chair; "is it not quite shocking, Tommy?" kissing her squirrel. "Oh! pray, Henry, do tell me what I am to put on; for I protest I don't know. Favolle always used to choose for me; and so did that odious Martin, for she had an exquisite taste."

"Not so exquisite as your own, I am sure; so for once choose for yourself," replied the good-humoured husband; "and pray make haste, for my father waits dinner."

Betwixt scolding, laughing, and blundering, the dress was at length completed; and Lady Juliana, in all the pomp of dress and pride of beauty, descended, leaning on her husband's arm.

On entering the drawing-room, which was now in a more comfortable state, Douglas led her to a lady who was sitting by the fire : and, placing her hand within that of the stranger, "Juliana, my love," said he, "this is a sister whom you have not yet seen, and with whom I am sure you will gladly make acquaintance."

The stranger received her noble sister with graceful ease ; and, with a sweet smile and pleasing accent, expressed herself happy in the introduction. Lady Juliana was surprised and somewhat disconcerted. She had arranged her plans, and made up her mind to be *condescending ;* she had resolved to enchant by her sweetness, dazzle by her brilliancy, and overpower by her affability. But there was a simple dignity in the air and address of the lady, before which even high-bred affectation sank abashed. Before she found a reply to the courteous yet respectful salutation of her sister-in-law Douglas introduced his brother ; and the old gentleman, impatient at any farther delay, taking Lady Juliana by the hand, pulled, rather than led her into the dining-room.

Even Lady Juliana contrived to make a meal of the roast mutton and moorfowl ; for the Laird piqued himself on the breed of his sheep, and his son was too good a sportsman to allow his friends to want for game.

"I think my darling Tommy would relish this

grouse very much," observed Lady Juliana, as she
secured the last remaining wing for her favourite.
"Bring him here!" turning to the tall, dashing lackey
who stood behind her chair, and whose handsome
livery and well-dressed hair formed a striking contrast to old Donald's tartan jacket and bob-wig.

"Come hither, my sweetest cherubs," extending
her arms towards the charming trio, as they entered,
barking, and chattering, and flying to their mistress.
A scene of noise and nonsense ensued.

Douglas remained silent, mortified and provoked
at the weakness of his wife, which not even the silver
tones of her voice or the elegance of her manners
could longer conceal from him. But still there was a
charm in her very folly, to the eye of love, which had
not yet wholly lost its power.

After the table was cleared, observing that he was
still silent and abstracted, Lady Juliana turned to her
husband, and, laying her hand on his shoulder, "You
are not well, love!" said she, looking up in his face,
and shaking back the redundant ringlets that shaded
her own.

"Perfectly so," replied her husband, with a sigh.

"What? dull? Then I must sing to enliven you."

And, leaning her head on his shoulder, she warbled
a verse of the beautiful little Venetian air, *La Bion-
dina in Gondoletta*. Then suddenly stopping, and
fixing her eyes on Mrs. Douglas, "I beg pardon,
perhaps you don't like music; perhaps my singing's a
bore."

"You pay us a bad compliment in saying so," said her sister-in-law, smiling; "and the only atonement you can make for such an injurious doubt is to proceed."

"Does anybody sing here?" asked she, without noticing this request. "Do, somebody, sing me a song."

"Oh! we all sing, and dance too," said one of the old young ladies; "and after tea we will show you some of our Scotch steps; but in the meantime Mrs. Douglas will favour us with her song."

Mrs. Douglas assented good-humouredly, though aware that it would be rather a nice point to please all parties in the choice of a song. The Laird reckoned all foreign music—*i.e.* everything that was not Scotch—an outrage upon his ears; and Mrs. Douglas had too much taste to murder Scotch songs with her English accent. She therefore compromised the matter as well as she could by selecting a Highland ditty clothed in her own native tongue; and sang with much pathos and simplicity the lamented Leyden's "Fall of Macgregor:"

> "In the vale of Glenorchy the night breeze was sighing
> O'er the tomb where the ancient Macgregors are lying;
> Green are their graves by their soft murmuring river,
> But the name of Macgregor has perished for ever.

> "On a red stream of light, by his gray mountains glancing,
> Soon I beheld a dim spirit advancing;
> Slow o'er the heath of the dead was its motion,
> Like the shadow of mist o'er the foam of the ocean.

" Like the sound of a stream through the still evening dying,—
   Stranger ! who treads where Macgregor is lying ?
   Darest thou to walk, unappall'd and firm-hearted,
   'Mid the shadowy steps of the mighty departed ?

" See ! round thee the caves of the dead are disclosing
   The shades that have long been in silence reposing ;
   Thro' their forms dimly twinkles the moon-beam descending,
   As upon thee their red eyes of wrath they are bending.

" Our gray stones of fame though the heath-blossom cover,
   Round the fields of our battles our spirits still hover ;
   Where we oft saw the streams running red from the moun-
     tains ;
   But dark are our forms by our blue native fountains.

" For our fame melts away like the foam of the river,
   Like the last yellow leaves on the oak-boughs that shiver :
   The name is unknown of our fathers so gallant ;
   And our blood beats no more in the breasts of the valiant.

" The hunter of red deer now ceases to number
   The lonely gray stones on the field of our slumber.—
   Fly, stranger ! and let not thine eye be reverted ;
   Why should'st thou see that our fame is departed ?"

"Pray, do you play on the harp?" asked the volatile lady, scarcely waiting till the first stanza was
ended ; "and, *apropos*, have you a good harp here?"

We've a very sweet spinnet," said Miss Jacky,
"which, in my opinion, is a far superior instrument :
and Bella will give us a tune upon it. Bella, my dear,
let Lady Juliana hear how well you can play."

Bella, blushing like a peony rose, retired to a
corner of the room, where stood the spinnet ; and with
great, heavy, trembling hands, began to belabour the
unfortunate instrument, while the aunts beat time,

and encouraged her to proceed with exclamations of admiration and applause.

"You have done very well, Bella," said Mrs. Douglas, seeing her preparing to *execute* another piece, and pitying the poor girl, as well as her auditors. Then whispering Miss Jacky that Lady Juliana looked fatigued, they arose to quit the room.

"Give me your arm, love, to the drawing-room," said her Ladyship languidly. "And now, pray, don't be long away," continued she, as he placed her on the sofa, and returned to the gentlemen.

CHAPTER V.

" You have displaced the mirth, broke the good meeting,
  With most admired disorder."

Macbeth.

THE interval, which seemed of endless duration to
the hapless Lady Juliana, was passed by the aunts in
giving sage counsel as to the course of life to be
pursued by married ladies. Worsted stockings and
quilted petticoats were insisted upon as indispensable
articles of dress; while it was plainly insinuated that
it was utterly impossible any child could be healthy
whose mother had not confined her wishes to barley
broth and oatmeal porridge.

"Only look at thae young lambs," said Miss Grizzy,
pointing to the five great girls; "see what picketrs
of health they are! I'm sure I hope, my dear niece,
your children will be just the same—only boys, for
we are sadly in want of boys. It's melancholy to
think we have not a boy among us, and that a fine
auntient race like ours should be dying away for want
of male heirs." And the tears streamed down the
cheeks of the good spinster as she spoke.

The entrance of the gentlemen put a stop to the
conversation.

Flying to her husband, Lady Juliana began to

whisper, in very audible tones, her inquiries, whether he had yet got any money—when they were to go away, etc. etc.

"Does your Ladyship choose any tea?" asked Miss Nicky, as she disseminated the little cups of coarse black liquid.

"Tea! oh no, I never drink tea. I'll take some coffee though; and Psyche doats on a dish of tea." And she tendered the beverage that had been intended for herself to her favourite.

"Here's no coffee," said Douglas, surveying the tea-table; "but I will ring for some," as he pulled the bell.

Old Donald answered the summons.

"Where's the coffee?" demanded Miss Nicky.

"The coffee!" repeated the Highlander; "troth, Miss Nicky, an' it's been clean forgot."

"Well, but you can get it yet?" said Douglas.

"'Deed, Maister Harry, the night's owre far gane for't noo; for the fire's a' ta'en up, ye see," reckoning with his fingers, as he proceeded; "there's parritch makin' for oor supper; and there's patatees boiling for the beasts; and—— "

"I'll see about it myself," said Miss Nicky, leaving the room, with old Donald at her back, muttering all the way.

The old Laird, all this while, had been enjoying his evening nap; but, that now ended, and the tea equipage being dismissed, starting up, he asked what they were about, that the dancing was not begun.

"Come, my Leddy, we'll set the example," snapping his fingers, and singing in a hoarse voice,

> " The mouse is a merry beastie,
>   And the moudiwort wants the een ;
> But folk sall ne'er get wit,
>   Sae merry as we twa ha'e been.'

"But whar's the girlies?" cried he. "Ho! Belle, Becky, Betty, Baby, Beeny—to your posts!"

The young ladies, eager for the delights of music and dancing, now entered, followed by Coil, the piper, dressed in the native garb, with cheeks seemingly ready blown for the occasion. After a little strutting and puffing, the pipes were fairly set agoing in Coil's most spirited manner. But vain would be the attempt to describe Lady Juliana's horror and amazement at the hideous sounds that for the first time assailed her ear. Tearing herself from the grasp of the old gentleman, who was just setting off in the reel, she flew shrieking to her husband, and threw herself trembling into his arms, while he called loudly to the self-delighted Coil to stop.

"What's the matter? what's the matter?" cried the whole family, gathering round.

"Matter!" repeated Douglas furiously; "you have frightened Lady Juliana to death with your infernal music. What did you mean," turning fiercely to the astonished piper, "by blowing that confounded bladder?"

Poor Coil gaped with astonishment; for never

before had his performance on the bagpipe been heard
but with admiration and applause.

"A bonny bargain, indeed, that canna stand the
pipes," said the old gentleman, as he went puffing up
and down the room. "She's no the wife for a Heeland-
man. Confoonded blather, indeed! By my faith,
ye're no blate!"

"I declare it's the most distressing thing I ever
met with," sighed Miss Grizzy. "I wonder whether
it could be the sight or the sound of the bagpipe that
frightened our dear niece. I wish to goodness Lady
Maclaughlan was here!"

"It's impossible the bagpipe could frighten anybody," said Miss Jacky, in a high key; "nobody
with common sense could be frightened at a bagpipe."

Mrs. Douglas here mildly interposed, and soothed
down the offended pride of the Highlanders by attri-
buting Lady Juliana's agitation entirely to *surprise*.
The word operated like a charm; all were ready to
admit that it was a surprising thing when heard for the
first time. Miss Jacky remarked that we are all liable
to be surprised; and the still more sapient Grizzy said
that, indeed, it was most surprising the effect that
surprise had upon some people. For her own part,
she could not deny but that she was very often
frightened when she was surprised.

Douglas, meanwhile, was employed in soothing the
terrors, real or affected, of his delicate bride, who
declared herself so exhausted with the fatigue she

had undergone, and the sufferings she had endured, that she must retire for the night. Henry, eager to escape from the questions and remarks of his family, gladly availed himself of the same excuse; and, to the infinite mortification of both aunts and nieces, the ball was broken up.

CHAPTER VI.

" What choice to choose for delicacy best."

MILTON.

OF what nature were the remarks passed in the parlour upon the new married couple has not reached the writer of these memoirs with as much exactness as the foregoing circumstances; but they may in part be imagined from the sketch already given of the characters which formed the Glenfern party. The conciliatory indulgence of Mrs. Douglas, when aided by the good-natured Miss Grizzy, doubtless had a favourable effect on the irritated pride but short-lived acrimony of the old gentleman. Certain it is that, before the evening concluded, they appeared all restored to harmony, and retired to their respective chambers in hopes of beholding a more propitious morrow.

Who has not perused sonnets, odes, and speeches in praise of that balmy blessing sleep; from the divine effusions of Shakespeare down to the drowsy notes of newspaper poets?

Yet cannot too much be said in its commendation. Sweet is its influence on the careworn eyes to tears

accustomed. In its arms the statesman forgets his
harassed thoughts; the weary and the poor are blessed
with its charms; and conscience—even conscience—
is sometimes soothed into silence, while the sufferer
sleeps. But nowhere, perhaps, is its influence more
happily felt than in the heart oppressed by the har-
assing accumulation of petty ills; like a troop of
locusts, making up by their number and their stings
what they want in magnitude.

Mortified pride in discovering the fallacy of our
own judgment; to be ashamed of what we love, yet
still to love, are feelings most unpleasant; and though
they assume not the dignity of deep distress, yet
philosophy has scarce any power to soothe their
worrying, incessant annoyance. Douglas was glad to
forget himself in sleep. He had thought a vast deal
that day, and of unpleasant subjects, more than the
whole of his foregoing life would have produced. If
he did not curse the fair object of his imprudence,
he at least cursed his own folly and himself; and
these were his last waking thoughts.

But Douglas could not repose as long as the seven
sleepers, and, in consequence of having retired sooner
to bed than he was accustomed to do, he waked at an
early hour in the morning.

The wonderful activity which people sometimes
feel when they have little to do with their bodies, and
less with their minds, caused him to rise hastily and
dress, hoping to pick up a new set of ideas by virtue
of his locomotive powers.

On descending to the dining-parlour he found his father seated at the window, carefully perusing a pamphlet written to illustrate the principle, *Let nothing be lost*, and containing many sage and erudite directions for the composition and dimensions of that ornament to a gentleman's farmyard, and a cottager's front door, ycleped, in the language of the country, a *midden*—with the signification of which we would not, for the world, shock the more refined feelings of our southern readers.

Many were the inquiries about dear Lady Juliana ; hoped she had rested well ; hoped they found the bed comfortable, etc. etc.   These inquiries were interrupted by the Laird, who requested his son to take a turn with him while breakfast was getting ready, that they might talk over past events and new plans ; that he might see the new planting on the hill ; the draining of the great moss ; with other agricultural concerns which we shall omit, not having the same power of commanding attention for our readers as the Laird had from his hearers.

After repeated summonses and many inquiries from the impatient party already assembled round the breakfast table, Lady Juliana made her appearance, accompanied by her favourites, whom no persuasions of her husband could prevail upon her to leave behind.

As she entered the room her olfactory nerves were smote with gales, not of " Araby the blest," but of old cheese and herrings, with which the hospitable board was amply provided.

The ladies having severally exchanged the salutations of the morning, Miss Nicky commenced the operation of pouring out tea, while the Laird laid a large piece of herring on her Ladyship's plate.

"Good heavens! what am I to do with this?" exclaimed she. "Do take it away, or I shall faint!"

"Brother, brother!" cried Miss Grizzy in a tone of alarm, "I beg you won't place any unpleasant object before the eyes of our dear niece. I declare! Pray, was it the sight or the smell of the beast[1] that shocked you so much, my dear Lady Juliana? I'm sure I wish to goodness Lady Maclaughlan was come!"

Mr. Douglas, or the Major, as he was styled, immediately rose and pulled the bell.

"Desire my gig to be got ready directly!" said he.

The aunts drew up stiffly, and looked at each other without speaking; but the old gentleman expressed his surprise that his son should think of leaving them so soon.

"May we inquire the reason of this sudden resolution?" at length said Miss Jacky in a tone of stifled indignation.

"Certainly, if you are disposed to hear it; it is because I find that there is company expected."

The three ladies turned up their hands and eyes in speechless horror.

---

[1] In Scotland everything that flies and swims ranks in the bestial tribe.

"Is it that virtuous woman Lady Maclaughlan you would shun, nephew?" demanded Miss Jacky.

"It is that insufferable woman I would shun," replied her nephew, with a heightened colour and a violence very unusual with him.

The good Miss Grizzy drew out her pocket-hand-kerchief, while Mrs. Douglas vainly endeavoured to silence her husband, and avert the rising storm.

"Dear Douglas!" whispered his wife in a tone of reproach.

"Oh, pray let him go on," said Miss Jacky, almost choking under the effort she made to appear calm. "Let him go on. Lady Maclaughlan's character, luckily, is far above the reach of calumny; nothing that Mr. Archibald Douglas can say will have power to change our opinions, or, I hope, to prejudice his brother and Lady Juliana against this most exemplary, virtuous woman—a woman of family—of fortune—of talents—of accomplishments; a woman of unblemished reputation—of the strictest morals, sweetest temper, charming heart, delightful spirits, so charitable—every year gives fifty flannel petticoats to the old people of the parish——"

"Then such a wife as she is!" sobbed out Miss Grizzy. "She has invented I don't know how many different medicines for Sir Sampson's complaint, and makes a point of his taking some of them every day; but for her I'm sure he would have been in his grave long ago."

"She's doing all she can to send him there, as

she has done many a poor wretch already, with her infernal compositions."

Here Miss Grizzy sank back in her chair, overcome with horror; and Miss Nicky let fall the teapot, the scalding contents of which discharged themselves upon the unfortunate Psyche, whose yells, mingling with the screams of its fair mistress, for a while drowned even Miss Jacky's oratory.

"Oh, what shall I do?" cried Lady Juliana, as she bent over her favourite. "Do send for a surgeon; pray, Henry, fly! Do fetch one directly, or she will die; and it would quite kill me to lose my darling. Do run, dearest Harry!"

"My dear Julia, how can you be so absurd? There's no surgeon within twenty miles of this."

"No surgeon within twenty miles!" exclaimed she, starting up. "How could you bring me to such a place? Good God! those dear creatures may die—I may die myself—before I can get any assistance!"

"Don't be alarmed, my dearest niece," said the good Miss Grizzy; "we are all doctors here. I understand something of physic myself; and our friend Lady Maclaughlan, who, I daresay, will be here presently, is perfect mistress of every disease of the human frame."

"Clap a cauld potatae to the brute's tae," cried the old Laird gruffly.

"I've a box of her scald ointment that will cure it in a minute."

"If it don't cure, it will kill," said Mr. Douglas, with a smile.

"Brother," said Miss Jacky, rising with dignity from her chair, and waving her hand as she spoke— "brother, I appeal to you to protect the character of this most amiable, respectable matron from the insults and calumny your son thinks proper to load it with. Sir Sampson Maclaughlan is your friend, and it therefore becomes your duty to defend his wife."

"Troth, but I'll hae aneugh to do if I am to stand up for a' my friends' wives," said the old gentleman. "But, however, Archie, you are to blame : Leddy Maclaughlan is a very decent woman—at least, as far as I ken—though she is a little free in the gab ; and out of respect to my auld friend Sir Sampson, it is my desire that you should remain here to receive him, and that you trait baith him and his Lady discreetly."

This was said in too serious a tone to be disputed, and his son was obliged to submit.

The ointment meanwhile having been applied to Psyche's paw, peace was restored, and breakfast recommenced.

"I declare our dear niece has not tasted a morsel," observed Miss Nicky.

"Bless me, here's charming barley meal scones," cried one, thrusting a plateful of them before her. "Here's tempting pease bannocks," interposed another, "and oat cakes. I'm sure your Ladyship never saw such cakes."

"I can't eat any of those things," said their delicate niece, with an air of disgust. "I should like some muffin and chocolate."

"You forget you are not in London, my love," said her husband reproachfully.

"No indeed, I do not forget it. Well then, give me some toast," with an air of languid condescension.

"Unfortunately, we happen be quite out of loaf bread at present," said Miss Nicky; "but we've sent to Drymsine for some. They bake excellent bread at Drymsine."

"Is there nothing within the bounds of possibility you would fancy, Julia?" asked Douglas. "Do think, love."

"I think I should like some grouse, or a beef-steak, if it was very nicely done," returned her Lady-ship in a languishing tone.

"Beef-steak!" repeated Miss Grizzy.

"Beef-steak!" responded Miss Jacky.

"Beef-steak!" reverberated Miss Nicky.

After much deliberation and consultation amongst the three spinsters, it was at length unanimously carried that the Lady's whim should be indulged.

"Only think, sisters," observed Miss Grizzy in an undertone, "what reflections we should have to make upon ourselves if the child was to resemble a moor-fowl!"

"Or have a face like a raw beef-steak!" said Miss Nicky.

These arguments were unanswerable; and a smoking steak and plump moor-fowl were quickly produced, of which Lady Juliana partook in company with her four-footed favourites.

CHAPTER VII.

" When winter soaks the fields, and female feet—
    Too weak to struggle with tenacious clay,
    Or ford the rivulets—are best at home."
                                            The Tusk.

THE meal being at length concluded, Glenfern desired Henry to attend him on a walk, as he wished to have a little more private conversation with him. Lady Juliana was beginning a remonstrance against the cruelty of taking Harry away from her, when her husband whispering her that he hoped to make something of the old gentleman, and that he should soon be back, she suffered him to depart in silence.

Old Donald having at length succeeded in clearing the table of its heterogeneous banquet, it was quickly covered with the young ladies' work.

Miss Nicky withdrew to her household affairs. Miss Jacky sat with one eye upon Lady Juliana, the other upon her five nieces. Miss Grizzy seated herself by her Ladyship, holding a spread letter of Lady Maclaughlan's before her as a screen.

While the young ladies busily plied their needles, the elder ones left no means untried to entertain their listless niece, whose only replies were exclamations of weariness, or expressions of affection bestowed upon her favourites.

At length even Miss Jacky's sense and Miss Grizzy's good nature were *at fault;* when a ray of sunshine darting into the room suggested the idea of a walk. The proposal was made, and assented to by her Ladyship, in the twofold hope of meeting her husband and pleasing her dogs, whose whining and scratching had for some time testified their desire of a change. The ladies therefore separated to prepare for their *sortie*, after many recommendations from the aunts to be sure to *hap*[1] well; but, as if distrusting her powers in that way, they speedily equipped themselves, and repaired to her chamber, arrayed *cap-à-pie* in the walking costume of Glenfern Castle. And, indeed, it must be owned their style of dress was infinitely more judicious than that of their fashionable niece; and it was not surprising that they, in their shrunk duffle greatcoats, vast poke-bonnets, red worsted neck-cloths, and pattens, should gaze with horror at her lace cap, lilac satin pelisse, and silk shoes. Ruin to the whole race of Glenfern, present and future, seemed inevitable from such a display of extravagance and imprudence. Having surmounted the first shock, Miss Jacky made a violent effort to subdue her rising wrath; and, with a sort of convulsive smile, addressed Lady Juliana: "Your Ladyship, I perceive, is not of the opinion of our inimitable bard, who, in his charming poem, 'The Seasons,' says 'Beauty needs not the

_____
[1] Wrap.

foreign aid of ornament; but is, when unadorned, adorned the most.' That is a truth that ought to be impressed on every young woman's mind."

Lady Juliana only stared. She was as little accustomed to be advised as she was to hear Thomson's "Seasons" quoted.

"I declare that's all quite true," said the more temporising Grizzy; "and certainly our girls are not in the least taken up about their dress, poor things! which is a great comfort. At the same time, I'm sure it's no wonder your Ladyship should be taken up about yours, for certainly that pelisse is most beautiful. Nobody can deny that; and I daresay it is the very newest fashion. At the same time, I'm just afraid that it's rather too delicate, and that it might perhaps get a little dirty on our roads; for although, in general, our roads are quite remarkable for being always dry, which is a great comfort in the country, yet you know the very best roads of course must be wet sometimes. And there's a very bad step just at the door almost, which Glenfern has been always speaking about getting mended. But, to be sure, he has so many things to think about that it's no wonder he forgets sometimes; but I daresay he will get it done very soon now."

The prospect of the road being mended produced no better effect than the quotation from Thomson's "Seasons." It was now Miss Nicky's turn.

"I'm afraid your Ladyship will frighten our stirks and stots with your finery. I assure you they are not accustomed to see such fine figures; and"—putting her hand out at the window—"I think it's spitting already."[1]

All three now joined in the chorus, beseeching Lady Juliana to put on something warmer and more wiselike.

"I positively have nothing," cried she, wearied with their importunities, "and I shan't get any winter things now till I return to town. My *roquelaire* does very well for the carriage."

The acknowledgment at the beginning of this speech was enough. All three instantly disappeared like the genii of Aladin's lamp, and, like that same person, presently returned, loaded with what, in their eyes, were precious as the gold of Arabia. One displayed a hard worsted shawl, with a flower-pot at each corner; another held up a tartan cloak, with a hood; and a third thrust forward a dark cloth Joseph, lined with flannel; while one and all showered down a variety of old bonnets, fur tippets, hair soles, clogs, pattens, and endless *et ceteras*. Lady Juliana shrank with disgust from these "delightful haps," and resisted all attempts to have them forced upon her, declaring, in a manner which showed her determined to have her own way, that she would either go out as she was or not go out at all. The aunts were therefore obliged to submit, and the party proceeded to what was termed the high road, though a stranger would have sought in vain for its pretensions to that

---

[1] A common expression in Scotland to signify slight rain.

title. Far as the eye could reach—and that was far
enough—not a single vehicle could be descried on it,
though its deep ruts showed that it was well frequented
by carts. The scenery might have had charms for
Ossian, but it had none for Lady Juliana, who would
rather have been entangled in a string of Bond Street
equipages than traversing "the lonely heath, with
the stream murmuring hoarsely, the old trees groan-
ing in the wind, the troubled lake," and the still more
troubled sisters. As may be supposed, she very soon
grew weary of the walk. The bleak wind pierced
her to the soul; her silk slippers and lace flounces
became undistinguishable masses of mud; her dogs
chased the sheep, and were, in their turn, pursued by
the "nowts," as the ladies termed the steers. One
sister expatiated on the great blessing of having a
peat moss at their door; another was at pains to
point out the purposed site of a set of new offices;
and the third lamented that her Ladyship had not on
thicker shoes, that she might have gone and seen the
garden. More than ever disgusted and wretched, the
hapless Lady Juliana returned to the house to fret
away the time till her husband's return.

CHAPTER VIII.

"On se rend insupportable dans la société par des défauts légers, mais qui se font sentir à tout moment."—VOLTAIRE.

THE family of Glenfern have already said so much for themselves that it seems as if little remained to be told by their biographer. Mrs. Douglas was the only member of the community who was at all conscious of the unfortunate association of characters and habits that had just taken place. She was a stranger to Lady Juliana; but she was interested by her youth, beauty, and elegance, and felt for the sacrifice she had made—a sacrifice so much greater than it was possible she ever could have conceived or anticipated. She could in some degree enter into the nature of her feelings towards the old ladies; for she too had felt how disagreeable people might contrive to render themselves without being guilty of any particular fault, and how much more difficult it is to bear with the weaknesses than the vices of our neighbours. Had these ladies' failings been greater in a moral point of view, it might not have been so arduous a task to put up with them. But to love such a set of little, trifling, tormenting foibles, all dignified with the name of virtues, required, from her elegant mind, an exertion of its highest principles—a continual remembrance of that difficult Christian precept, "to bear with one another." A person of less sense than Mrs. Douglas would have endeavoured to open the eyes of their understandings on what appeared to be the folly and narrowmindedness of their ways; but she refrained from the attempt, not from want of benevolent exertion, but from an innate conviction that their foibles all originated in what was now incurable, viz. the natural weakness of their minds, together with their ignorance of the world and the illiberality and prejudices of a vulgar education. "These poor women," reasoned the charitable Mrs. Douglas, "are perhaps, after all, better characters in the sight of God than I am. He who has endowed us all as His wisdom has seen fit, and has placed me amongst them, oh, may He teach me to remember that we are all His children, and enable me to bear with their faults, while I study to correct my own."

Thus did this amiable woman contrive not only to live in peace, but, without sacrificing her own liberal ideas, to be actually beloved by those amongst whom her lot had been cast, however dissimilar to herself. But for that Christian spirit (in which must ever be included a liberal mind and gentle temper), she must have felt towards her connexions a still stronger repugnance than was even manifested by Lady Juliana; for Lady Juliana's superiority over them was merely that of refined habits and elegant

manners ; whereas Mrs. Douglas's was the superiority
of a noble and highly-gifted mind, which could hold
no intercourse with theirs except by stooping to the
level of their low capacities. But, that the merit of
her conduct may be duly appreciated, I shall endeavour to give a slight sketch of the female *dramatis
personæ* of Glenfern Castle.

Miss Jacky, the senior of the trio, was what is
reckoned a very sensible woman—which generally
means, a very disagreeable, obstinate, illiberal director
of all men, women, and children—a sort of superin-
tendent of all actions, time, and place—with unques-
tioned authority to arraign, judge, and condemn upon
the statutes of her own supposed sense. Most country
parishes have their sensible woman, who lays down
the law on all affairs, spiritual and temporal. Miss
Jacky stood unrivalled as the sensible woman of
Glenfern. She had attained this eminence partly
from having a little more understanding than her
sisters, but principally from her dictatorial manner,
and the pompous decisive tone in which she delivered
the most commonplace truths. At home her supremacy
in all matters of sense was perfectly established ; and
thence the infection, like other superstitions, had
spread over the whole neighbourhood. As sensible
woman she regulated the family, which she took care
to let everybody see ; she was conductor of her nieces'
education, which she took care to let everybody hear ;
she was a sort of postmistress general—a detector of
all abuses and impositions ; and deemed it her pre-

rogative to be consulted about all the useful and useless things which everybody else could have done as
well. She was liberal of her advice to the poor,
always enforcing upon them the iniquity of idleness,
but doing nothing for them in the way of employment
—strict economy being one of the many points in which
she was particularly sensible. The consequence was,
while she was lecturing half the poor women in the
parish for their idleness, the bread was kept out of
their mouths by the incessant carding of wool and
knitting of stockings, and spinning, and reeling, and
winding, and pirning, that went on amongst the
ladies themselves. And, by-the-bye, Miss Jacky is
not the only sensible woman who thinks she is acting
a meritorious part when she converts what ought to
be the portion of the poor into the employment of
the affluent.

In short, Miss Jacky was all over sense. A skilful
physiognomist would, at a single glance, have detected
the sensible woman, in the erect head, the compressed
lips, square elbows, and firm judicious step. Even
her very garments seemed to partake of the prevailing
character of their mistress : her ruff always looked
more sensible than any other body's ; her shawl sat
most sensibly on her shoulders ; her walking shoes
were acknowledged to be very sensible ; and she
drew on her gloves with an air of sense, as if the one
arm had been Seneca, the other Socrates. From
what has been said it may easily be inferred that
Miss Jacky was in fact anything but a sensible woman ;

as indeed no woman can be who bears such visible outward marks of what is in reality the most quiet and unostentatious of all good qualities. But there is a spurious sense, which passes equally well with the multitude; it is easily assumed, and still more easily maintained; common truths and a grave dictatorial air being all that is necessary for its support.

Miss Grizzy's character will not admit of so long a commentary as that of her sister. She was merely distinguishable from nothing by her simple good nature, the inextricable entanglement of her thoughts, her love of letter-writing, and her friendship with Lady Maclaughlan. Miss Nicky had about as much sense as Miss Jacky; but, as no kingdom can maintain two kings, so no family can admit of two sensible women; and Nicky was therefore obliged to confine hers to the narrowest possible channels of housekeeping, mantua-making, etc., and to sit down for life (or at least till Miss Jacky should be married) with the dubious character of "not wanting for sense either." With all these little peccadilloes the sisters possessed some good properties. They were well-meaning, kind-hearted, and, upon the whole, good-tempered; they loved one another, revered their brother, doated upon their nephews and nieces, took a lively interest in the poorest of their poor cousins, a hundred degrees removed, and had a firm conviction of the perfectibility of human nature, as exemplified in the persons of all their own friends. "Even their failings leaned to virtue's side;" for whatever they did was with the

intention of doing good, though the means they made
use of generally produced an opposite effect. But
there are so many Miss Douglases in the world, that
doubtless every one of my readers is as well acquainted
with them as I am myself. I shall therefore leave
them to finish the picture according to their own
ideas, while I return to the parlour, where the worthy
spinsters are seated in expectation of the arrival of
their friend.

CHAPTER IX.

"Though both
Not equal, as their sex not equal seemed—
For contemplation he, and valour formed;
For softness she, and sweet attractive grace."

MILTON.

"WHAT *can* have come over Lady Maclaughlan?" said Miss Grizzy, as she sat at the window in a dejected attitude.

"I think I hear a carriage at last," cried Miss Jacky, turning up her ears. "Wisht! let us listen."

"It's only the wind," sighed Miss Grizzy.

"It's the cart with the bread," said Miss Nicky.

"It's Lady Maclaughlan, I assure you," pronounced Miss Jacky.

The heavy rumble of a ponderous vehicle now proclaimed the approach of the expected visitor; which pleasing anticipation was soon changed into blissful certainty by the approach of a high-roofed, square-bottomed, pea-green chariot, drawn by two long-tailed white horses, and followed by a lackey in the Highland garb. Out of this equipage issued a figure, clothed in a light-coloured, large-flowered chintz raiment, carefully drawn through the pocket-holes,

either for its own preservation, or the more disinterested purpose of displaying a dark short stuff petticoat,
which, with the same liberality, afforded ample scope
for the survey of a pair of worsted stockings and black
leather shoes, something resembling buckets.   A
faded red cloth jacket, which bore evident marks of
having been severed from its native skirts, now acted
in the capacity of a spencer.   On the head rose a
stupendous fabric, in the form of a cap, on the summit
of which was placed a black beaver hat, tied *à la pois-
sarde.*   A small black satin muff in one hand, and a
gold-headed walking-stick in the other, completed the
dress and decoration of this personage.

The lackey, meanwhile, advanced to the carriage;
and, putting in both his hands, as if to catch something, he pulled forth a small bundle, enveloped in a
military cloak, the contents of which would have baffled
conjecture, but for the large cocked hat and little
booted leg which protruded at opposite extremities.

A loud but slow and well-modulated voice now
resounded through the narrow stone passage that conducted to the drawing-room.

"Bring him in—bring him in, Philistine!   I
always call my man Philistine, because he has Sampson in his hands.   Set him down there," pointing to
an easy chair, as the group now entered, headed by
Lady Maclaughlan.

"Well, girls!" addressing the venerable spinsters,
as they severally exchanged a tender salute; "so
you're all alive, I see;—humph!"

"Dear Lady Maclaughlan, allow me to introduce our beloved niece, Lady Juliana Douglas," said Miss Grizzy, leading her up, and bridling as she spoke with ill-suppressed exultation.

"So—you're very pretty—yes, you are very pretty!" kissing the forehead, cheeks, and chin of the youthful beauty between every pause. Then, holding her at arm's length, she surveyed her from head to foot, with elevated brows, and a broad fixed stare.

"Pray sit down, Lady Maclaughlan," cried her three friends all at once, each tendering a chair.

"Sit down!" repeated she; "why, what should I sit down for? I choose to stand—I don't like to sit —I never sit at home—do I, Sir Sampson?" turning to the little warrior, who, having been seized with a violent fit of coughing on his entrance, had now sunk back, seemingly quite exhausted, while the *Philistine* was endeavouring to disencumber him of his military accoutrements.

"How very distressing Sir Sampson's cough is!" said the sympathising Miss Grizzy.

"Distressing, child! No—it's not the least distressing. How can a thing be distressing that does no harm? He's much the better of it—it's the only exercise he gets."

"Oh! well, indeed, if that's the case, it would be a thousand pities to stop it," replied the accommodating spinster.

"No, it wouldn't be the least pity to stop it!"

returned Lady Maclaughlan, in her loud authoritative tone; "because, though it's not distressing, it's very disagreeable. But it cannot be stopped—you might as well talk of stopping the wind—it is a cradle cough."

"My dear Lady Maclaughlan!" screamed Sir Sampson in a shrill pipe, as he made an effort to raise himself, and rescue his cough from this aspersion; "how can you persist in saying so, when I have told you so often it proceeds entirely from a cold caught a few years ago, when I attended his Majesty at——" Here a violent relapse carried the conclusion of the sentence along with it.

"Let him alone—don't meddle with him," called his lady to the assiduous nymphs who were bustling around him; "leave him to Philistine; he's in very good hands when he is in Philistine's." Then resting her chin upon the head of her stick, she resumed her scrutiny of Lady Juliana.

"You really are a pretty creature! You've got a very handsome nose, and your mouth's very well, but I don't like your eyes; they're too large and too light; they're saucer eyes, and I don't like saucer eyes. Why ha'nt you black eyes? You're not a bit like you're father—I knew him very well. Your mother was an heiress; your father married her for her money, and she married him to be a Countess; and so that's the history of their marriage—humph."

This well-bred harangue was delivered in an unvarying tone, and with unmoved muscles; for though the lady seldom failed of calling forth some conspicuous emotion, either of shame, mirth, or anger, on the countenances of her hearers, she had never been known to betray any correspondent feelings on her own ; yet her features were finely formed, marked, and expressive ; and, in spite of her ridiculous dress and eccentric manners, an air of dignity was diffused over her whole person, that screened her from the ridicule to which she must otherwise have been exposed. Amazement at the uncouth garb and singular address of Lady Maclaughlan was seldom unmixed with terror at the stern imperious manner that accompanied all her actions. Such were the feelings of Lady Juliana as she remained subjected to her rude gaze and impertinent remarks.

"My Lady !" squeaked Sir Sampson from forth his easy chair.

"My love ?" interrogated his lady as she leant upon her stick.

"I want to be introduced to my Lady Juliana Douglas ; so give me your hand," attempting, at the same time, to emerge from the huge leathern receptacle into which he had been plunged by the care of the kind sisters.

"Oh, pray sit still, dear Sir Sampson," cried they as usual all at once ; "our sweet niece will come to you, don't take the trouble to rise ; pray don't," each putting a hand on this man of might, as he was half risen, and pushing him down.

"Ay, come here, my dear," said Lady Maclaughlan ;

"you're abler to walk to Sir Sampson than he to you,"
pulling Lady Juliana in front of the easy chair;
"there—that's her; you see she is very pretty."

"Zounds, what is the meaning of all this?" screamed
the enraged baronet. "My Lady Juliana Douglas, I
am shocked beyond expression at this freedom of my
lady's. I beg your ladyship ten thousand pardons;
pray be seated. I'm shocked; I am ready to faint at
the impropriety of this introduction, so contrary to
all rules of etiquette. How *could* you behave in such
a manner, my Lady Maclaughlan?"

"Why, you know, my dear, your legs may be very
good legs, but they can't walk," replied she, with her
usual *sang froid.*

"My Lady Maclaughlan, you perfectly confound
me," stuttering with rage. "My Lady Juliana
Douglas, see here," stretching out a meagre shank, to
which not even the military boot and large spur could
give a respectable appearance: "You see that leg
strong and straight," stroking it down; "now, behold the fate of war!" dragging forward the other,
which was shrunk and shrivelled to almost one half
its original dimensions. "These legs were once the
same; but I repine not—I sacrificed it in a noble
cause: to that leg my Sovereign owes his life!"

"Well, I declare, I had no idea; I thought always
it had been rheumatism," burst from the lips of the
astonished spinsters, as they crowded round the illustrious limb, and regarded it with looks of veneration.

"Humph!" emphatically uttered his lady.

"The story's a simple one, ladies, and soon told: I happened to be attending his Majesty at a review; I was then aid-de-camp to Lord ——. His horse took fright, I—I—I,"—here, in spite of all the efforts that could be made to suppress it, the *royal cough* burst forth with a violence that threatened to silence its brave owner for ever.

"It's very strange you will talk, my love," said his sympathising lady, as she supported him; "talking never did, nor never will agree with you; it's very strange what pleasure people take in talking—humph!"

"Is there anything dear Sir Sampson could take?" asked Miss Grizzy.

"*Could* take? I don't know what you mean by *could* take. He couldn't take the moon, if you mean that; but he must take what I give him; so call Philistine; he knows where my cough tincture is."

"Oh, we have plenty of it in this press," said Miss Grizzy, flying to a cupboard, and, drawing forth a bottle, she poured out a bumper, and presented it to Sir Sampson.

"I'm poisoned!" gasped he feebly; "that's not my lady's cough-tincture."

"Not cough-tincture!" repeated the horror-struck doctress, as for the first time she examined the label; "Oh! I declare, neither it is—it's my own stomach lotion. Bless me, what will be done?" and she wrung her hands in despair. "Oh, Murdoch," flying to the *Philistine*, as he entered with the real cough-tincture,

"I've given Sir Sampson a dose of my own stomach lotion by mistake, and I am terrified for the consequences!"

"Oo, but hur need na be feared, hur will no be a hair the war o't; for hurs wad na tak' the feesick that the leddie ordered hur yestreen."

"Well, I declare things are wisely ordered," observed Miss Grizzy; "in that case it may do dear Sir Sampson a great deal of good."

Just as this pleasing idea was suggested, Douglas and his father entered, and the ceremony of presenting her nephew to her friend was performed by Miss Grizzy in her most conciliating manner.

"Dear Lady Maclaughlan, this is our nephew Henry, who, I know, has the highest veneration for Sir Sampson and you. Henry, I assure you, Lady Maclaughlan takes the greatest interest in everything that concerns Lady Juliana and you."

"Humph!" rejoined her ladyship, as she surveyed him from head to foot. "So your wife fell in love with you, it seems; well, the more fool she; I never knew any good come of love marriages."

Douglas coloured, while he affected to laugh at this extraordinary address, and withdrawing himself from her scrutiny, resumed his station by the side of his Juliana.

"Now, girls, I must go to my toilet; which of you am I to have for my handmaid?"

"Oh, we'll all go," eagerly exclaimed the three nymphs; "our dear niece will excuse us for a little;

young people are never at a loss to amuse one another."

"Venus and the Graces, by Jove!" exclaimed Sir Sampson, bowing with an air of gallantry; "and now I must go and adonise a little myself."

The company then separated to perform the important offices of the toilet.

CHAPTER X.

" Nature here
Wanton'd as in her prime, and played at will
Her virgin fancies."

MILTON.

THE gentlemen were already assembled round the drawing-room fire, impatiently waiting the hour of dinner, when Lady Maclaughlan and her three friends entered. The masculine habiliments of the morning had been exchanged for a more feminine costume. She was now arrayed in a pompadour satin *négligée*, and petticoat trimmed with Brussels lace. A high starched handkerchief formed a complete breastwork, on which, amid a large bouquet of truly artificial roses, reposed a miniature of Sir Sampson, *à la militaire*. A small fly cap of antique lace was scarcely perceptible on the summit of a stupendous frizzled toupee, hemmed in on each side by large curls. The muff and stick had been relinquished for a large fan, something resembling an Indian screen, which she waved to and fro in one hand, while a vast brocaded workbag was suspended from the other.

"So, Major Douglas, your servant," said she, in answer to the constrained formal bow with which he saluted her on her entrance. "Why, it's so long since I've seen you that you may be a grandfather for ought I know."

The poor awkward Misses at that moment came sneaking into the room: "As for you, girls, you'll never be grandmothers; you'll never be married, unless to wild men of the woods. I suppose you'd like that; it would save you the trouble of combing your hair, and tying your shoes, for then you could go without clothes altogether—humph! You'd be much better without clothes than to put them on as you do," seizing upon the luckless Miss Baby, as she endeavoured to steal behind backs.

And here, in justice to the lady, it must be owned that, for once, she had some grounds for animadversion in the dress and appearance of the Misses Douglas.

They had stayed out, running races and riding on a pony, until near the dinner hour; and, dreading their father's displeasure should they be too late, they had, with the utmost haste, exchanged their thick morning dresses for thin muslin gowns, made by a mantuamaker of the neighbourhood in the extreme of a two-year-old fashion, when waists *were not*.

But as dame Nature had been particularly lavish in the length of theirs, and the staymaker had, according to their aunt's direction, given them *full measure* of their new dark stays, there existed a visible breach between the waists of their gowns and the bands of their petticoats, which they had vainly sought to adjust by a meeting. Their hair had been curled, but not combed, and dark gloves had been hastily drawn on to hide red arms.

"I suppose," continued the stern Lady Maclaughlan, as she twirled her victim round and round; "I suppose you think yourself vastly smart and well dressed. Yes, you are very neat, very neat indeed; one would suppose Ben Jonson had you in his eye when he composed that song." Then in a voice like thunder, she chanted forth—

> " Give me a look, give me a face
> That makes simplicity a grace ;
> Robes loosely flowing, hair as free,
> Such sweet neglect more taketh me."

Miss Grizzy was in the utmost perplexity between her inclination to urge something in extenuation for the poor girls, and her fear of dissenting from Lady Maclaughlan, or rather of not immediately agreeing with her; she therefore steered, as usual, the middle course, and kept saying, "Well, children, really what Lady Maclaughlan says is all very true; at the same time"—turning to her friend—"I declare it's not much to be wondered at; young people are so thoughtless, poor lambs !"

"What's aw this wark aboot?" said the old gentleman angrily; "the girlies are weel eneugh; I see naething the matter wi' them; they're no dressed like auld queens or stage-actresses;" and he glanced his eye from Lady Maclaughlan to his elegant daughter-in-law, who just then entered, hanging, according to custom, on her husband, and preceded by Cupid.

Mrs. Douglas followed, and the sound of the dinner bell put a stop to the dispute.

"Come, my leddie, we'll see how the dinner's dressed," said the Laird, as he seized Lady Maclaughlan by the tip of the finger, and holding it up aloft, they marched into the dining-room.

"Permit me, my Lady Juliana Douglas," said the little Baronet, with much difficulty hobbling towards her, and attempting to take her hand. "Come, Harry, love; here, Cupid," cried she; and without noticing the enraged Sir Sampson, she passed on, humming a tune, and leaning upon her husband.

"Astonishing! perfectly astonishing!" exclaimed the Baronet; "how a young woman of Lady Juliana's rank and fashion should be guilty of such a solecism in good breeding."

"She is very young," said Mrs. Douglas, smiling, as he limped along with her, "and you must make allowances for her; but, indeed, I think her beauty must ever be a sufficient excuse for any little errors she may commit with a person of such taste and gallantry as Sir Sampson Maclaughlan."

The little Baronet smiled, pressed the hand he held; and, soothed by the well-timed compliment, he seated himself next to Lady Juliana with some complacency. As she insisted on having her husband on the other side of her, Mr. Douglas was condemned to take his station by the hated Lady Maclaughlan, who, for the first time observing Mrs. Douglas, called to her—

"Come here, my love; I haven't seen you these hundred years;" then seizing her face between her hands, she saluted her in the usual style. "There," at length releasing Mrs. Douglas from her gripe—"there's for you! I love you very much; you're neither a fool nor a hoyden; you're a fine intelligent being."

Having carefully rolled up and deposited her gloves in her pocket, she pulled out a pin-cushion, and calling Miss Bella, desired her to pin her napkin over her shoulders; which done, she began to devour her soup in silence.

Peace was, however, of short duration. Old Donald, in removing a dish of whipt cream, unfortunately overturned one upon Lady Maclaughlan's pompadour satin petticoat—the only part of her dress that was unprotected.

"Do you see what you have done, you old Donald, you?" cried she, seizing the culprit by the sleeve; "why, you've got St. Vitus's dance. A fit hand to carry whipt cream, to be sure! Why, I could as well carry a custard on the point of a bayonet—humph!"

"Dear me, Donald, how could you be so senseless?" cried Miss Jacky.

"Preserve me, Donald, I thought you had more sense!" squeaked Miss Nicky.

"I am sure, Donald, that was na like you!" said Miss Grizzy, as the friends all flocked around the petticoat, each suggesting a different remedy.

"It's all of you, girls, that this has happened.

Why can't you have a larger tablecloth upon your table! And that old man has the palsy. Why don't you electrify him?" in a tone admirably calculated to have that effect.

"I declare, it's all very true," observed Miss Grizzy; "the tablecloth *is* very small, and Donald certainly *does* shake, that cannot be denied;" but, lowering her voice, "he is so obstinate, we really don't know what to do with him. My sisters and I attempted to use the flesh-brush with him."

"Oh, and an excellent thing it is; I make Philistine rub Sir Sampson every morning and night. If it was not for that and his cough, nobody would know whether he were dead or alive; I don't believe he would know himself—humph!"

Sir Sampson's lemon face assumed an orange hue as he overheard this domestic detail; but not daring to contradict the facts, he prudently turned a deaf ear to them, and attempted to carry on a flirtation with Lady Juliana through the medium of Cupid, whom he had coaxed upon his knee.

Dinner being at length ended, toasts succeeded: and each of the ladies having given her favourite laird, the signal of retreat was given, and a general movement took place.

Lady Juliana, throwing herself upon a sofa with her pugs, called Mrs. Douglas to her. "Do sit down here and talk with me," yawned she.

Her sister-in-law, with great good-humour, fetched her work, and seated herself by the spoilt child.

"What strange thing is that you are making?" asked she, as Mrs. Douglas pulled out her knitting.

"It's a child's stocking," replied her sister-in-law.

"A child's stocking! Oh, by-the-bye, have you a great many children?"

"I have none," answered Mrs. Douglas, with a half-stifled sigh.

"None at all?" repeated Lady Juliana, with surprise; "then, why do you make children's stockings?"

"I make them for those whose parents cannot afford to purchase them."

"La! what poor wretches they must be, that can't afford to buy stockings," rejoined Lady Juliana, with a yawn. "It's monstrous good of you to make them, to be sure; but it must be a shocking bore! and such a trouble!" and another long yawn succeeded.

"Not half such a bore to me as to sit idle," returned Mrs. Douglas, with a smile, "nor near so much trouble as you undergo with your favourites."

Lady Juliana made no reply, but turning from her sister-in-law, soon was, or affected to be, sound asleep, from which she was only roused by the entrance of the gentlemen. "A rubber or a reel, my Leddie?" asked the Laird, going up to his daughter-in-law.

"Julia, love," said her husband, "my father asks you if you choose cards or dancing."

"There's nobody to dance with," said she, casting a languid glance around; "I'll play at cards."

"Not whist, surely!" said Henry.

"Whist! Oh, heavens, no."

"Weel, weel, you youngsters will get a round game; come, my Leddy Maclaughlan, Grizzy, Mrs. Douglas, hey for the odd trick and the honours!"

"What would your Ladyship choose to play at?" asked Miss Jacky, advancing with a pack of cards in one hand, and a box of counters in the other.

"Oh, anything; I like loo very well, or quadrille, or—I really don't care what."

The Misses, who had gathered round, and were standing gaping in joyful expectation of Pope Joan, or a pool at commerce, here exchanged sorrowful glances.

"I am afraid the young people don't play these games," replied Miss Jacky; "but we've counters enough," shaking her little box, "for Pope Joan, and we all know that."

"Pope Joan! I never heard of such a game," replied Lady Juliana.

"Oh, we can soon learn you," said Miss Nicky, who having spread the green cloth on the tea-table, now advanced to join the consultation.

"I hate to be taught," said Lady Juliana, with a yawn; "besides, I am sure it must be something very stupid."

"Ask if she plays commerce," whispered Miss Bella to Miss Baby.

The question was put, but with no better success, and the young ladies' faces again bespoke their disappointment, which their brother observing, he good-naturedly declared his perfect knowledge of commerce;

"and I must insist upon teaching you, Juliana," gently dragging her to the table.

"What's the pool to be?" asked one of the young ladies.

"I'm sure I don't know," said the aunts, looking to each other.

"I suppose we must make it sixpence," said Miss Jacky, after a whispering consultation with her sister.

"In that case we can afford nothing to the best hand," observed Miss Nicky.

"And we ought to have five lives and grace," added one of the nieces.

These points having been conceded, the preliminaries were at length settled. The cards were slowly *doled* out by Miss Jacky; and Lady Juliana was carefully instructed in the rules of the game, and strongly recommended always to try for a sequence, or pairs, etc. "And if you win," rejoined Miss Nicky, shaking the snuffer-stand in which were deposited the sixpences, "you get all this."

As may be conjectured, Lady Juliana's patience could not survive more than one life; she had no notion of playing for sixpences, and could not be at the trouble to attend to any instructions; she therefore quickly retired in disgust, leaving the aunts and nieces to struggle for the glorious prize. "My dear child, you played that last stroke like a perfect natural," cried Lady Maclaughlan to Miss Grizzy, as, the rubber ended, they arose from the table.

"Indeed, I declare, I daresay I did," replied her friend in a deprecating tone.

"Daresay you did! I know you did—humph! I knew the ace lay with you; I knew that as well as if I had seen it. I suppose you have eyes—but I don't know; if you have, didn't you see Glenfern turn up the king, and yet you returned his lead—returned your adversary's lead in the face of his king. I've been telling you these twenty years not to return your adversary's lead; nothing can be more despicable; nothing can be a greater proof of imbecility of mind—humph!" Then, seating herself, she began to exercise her fan with considerable activity. "This has been the most disagreeable day I ever spent in this house, girls. I don't know what's come over you, but you are all wrong; my petticoat's ruined; my pockets picked at cards. It won't do, girls; it won't do—humph!"

"I am sure I can't understand it," said Miss Grizzy in a rueful accent; "there really appears to have been some fatality."

"Fatality!—humph! I wish you would give everything its right name. What do you mean by fatality?"

"I declare—I am sure—I—I really don't know," stammered the unfortunate Grizzy.

"Do you mean that the spilling of the custard was the work of an angel?" demanded her unrelenting friend.

"Oh, certainly not."

"Or that it was the devil tempted you to throw

away your ace there? I suppose there's a fatality in
our going to supper just now," continued she, as her
deep-toned voice resounded through the passage that
conducted to the dining-room; "and I suppose it will
be called a fatality if that old Fate," pointing to
Donald, "scalds me to death with that mess of porridge he's going to put on the table—humph !"

No such fatality, however, occurred; and the rest
of the evening passed off in as much harmony as could
be expected from the very heterogeneous parts of which
the society was formed.

The family group had already assembled round the
breakfast-table, with the exception of Lady Juliana,
who chose to take that meal in bed; but, contrary to
her usual custom, no Lady Maclaughlan had yet made
her appearance.

"The scones will be like leather," said Miss Grizzy,
as she wrapped another napkin round them.

"The eggs will be like snowballs," cried Miss
Jacky, popping them into the slop-basin.

"The tea will be like brandy," observed Miss
Nicky, as she poured more water to the three tea-
spoonfuls she had infused.

"I wish we saw our breakfast," said the Laird, as
he finished the newspapers, and deposited his spectacles in his pocket.

At that moment the door opened, and the person
in question entered in her travelling dress, followed
by Sir Sampson, Philistine bringing up the rear with
a large green bag and a little band-box.

"I hope your bed was warm and comfortable. I hope you rested well. I hope Sir Sampson's quite well!" immediately burst as if from a thousand voices, while the sisters officiously fluttered round their friend.

"I rested very ill; my bed was very uncomfortable; and Sir Sampson's as sick as a cat—humph!"

Three disconsolate "Bless me's!" here burst forth.

"Perhaps your bed was too hard?" said Miss Grizzy.

"Or too soft?" suggested Miss Jacky.

"Or too hot?" added Miss Nicky.

"It was neither too hard, nor too soft, nor too hot, nor too cold," thundered the Lady, as she seated herself at the table; "but it was all of them."

"I declare, that's most distressing," said Miss Grizzy, in a tone of sorrowful amazement. "Was your head high enough, dear Lady Maclaughlan?"

"Perhaps it was too high," said Miss Jacky.

"I know nothing more disagreeable than a high head," remarked Miss Nicky.

"Except a fool's head—humph!"

The sound of a carriage here set all ears on full stretch, and presently the well-known pea-green drew up.

"Dear me! Bless me! Goodness me!" shrieked the three ladies at once. "Surely, Lady Maclaughlan, you can't—you don't—you won't; this must be a mistake."

"There's no mistake in the matter, girls," replied their friend, with her accustomed *sang froid*. "I'm

going home; so I ordered the carriage; that's all—
humph!"

"Going home!" faintly murmured the disconsolate
spinsters.

"What! I suppose you think I ought to stay here
and have another petticoat spoiled; or lose another
half-crown at cards; or have the finishing stroke put
to Sir Sampson—humph!"

"Oh! Lady Maclaughlan!" was three times uttered
in reproachful accents.

"I don't know what else I should stay for; you
are not yourselves, girls; you've all turned topsy-turvy.
I've visited here these twenty years, and I never saw
things in the state they are now—humph!"

"I declare it's very true," sighed Miss Grizzy;
"we certainly are a little in confusion, that can't be
denied."

"Denied! Why, can you deny that my petticoat's
ruined? Can you deny that my pocket was picked
of half-a-crown for nothing? Can you deny that Sir
Sampson has been half-poisoned? and——"

"My Lady Maclaughlan," interrupted the enraged
husband, "I—I—I am surprised—I am shocked!
Zounds, my Lady, I won't suffer this! I cannot stand
it;" and pushing his tea-cup away, he arose, and
limped to the window. Philistine here entered to
inform his mistress that "awthing was ready."
"Steady, boys, steady! I always am ready," responded the Lady in a tone adapted to the song.
"Now I am ready; say nothing, girls—you know my

rules. Here, Philistine, wrap up Sir Sampson, and put him in. Get along, my love. Good-bye, girls; and I hope you will all be restored to your right senses soon."

"Oh, Lady Maclaughlan!" whined the weeping Grizzy, as she embraced her friend, who, somewhat melted at the signs of her distress, bawled out from the carriage, as the door was shut, "Well, God bless you, girls, and make you what you have been; and come to Lochmarlie Castle soon, and bring your wits along with you."

The carriage then drove off, and the three disconsolate sisters returned to the parlour to hold a cabinet council as to the causes of the late disasters.

CHAPTER XI.

"If there be cure or charm
To respite or relieve, or slack the pain
Of this ill mansion."
MILTON.

TIME, which generally alleviates ordinary distresses, served only to augment the severity of Lady Juliana's, as day after day rolled heavily on, and found her still an inmate of Glenfern Castle. Destitute of every resource in herself, she yet turned with contempt from the scanty sources of occupation or amusement that were suggested by others; and Mrs. Douglas's attempts to teach her to play at chess and read Shakespeare were as unsuccessful as the endeavours of the good aunts to persuade her to study Fordyce's Sermons and make baby linen.

In languid dejection or fretful repinings did the unhappy beauty therefore consume the tedious hours, while her husband sought alternately to soothe with fondness he no longer felt, or flatter with hopes which he knew to be groundless. To his father alone could he now look for any assistance, and from him he was not likely to obtain it in the form he desired; as the old gentleman repeatedly declared his utter inability to advance him any ready money, or to allow him more than a hundred a year—moreover, to be paid quarterly—a sum which could not defray their expenses to London.

Such was the state of affairs when the Laird one morning entered the dining-room with a face of much importance, and addressed his son with, "Weel, Harry, you're a lucky man; and it's an ill wind that blaws naebody gude : here's puir Macglashan gane like snaw aff a dyke."

"Macglashan gone !" exclaimed Miss Grizzy. "Impossible, brother; it was only yesterday I sent him a blister for his back !"

"And I," said Miss Jacky, "talked to him for upwards of two hours last night on the impropriety of his allowing his daughter to wear white gowns on Sunday."

"By my troth, an' that was eneugh to kill ony man," muttered the Laird.

"How I am to derive any benefit from this important demise is more than I can perceive," said Henry in a somewhat contemptuous tone.

"You see," replied his father, "that by our agreement his farm falls vacant in consequence."

"And I hope I am to succeed to it?" replied the son, with a smile of derision.

"Exactly! By my faith, but you have a bein downset. There's three thousand and seventy-five acres of as good sheepwalk as any in the whole country-side; and I shall advance you stocking and

stedding, and everything complete, to your very peat-
stacks. What think ye of that?" slapping his son's
shoulder, and rubbing his own hands with delight as
he spoke.

Horrorstruck at a scheme which appeared to him
a thousand times worse than anything his imagination
had ever painted, poor Henry stood in speechless
consternation; while "Charming! Excellent! Delightful!" was echoed by the aunts, as they crowded
round, wishing him joy, and applauding their brother's
generosity.

"What will our sweet niece say to this, I wonder?"
said the innocent Grizzy, who in truth wondered none.
"I would like to see her face when she hears it;" and
her own was puckered into various shapes of delight.

"I have no doubt but her good sense will teach
her to appreciate properly the blessings of her lot,"
observed the more reflecting Jacky.

"She has had her own good luck," quoth the
sententious Nicky, "to find such a downset all cut
and dry."

At that instant the door opened, and the favoured
individual in question entered. In vain Douglas
strove to impose silence on his father and aunts. The
latter sat, bursting with impatience to break out into
exclamation, while the former, advancing to his fair
daughter-in-law, saluted her as "Lady Clackandow?"
Then the torrent burst forth, and, stupefied with surprise, Lady Juliana suffered herself to be kissed and
hugged by the whole host of aunts and nieces, while

the very walls seemed to reverberate the shouts, and the pugs and mackaw, who never failed to take part in every commotion, began to bark and scream in chorus.

The old gentleman, clapping his hands to his ears, rushed out of the room. His son, cursing his aunts, and everything around him, kicked Cupid, and gave the mackaw a box on the ear, as he also quitted the apartment, with more appearance of anger than he had ever yet betrayed.

The tumult at length began to subside. The mackaw's screams gave place to a low quivering croak; and the insulted pug's yells yielded to a gentle whine. The aunts' obstreperous joy began to be chastened with fear for the consequences that might follow an abrupt disclosure; and, while Lady Juliana condoled with her favourites, it was concerted between the prudent aunts that the joyful news should be broke to their niece in the most cautious manner possible. For that purpose Misses Grizzy and Jacky seated themselves on each side of her; and, after duly preparing their voices by sundry small hems, Miss Grizzy thus began:

"I'm sure—I declare—I dare say, my dear Lady Juliana, you must think we are all distracted."

Her auditor made no attempt to contradict the supposition.

"We certainly ought, to be sure, to have been more cautious, considering your delicate situation; but the joy—though, indeed, it seems cruel to say so.

And I am sure you will sympathise, my dear niece, in the cause, when you hear that it is occasioned by our poor neighbour Macglashan's death, which, I'm sure, was quite unexpected. Indeed, I declare I can't conceive how it came about; for Lady Maclaughlan, who is an excellent judge of these things, thought he was really a remarkably stout-looking man for his time of life; and indeed, except occasional colds, which you know we are all subject to, I really never knew him complain. At the same time——"

"I don't think, sister, you are taking the right method of communicating the intelligence to our niece," said Miss Jacky.

"You cannot communicate anything that would give me the least pleasure, unless you could tell me that I was going to leave this place," cried Lady Juliana in a voice of deep despondency.

"Indeed! if it can afford your Ladyship so much pleasure to be at liberty to quit the hospitable mansion of your amiable husband's respectable father," said Miss Jacky, with an inflamed visage and outspread hands, "you are at perfect liberty to depart when you think proper. The generosity, I may say the munificence, of my excellent brother, has now put it in your power to do as you please, and to form your own plans."

"Oh, delightful!" exclaimed Lady Juliana, starting up; "now I shall be quite happy. Where's Harry? Does he know? Is he gone to order the carriage? Can we get away to-day?" And she was flying out

of the room when Miss Jacky caught her by one
hand, while Miss Grizzy secured the other.

"Oh, pray don't detain me! I must find Harry;
and I have all my things to put up," struggling to
release herself from the gripe of the sisters; when the
door opened, and Harry entered, eager, yet dreading
to know the effects of the *éclaircissement*. His surprise
extreme at beholding his wife, with her eyes sparkling, her cheeks glowing, and her whole countenance
expressing extreme pleasure. Darting from her
keepers, she bounded towards him with the wildest
ejaculations of delight; while he stood alternately
gazing at her and his aunts, seeking by his eyes the
explanation he feared to demand.

"My dearest Juliana, what is the meaning of all
this?" he at length articulated.

"Oh, you cunning thing! So you think I don't
know that your father has given you a great, great
quantity of money, and that we may go away whenever
we please, and do just as we like, and live in London,
and—and—oh, delightful!" And she bounded and
skipped before the eyes of the petrified spinsters.

"In the name of heaven, what does all this mean?"
asked Henry, addressing his aunts, who, for the first
time in their lives, were struck dumb by astonishment.
But Miss Jacky, at length recollecting herself, turned
to Lady Juliana, who was still testifying her delight
by a variety of childish but graceful movements, and
thus addressed her:

"Permit me to put a few questions to your Ladyship, in presence of those who were witnesses of what has already passed."

"Oh, I can't endure to be asked questions; besides, I have no time to answer them."

"Your Ladyship must excuse me; but I can't permit you to leave this room under the influence of an error. Have the goodness to answer me the following questions, and you will then be at liberty to depart. Did I inform your Ladyship that my brother had given my nephew a great quantity of money?"

"Oh yes! a great, great deal; I don't know how much, though——"

"Did I?" returned her interrogator.

"Come, come, have done with all this confounded nonsense!" exclaimed Henry passionately. "Do you imagine I will allow Lady Juliana to stand here all day, to answer all the absurd questions that come into the heads of three old women? You stupefy and bewilder her with your eternal tattling and roundabout harangues." And he paced the room in a paroxysm of rage, while his wife suspended her dancing, and stood in breathless amazement.

"I declare—I'm sure—it's a thousand pities that there should have been any mistake made," whined poor Miss Grizzy.

"The only remedy is to explain the matter quickly," observed Miss Nicky; "better late than never."

"I have done," said Miss Jacky, seating herself with much dignity.

"The short and the long of it is this," said Miss

Nicky, "My brother has not made Henry a present
of money. I assure you money is not so rife; but
he has done what is much better for you both,—he
has made over to him that fine thriving farm of poor
Macglashan's."

"No money!" repeated Lady Juliana in a disconsolate tone: then quickly brightening up, "It would
have been better, to be sure, to have had the money
directly; but you know we can easily sell the estate.
How long will it take?—a week?"

"Sell Clackandow!" exclaimed the three horror-struck daughters of the house of Douglas. "Sell
Clackandow! Oh! oh! oh!"

"What else could we do with it?" inquired her
Ladyship.

"Live at it, to be sure," cried all three.

"Live at it!" repeated she, with a shriek of horror
that vied with that of the spinsters—"Live at it!
Live on a thriving farm! Live all my life in such a
place as this! Oh! the very thought is enough to
kill me!"

"There is no occasion to think or say any more
about it," interrupted Henry in a calmer tone; and,
glancing round on his aunts, "I therefore desire no
more may be said on the subject."

"And is this really all? And have you got no
money? And are we not going away?" gasped the
disappointed Lady Juliana, as she gave way to a
violent burst of tears, that terminated in a fit of
hysterics; at sight of which, the good spinsters

entirely forgot their wrath; and while one burnt
feathers under her nose, and another held her hands,
a third drenched her in floods of Lady Maclaughlan's
hysteric water.   After going through the regular
routine, the lady's paroxsym subsided; and being
carried to bed, she soon sobbed herself into a feverish
slumber; in which state the harassed husband left
her to attend a summons from his father.

CHAPTER XII.

"See what delight in sylvan scenes appear!"

POPE.

"Haply this life is best,
Sweetest to you, well corresponding
With your stiff age; but unto us it is
A cell of ignorance, a prison for a debtor."

Cymbeline.

HE found the old gentleman in no very complaisant humour, from the disturbances that had taken place, but the chief cause of which he was still in ignorance of. He therefore accosted his son with:

"What was the meaning o' aw that skirling and squeeling I heard a while ago? By my faith, there's nae bearing this din! Thae beasts o' your wife's are enugh to drive a body oot o' their judgment. But she maun gi'e up thae maggots when she becomes a farmer's wife. She maun get stirks and stots to mak' pets o', if she maun ha'e *four-fitted* favourites; but, to my mind, it wad set her better to be carrying a wise-like wean in her arms, than trailing aboot wi' thae confoonded dougs an' paurits."

Henry coloured, bit his lips, but made no reply to this elegant address of his father's, who continued, "I sent for you, sir, to have some conversation about

this farm of Macglashan's; so sit down there till I
show you the plans."

Hardly conscious of what he was doing, poor
Henry gazed in silent confusion, as his father pointed
out the various properties of this his future possession.
Wholly occupied in debating within himself how he
was to decline the offer without a downright quarrel,
he heard, without understanding a word, all the old
gentleman's plans and proposals for building dikes,
draining moss, etc.; and, perfectly unconscious of
what he was doing, yielded a ready assent to all the
improvements that were suggested.

"Then as for the hoose and offices,—let me see,"
continued the Laird, as he rolled up the plans of the
farm, and pulled forth that of the dwelling-house
from a bundle of papers. "Ay, here it is. By my
troth, ye'll be weel lodged here. The hoose is in a
manner quite new, for it has never had a brush upon
it yet. And there's a byre—fient a bit, if I would
mean the best man i' the country to sleep there
himsel.'"

A pause followed, during which Glenfern was busily
employed in poring over his parchment; then taking
off his spectacles, and surveying his son, "And now,
sir, that you've heard a' the oots an' ins o' the business, what think you your farm should bring you at
the year's end?"

"I—I—I'm sure—I—I don't know," stammered
poor Henry, awakening from his reverie.

"Come, come, gi'e a guess."

"I really—I cannot—I haven't the least idea."

"I desire, sir, ye'll say something directly, that I may judge whether or no ye ha'e common sense," cried the old gentleman angrily.

"I should suppose—I imagine—I don't suppose it will exceed seven or eight hundred a year," said his son, in the greatest trepidation at this trial of his intellect.

"Seven or eight hunder deevils!" cried the incensed Laird, starting up and pushing his papers from him. "By my faith, I believe ye're a born idiot! Seven or eight hunder pounds!" repeated he, at least a dozen times, as he whisked up and down the little apartment with extraordinary velocity, while poor Henry affected to be busily employed in gathering up the parchments with which the floor was strewed.

"I'll tell you what, sir," continued he, stopping; "you're no fit to manage a farm; you're as ignorant as yon coo, an' as senseless as its cauf. Wi' gude management, Clackandow should produce you twa hunder and odd pounds yearly; but in your guiding I doot if it will yield the half. However, tak' it or want it, mind me, sir, that it's a' ye ha'e to trust to in my lifetime; so ye may mak' the maist o't."

Various and painful were the emotions that struggled in Henry's breast at this declaration. Shame, regret, indignation, all burned within him; but the fear he entertained of his father, and the consciousness of his absolute dependence, chained his tongue, while the bitter emotions that agitated him painted themselves

legibly in his countenance. His father observed his
agitation; and, mistaking the cause, felt somewhat
softened at what he conceived his son's shame and
penitence for his folly. He therefore extended his
hand towards him, saying, "Weel, weel, nae mair
aboot it; Clackandow's yours, as soon as I can put
you in possession. In the meantime, stay still here,
and welcome."

"I—am much obliged to you for the offer, sir; I
—feel very grateful for your kindness," at length
articulated his son; "but—I—am, as you observe, so
perfectly ignorant of country matters, that I—I—in
short, I am afraid I should make a bad hand of the
business."

"Nae doot, nae doot ye would, if ye was left to
your ain discretion; but ye'll get mair sense, and I
shall put ye upon a method, and provide ye wi' a
grieve; an' if you are active, and your wife managing,
there's nae fear o' you."

"But Lady Juliana, sir, has never been accustomed——"

"Let her serve an apprenticeship to your aunts;
she couldna be in a better school."

"But her education, sir, has been so different from
what would be required in that station," resumed her
husband, choking with vexation, at the idea of his
beauteous high-born bride being doomed to the
drudgery of household cares.

"Edication! what has her edication been, to mak'
her different frae other women? If a woman can

nurse her bairns, mak' their claes, and manage her hoose, what mair need she do? If she can play a tune on the spinnet, and dance a reel, and play a rubber at whist—nae doot these are accomplishments, but they're soon learnt. Edication! pooh!—I'll be bound Leddy Jully Anie wull mak' as gude a figure by-and-by as the best edicated woman in the country."

"But she dislikes the country, and——"

"She'll soon come to like it. Wait a wee till she has a wheen bairns, an' a hoose o' her ain, an' I'll be bound she'll be happy as the day's lang."

"But the climate does not agree with her," continued the tender husband, almost driven to extremities by the persevering simplicity of his father.

"Stay a wee till she gets to Clackandow! There's no a finer, freer-aired situation in a' Scotland. The air's sharpish, to be sure, but fine and bracing; and you have a braw peat-moss at your back to keep you warm."

Finding it in vain to attempt *insinuating* his objections to a pastoral life, poor Henry was at length reduced to the necessity of coming to the point with the old gentleman, and telling him plainly that it was not at all suited to his inclinations, or Lady Juliana's rank and beauty.

Vain would be the attempt to paint the fiery wrath and indignation of the ancient Highlander as the naked truth stood revealed before him :—that his son despised the occupation of his fathers, even the feeding of sheep and the breeding of black cattle; and

that his high-born spouse was above fulfilling those
duties which he had ever considered the chief end
for which woman was created. He swore, stamped,
screamed, and even skipped with rage, and, in short,
went through all the evolutions as usually performed
by testy old gentlemen on first discovering that they
have disobedient sons and undutiful daughters. Henry,
who, though uncommonly good-tempered, inherited a
portion of his father's warmth, became at length irritated at the invectives that were so liberally bestowed
on him, and replied in language less respectful than
the old Laird was accustomed to hear; and the altercation became so violent that they parted in mutual
anger; Henry returning to his wife's apartment in a
state of the greatest disquietude he had ever known.
To her childish complaints, and tiresome complaints,
he no longer vouchsafed to reply, but paced the
chamber with a disordered mien, in sullen silence;
till at length, distracted by her reproaches, and disgusted with her selfishness, he rushed from the apartment and quitted the house.

CHAPTER XIII.

" Never talk to me ; I will weep."

As You Like It.

TWICE had the dinner bell been loudly sounded by old Donald, and the family of Glenfern were all assembled, yet their fashionable guests had not appeared. Impatient of delay, Miss Jacky hastened to ascertain the cause. Presently she returned in the utmost perturbation, and announced that Lady Juliana was in bed in a high fever, and Henry nowhere to be found. The whole eight rushed upstairs to ascertain the fact, leaving the old gentleman much discomposed at this unseasonable delay.

Some time elapsed ere they again returned, which they did with lengthened faces, and in extreme perturbation. They had found their noble niece, according to Miss Jacky's report, in bed—according to Miss Grizzy's opinion, in a brain fever; as she no sooner perceived them enter, than she covered her head with the bedclothes, and continued screaming for them to be gone, till they had actually quitted the apartment.

"And what proves beyond a doubt that our sweet niece is not herself," continued poor Miss Grizzy, in a lamentable tone, "is that we appeared to her in every form but our own! She sometimes took us for cats; then thought we were ghosts haunting her; and, in short, it is impossible to tell all the things she called us; and she screams so for Harry to come and take her away that I am sure—I declare—I don't know what's come over her!"

Mrs. Douglas could scarce suppress a smile at the simplicity of the good spinsters. Her husband and she had gone out immediately after breakfast to pay a visit a few miles off, and did not return till near the dinner hour. They were therefore ignorant of all that had been acted during their absence; but as she suspected something was amiss, she requested the rest of the company would proceed to dinner, and leave her to ascertain the nature of Lady Juliana's disorder.

"Don't come near me!" shrieked her Ladyship, on hearing the door open. "Send Harry to take me away; I don't want anybody but Harry!"—and a torrent of tears, sobs, and exclamations followed.

"My dear Lady Juliana," said Mrs. Douglas, softly approaching the bed, "compose yourself; and if my presence is disagreeable to you I shall immediately withdraw."

"Oh, is it you?" cried her sister-in-law, uncovering her face at the sound of her voice. "I thought it had been these frightful old women come to torment me; and I shall die—I know I shall—if ever I look at them again. But I don't dislike *you;* so you may stay if you choose, though I don't want anybody but Harry to come and take me away."

A fresh fit of sobbing here impeded her utterance; and Mrs. Douglas, compassionating her distress, while she despised her folly, seated herself by the bedside, and taking her hand, in the sweetest tone of complacency attempted to soothe her into composure.

"The only way in which you can be less miserable," said Mrs. Douglas in a soothing tone, "is to support your present situation with patience, which you may do by looking forward to brighter prospects. It is *possible* that your stay here may be short; and it is *certain* that it is in your own power to render your life more agreeable by endeavouring to accommodate yourself to the peculiarities of your husband's family. No doubt they are often tiresome and ridiculous; but they are always kind and well-meaning."

"You may say what you please, but I think them all odious creatures; and I won't live here with patience; and I shan't be agreeable to them; and all the talking in the world won't make me less miserable. If you were me, you would be just the same; but you have never been in London—that's the reason."

"Pardon me," replied her sister-in-law, "I spent many years of my life there."

"You lived in London!" repeated Lady Juliana in astonishment. "And how, then, can you contrive to exist here?"

"I not only contrive to exist, but to be extremely contented with existence," said Mrs. Douglas, with a

smile.   Then assuming a more serious air, "I possess
health, peace of mind, and the affections of a worthy
husband; and I should be very undeserving of these
blessings were I to give way to useless regrets or
indulge in impious repinings because my happiness
might once have been more perfect, and still admits
of improvement."

"I don't understand you," said Lady Juliana, with
a peevish yawn.   "Who did you live with in London?"

"With my aunt, Lady Audley."

"With Lady Audley!" repeated her sister-in-law
in accents of astonishment.   "Why, I have heard of
her; she lived quite in the world; and gave balls and
assemblies; so that's the reason you are not so disagreeable as the rest of them.   Why did you not
remain with her, or marry an Englishman?   But I
suppose, like me, you didn't know what Scotland
was!"

Happy to have excited an interest, even through
the medium of childish curiosity, in the bosom of her
fashionable relative, Mrs. Douglas briefly related such
circumstances of her past life as she judged proper
to communicate; but as she sought rather to amuse
than instruct by her simple narrative, we shall allow
her to pursue her charitable intentions, while we
do more justice to her character by introducing her
regularly to the acquaintance of our readers.

History of Mrs. Douglas.

" The selfish heart deserves the pang it feels ;
More generous sorrow, while it sinks, exalts,
And conscious virtue mitigates the pang."

YOUNG.

MRS. DOUGLAS was, on the maternal side, related to
an English family. Her mother had died in giving
birth to her ; and her father, shortly after, falling in
the service of his country, she had been consigned in
infancy to the care of her aunt. Lady Audley had
taken charge of her, on condition that she should
never be claimed by her Scottish relations, for whom
that lady entertained as much aversion as contempt.
A latent feeling of affection for her departed sister,
and a large portion of family pride, had prompted her
wish of becoming the protectress of her orphan niece ;
and, possessed of a high sense of rectitude and honour,
she fulfilled the duty thus voluntarily imposed in a
manner that secured the unshaken gratitude of the
virtuous Alicia.

Lady Audley was a character more esteemed and
feared than loved, even by those with whom she was
most intimate. Firm, upright, and rigid, she exacted
from others those inflexible virtues which in herself

she found no obstacle to performing. Neglecting the softer attractions which shed their benign influence over the commerce of social life, she was content to enjoy the extorted esteem of her associates; for friends she had none. She sought in the world for objects to fill up the void which her heart could not supply. She loved éclat, and had succeeded in creating herself an existence of importance in the circles of high life, which she considered more as due to her consequence than essential to her enjoyment. She had early in life been left a widow, with the sole tutelage and management of an only son, whose large estate she regulated with the most admirable prudence and judgment.

Alicia Malcolm was put under the care of her aunt at two years of age. A governess had been procured for her, whose character was such as not to impair the promising dispositions of her pupil. Alicia was gifted by nature with a warm affectionate heart, and a calm imagination attempered its influence. Her governess, a woman of a strong understanding and enlarged mind, early instilled into her a deep and strong sense of religion; and to it she owed the support which had safely guided her through the most trying vicissitudes.

When at the age of seventeen Alicia Malcolm was produced in the world. She was a rational, cheerful, and sweet-tempered girl, with a finely formed person, and a countenance in which was so clearly painted the sunshine of her breast, that it attracted the *bienveill-*

ance even of those who had not taste or judgment to define the charm. Her open natural manner, blending the frankness of the Scotch with the polished reserve of the English woman, her total exemption from vanity, calculated alike to please others and maintain her own cheerfulness undimmed by a single cloud.

Lady Audley felt for her niece a sentiment which she mistook for affection; her self-approbation was gratified at the contemplation of a being who owed every advantage to her, and whom she had rescued from the coarseness and vulgarity which she deemed inseparable from the manners of every Scotchwoman.

If Lady Audley really loved any human being it was her son. In him were centred her dearest interests; on his aggrandisement and future importance hung her most sanguine hopes. She had acted contrary to the advice of her male relations, and followed her own judgment, by giving her son a private education. He was brought up under her own eye by a tutor of deep erudition, but who was totally unfitted for forming the mind, and compensating for those advantages which may be derived from a public education. The circumstances of his education, however, combined rather to stifle the exposure than to destroy the existence of some very dangerous qualities that seemed inherent in Sir Edmund's nature. He was ardent, impetuous, and passionate, though these propensities were cloaked by a reserve, partly natural, and partly arising from the repelling manners of his mother and tutor.

His was not the effervescence of character which bursts forth on every trivial occasion; but when any powerful cause awakened the slumbering inmates of his breast, they blazed with an uncontrolled fury that defied all opposition, and overleaped all bounds of reason and decorum.

Experience often shows us that minds formed of the most opposite attributes more forcibly attract each other than those which appear cast in the same mould. The source of this fascination is difficult to trace; it possesses not reason for its basis, yet it is perhaps the more tyrannical in its influence from that very cause. The weakness of our natures occasionally makes us feel a potent charm in "errors of a noble mind."

Sir Edmund Audley and Alicia Malcolm proved examples of this observation. The affection of childhood had so gradually ripened into a warmer sentiment, that neither was conscious of the nature of that sentiment till after it had attained strength to cast a material influence on their after lives. The familiarity of near relatives associating constantly together produced a warm sentiment of affection, cemented by similarity of pursuits, and enlivened by diversity of character; while the perfect tranquillity of their lives afforded no event that could withdraw the veil of ignorance from their eyes.

Could a woman of Lady Audley's discernment, it may be asked, place two young persons in such a situation, and doubt the consequences? Those who are no longer young are liable to forget that love is a plant of early growth, and that the individuals that they have but a short time before beheld placing their supreme felicity on a rattle and a go-cart can so soon be actuated by the strongest passions of the human breast.

Sir Edmund completed his nineteenth year, and Alicia entered her eighteenth, when this happy state of unconscious security was destroyed by a circumstance which rent the veil from her eyes, and disclosed his sentiments in all their energy and warmth. This circumstance was no other than a proposal of marriage to Alicia from a gentleman of large fortune and brilliant connexions who resided in their neighbourhood. His character was as little calculated as his appearance to engage the affections of a young woman of delicacy and good sense. But he was a man of consequence; heir to an earldom; member for the county; and Lady Audley, rejoicing at what she termed Alicia's good fortune, determined that she should become his wife.

With mild firmness she rejected the honour intended her; but it was with difficulty that Lady Audley's mind could adopt or understand the idea of an opposition to her wishes. She could not seriously embrace the conviction that Alicia was determined to disobey her; and in order to bring her to a right understanding she underwent a system of persecution that tended naturally to increase the antipathy her suitor had inspired. Lady Audley, with the indiscriminating zeal of prejudiced and overbearing persons,

strove to recommend him to her niece by all those
attributes which were of value in her own eyes;
making allowance for a certain degree of indecision
in her niece, but never admitting a doubt that in due
time her will should be obeyed, as it had always
hitherto been.

At this juncture Sir Edmund came down to the
country, and was struck by the altered looks and
pensive manners of his once cheerful cousin. About
a week after his arrival he found Alicia one morning
in tears, after a long conversation with Lady Audley.
Sir Edmund tenderly soothed her, and entreated to
be made acquainted with the cause of her distress.
She was so habituated to impart every thought to her
cousin, the intimacy and sympathy of their souls were
so entire, that she would not have concealed the late
occurrence from him had she not been withheld by
the natural timidity and delicacy a young woman feels
in making her own conquests the subject of conversation. But now so pathetically and irresistibly per-
suaded by Sir Edmund, and sensible that every distress of hers wounded his heart, Alicia candidly
related to him the pursuit of her disagreeable suitor,
and the importunities of Lady Audley in his favour.
Every word she had spoken had more and more dispelled the mist that had so long hung over Sir
Edmund's inclinations. At the first mention of a
suitor, he had felt that to be hers was a happiness
that comprised all others; and that the idea of losing
her made the whole of existence appear a frightful

blank. These feelings were no sooner known to himself than spontaneously poured into her delighted
ears; while she felt that every sentiment met a
kindred one in her breast. Alicia sought not a
moment to disguise those feelings, which she now, for
the first time, became aware of; they were known to
the object of her innocent affection as soon as to herself, and both were convinced that, though not conscious before of the nature of their sentiments, love
had long been mistaken for friendship in their hearts.

But this state of blissful serenity did not last long.
On the evening of the following day Lady Audley
sent for her to her dressing-room. On entering,
Alicia was panic-struck at her aunt's pale countenance,
fiery eyes, and frame convulsed with passion. With
difficulty Lady Audley, struggling for calmness, demanded an instant and decided reply to the proposals
of Mr. Compton, the gentleman who had solicited
her hand. Alicia entreated her aunt to waive the
subject, as she found it impossible ever to consent to
such a union.

Scarcely was her answer uttered when Lady
Audley's anger burst forth uncontrollably. She accused her niece of the vilest ingratitude in having
seduced her son from the obedience he owed his
mother; of having plotted to ally her base Scotch
blood to the noble blood of the Audleys; and, having
exhausted every opprobrious epithet, she was forced
to stop from want of breath to proceed. As Alicia
listened to the cruel, unfounded reproaches of her

aunt, her spirit rose under the unmerited ill-usage,
but her conscience absolved her from all intention of
injuring or deceiving a human being ; and she calmly
waited till Lady Audley's anger should have exhausted
itself, and then entreated to know what part of her
conduct had excited her aunt's displeasure.

Lady Audley's reply was diffuse and intemperate.
Alicia gathered from it that her rage had its source in
a declaration her son had made to her of his affection
for his cousin, and his resolution of marrying her as
soon as he was of age ; which open avowal of his
sentiments had followed Lady Audley's injunctions to
him to forward the suit of Mr. Compton.

That her son, for whom she had in view one of the
first matches in the kingdom, should dare to choose
for himself ; and, above all, to choose one whom she
considered as much his inferor in birth as she was in
fortune, was a circumstance quite insupportable to her
feelings.

Of the existence of love Lady Audley had little
conception ; and she attributed her son's conduct to
wilful disobedience and obstinacy. In proportion as
she had hitherto found him complying and gentle, her
wrath had kindled at his present firmness and inflexibility. So bitter were her reflections on his conduct,
so severe her animadversions on the being he loved,
that Sir Edmund, fired with resentment, expressed
his resolution of acting according to the dictates of
his own will ; and expressed his contempt for her
authority in terms the most unequivocal. Lady

Audley, ignorant of the arts of persuasion, by every word she uttered more and more widened the breach her imperiousness had occasioned, until Sir Edmund, feeling himself no longer master of his temper, announced his intention of leaving the house, to allow his mother time to reconcile herself to the inevitable misfortune of beholding him the husband of Alicia Malcolm.

He instantly ordered his horses and departed, leaving the following letter for his cousin :—

"I have been compelled by motives of prudence, of which you are the sole object, to depart without seeing you. My absence became necessary from the unexpected conduct of Lady Audley, which has led me so near to forgetting that she was my mother, that I dare not remain, and subject myself to excesses of temper which I might afterwards repent. Two years must elapse before I can become legally my own master, and should Lady Audley so far depart from the dictates of cool judgment as still to oppose what she knows to be inevitable, I fear that we cannot meet till then. My heart is well known to you; therefore I need not enlarge on the pain I feel at this unlooked-for separation. At the same time, I am cheered with the prospect of the unspeakable happiness that awaits me—the possession of your hand; and the confidence I feel in your constancy is in proportion to the certainty I experience in my own; I cannot, therefore, fear that any of the means which

may be put in practice to disunite us will have more
effect on you than on me.

"Looking forward to the moment that shall make
you mine for ever, I remain with steady confidence
and unspeakable affection, your

"EDMUND AUDLEY."

With a trembling frame Alicia handed the note to
Lady Audley, and begged leave to retire for a short
time; expressing her willingness to reply at another
moment to any question her aunt might choose to
put to her with regard to her engagement with Sir
Edmund.

In the solitude of her own chamber Alicia gave
way to those feelings of wretchedness which she had
with difficulty stifled in the presence of Lady Audley,
and bitterly wept over the extinction of her bright
and newly-formed visions of felicity. To yield to
unmerited ill-usage, or to crouch beneath imperious
and self-arrogated power, was not in the nature of
Alicia; and had Lady Audley been a stranger to her,
the path of duty would have been less intricate.
However much her own pride might have been
wounded by entering into a family which considered
her as an intruding beggar, never would she have
consented to sacrifice the virtuous inclinations of the
man she loved to the will of an arrogant and imperious
mother. But alas! the case was far different. The
recent ill-treatment she had experienced from Lady
Audley could not efface from her noble mind the

recollection of benefits conferred from the earliest period of her life, and of unvarying attention to her welfare. To her aunt she owed all but existence: she had wholly supported her; bestowed on her the most liberal education; and from Lady Audley sprang every pleasure she had hitherto enjoyed.

Had she been brought up by her paternal relations, she would in all probability never have beheld her cousin; and the mother and son might have lived in uninterrupted concord. Could she be the person to inflict on Lady Audley the severest disappointment she could experience? The thought was too dreadful to bear; and, knowing that procrastination could but increase her misery, no sooner had she felt convinced of the true nature of her duty than she made a steady resolution to perform and to adhere to it. Lady Audley had *vowed that while she had life she would never give her consent and approbation to her son's marriage;* and Alicia was too well acquainted with her disposition to have the faintest expectation that she would relent.

But to remain any longer under her protection was impossible; and she resolved to anticipate any proposal of that sort from her protectress.

When Lady Audley's passion had somewhat cooled, she again sent for Alicia. She began by repeating her *eternal enmity* to the marriage in a manner impressive to the greatest degree, and still more decisive in its form by the cool collectedness of her manner. She then desired to hear what Alicia had to say in exculpation of her conduct.

The profound sorrow which filled the heart of Alicia left no room for timidity or indecision. She answered her without hesitation and embarrassment, and asserted her innocence of all deceit in such a manner as to leave no doubt at least of honourable proceeding. In a few impressive words she proved herself sensible of the benefits her aunt had through life conferred upon her; and, while she openly professed to think herself, in the present instance, deeply wronged, she declared her determination of never uniting herself to her cousin without Lady Audley's permission, which she felt convinced was unattainable.

She then proceeded to ask where she should deem it most advisable for her to reside in future.

Happy to find her wishes thus prevented, the unfeeling aunt expressed her satisfaction at Alicia's good sense and discretion; represented, in what she thought glowing colours, the unheard-of presumption it would have been in her to take advantage of Sir Edmund's momentary infatuation; and then launched out into details of her ambitious views for him in a matrimonial alliance—views which she affected now to consider without obstacle.

Alicia interrupted the painful and unfeeling harangue. It was neither, she said, for Sir Edmund's advantage nor to gratify his mother's pride, but to perform the dictates of her own conscience, that she had resigned him; she even ventured to declare that the sharpest pang which that resignation had cost her was the firm conviction that it would inflict upon him a deep and lasting sorrow.

Lady Audley, convinced that moderate measures would be most likely to ensure a continuation of Alicia's obedience, expressed herself grieved at the necessity of parting with her, and pleased that she should have the good sense to perceive the propriety of such a separation.

Sir Duncan Malcolm, the grandfather of Alicia, had, in the few communications that had passed between Lady Audley and him, always expressed a wish to see his granddaughter before he died. Her ladyship's antipathy to Scotland was such that she would have deemed it absolute contamination for her niece to have entered the country; and she had therefore always eluded the request.

It was now, of all plans, the most eligible; and she graciously offered to convey her niece as far as Edinburgh. The journey was immediately settled; and before Alicia left her aunt's presence a promise was exacted with unfeeling tenacity, and given with melancholy firmness, never to unite herself to Sir Edmund unsanctioned by his mother.

Alas! how imperfect is human wisdom! Even in seeking to do right how many are the errors we commit! Alicia judged wrong in thus sacrificing the happiness of Sir Edmund to the pride and injustice of his mother; but her error was that of a noble, self-denying spirit, entitled to respect, even though it cannot claim approbation. The honourable open con-

duct of her niece had so far gained upon Lady Audley
that she did not object to her writing to Sir Edmund,
which she did as follows :—

"Dear Sir Edmund—A painful line of conduct
is pointed out to me by duty; yet of all the regrets
I feel not one is so poignant as the consciousness of
that which you will feel at learning that I have for
ever resigned the claims you so lately gave me to your
heart and hand. It was not weakness—it could not
be inconstancy—that produced the painful sacrifice of
a distinction still more gratifying to my heart than
flattering to my pride.

"Need I remind you that to your mother I owe
every benefit in life? Nothing can release me from
the tribute of gratitude which would be ill repaid by
braving her authority and despising her will. Should
I give her reason to regret the hour she received me
under her roof, to repent of every benefit she has
hitherto bestowed on me; should I draw down a
mother's displeasure, what reasonable hopes could we
entertain of solid peace through life? I am not in a
situation which entitles me to question the justice of
Lady Audley's will; and that will has pronounced
that I shall never be Sir Edmund's wife.

"Your first impulse may perhaps be to accuse me
of coldness and ingratitude in quitting the place and
country you inhabit, and resigning you back to yourself, without personally taking leave of you; but I trust
that you will, on reflection, absolve me from the charge.

"Could I have had any grounds to suppose that a personal interview would be productive of comfort to you, I would have joyfully supported the sufferings it would have inflicted on myself. But question your own heart as to the use you would have made of such a meeting; bear in mind that Lady Audley has my solemn promise never to be yours—a promise not lightly given; then imagine what must have been an interview between us under such circumstances.

"In proof of an affection which I can have no reason to doubt, I conjure you to listen to the last request I shall ever make to my dear cousin. Give me the heartfelt satisfaction to know that my departure has put an end to those disagreements between mother and son of which I have been the innocent cause.

"You have no reason to blame Lady Audley for this last step of mine. I have not been intimidated—threats, believe me, never would have extorted from me a promise to renounce you, had not Virtue herself dictated the sacrifice; and my reward will spring from the conviction that, as far as my judgment could discern, I have acted right.

"Forget, I entreat you, this inauspicious passion. Resolve, like me, to resign yourself, without murmuring, to what is now past recall; and, instead of indulging melancholy, regain, by a timely exertion of mind and body, that serenity which is the portion of those who have obeyed the dictates of rectitude.

"Farewell, Sir Edmund. May every happiness

attend your future life ! While I strive to forget my
ill-fated affection, the still stronger feelings of gratitude and esteem for you can never fade from the
heart of   "ALICIA MALCOLM."

To say that no tears were shed during the composition of this letter would be to overstrain fortitude beyond natural bounds. With difficulty Alicia
checked the effusions of her pen. She wished to have
said much more, and to have soothed the agony of
renunciation by painting with warmth her tenderness
and her regret; but reason urged that, in exciting
his feelings and displaying her own, she would defeat
the chief purpose of her letter. She hastily closed
and directed it, with a feeling almost akin to despair.

The necessary arrangements for the journey having
been hastily made, the ladies set out two days after
Sir Edmund had so hastily quitted them. The un-
complaining Alicia buried her woes in her own bosom;
and neither murmurs on the one hand, nor reproaches
on the other, were heard.

At the end of four days the travellers entered
Scotland; and when they stopped for the night,
Alicia, fatigued and dispirited, retired immediately to
her apartment.

She had been there but a few minutes when the
chambermaid knocked at the door, and informed her
that she was wanted below.

Supposing that Lady Audley had sent for her, she
followed the girl without observing that she was con-

ducted in an opposite direction; when, upon entering
an apartment, what was her astonishment at finding
herself, not in the presence of Lady Audley, but in
the arms of Sir Edmund! In the utmost agitation,
she sought to disengage herself from his almost frantic
embrace; while he poured forth a torrent of rapturous
exclamations, and swore that no human power should
ever divide them again.

"I have followed your steps, dearest Alicia, from
the moment I received your letter. We are now in
Scotland—in this blessed land of liberty. Everything
is arranged; the clergyman is now in waiting; and
in five minutes you shall be my own beyond the
power of fate to sever us."

Too much agitated to reply, Alicia wept in silence;
and in the delight of once more beholding him she
had thought never more to behold, forgot, for a
moment, the duty she had imposed upon herself.
But the native energy of her character returned.
She raised her head, and attempted to withdraw from
the encircling arms of her cousin.

"Never until you have vowed to be mine! The
clergyman—the carriage—everything is in readiness.
Speak but the word, dearest." And he knelt at her
feet.

At this juncture the door opened, and, pale with
rage, her eyes flashing fire, Lady Audley stood before
them. A dreadful scene now ensued. Sir Edmund
disdained to enter into any justification of his conduct, or even to reply to the invectives of his mother,

but lavished the most tender assiduities on Alicia; who, overcome more by the conflicts of her own heart than with alarm at Lady Audley's violence, sat the pale and silent image of consternation.

Baffled by her son's indignant disregard, Lady Audley turned all her fury on her niece; and, in the most opprobrious terms that rage could invent, upbraided her with deceit and treachery—accusing her of making her pretended submission instrumental to the more speedy accomplishment of her marriage. Too much incensed to reply, Sir Edmund seized his cousin's hand, and was leading her from the room.

"Go, then—go, marry her; but first hear me swear, solemnly swear"—and she raised her hand and eyes to heaven—"that my malediction shall be your portion! Speak but the word, and no power shall make me withhold it!"

"Dear Edmund!" exclaimed Alicia, distractedly, "never ought I to have allowed time for the terrifying words that have fallen from Lady Audley's lips; never for me shall your mother's malediction fall on you. Farewell for ever!" and, with the strength of desperation, she rushed past him, and quitted the room. Sir Edmund madly followed, but in vain. Alicia's feelings were too highly wrought at that moment to be touched even by the man she loved; and, without an additional pang, she saw him throw himself into the carriage which he had destined for so different a purpose, and quit for ever the woman he adored.

It may easily be conceived of how painful a nature must have been the future intercourse betwixt Lady Audley and her niece. The former seemed to regard her victim with that haughty distance which the unrelenting oppressor never fails to entertain towards the object of his tyranny; while even the gentle Alicia, on her part, shrank, with ill-concealed abhorrence, from the presence of that being whose stern decree had blasted all the fairest blossoms of her happiness.

Alicia was received with affection by her grandfather; and she laboured to drive away the heavy despondency which pressed on her spirits by studying his taste and humours, and striving to contribute to his comfort and amusement.

Sir Duncan had chosen the time of Alicia's arrival to transact some business; and instead of returning immediately to the Highlands, he determined to remain some weeks in Edinburgh for her amusement.

But, little attractive as dissipation had been, it was now absolutely repugnant to Alicia. She loathed the idea of mixing in scenes of amusement with a heart incapable of joy, a spirit indifferent to every object that surrounded her; and in solitude alone she expected gradually to regain her peace of mind.

In the amusements of the gay season of Edinburgh Alicia expected to find all the vanity, emptiness, and frivolity of London dissipation, without its varied brilliancy and elegant luxury; yet, so much was it the habit of her mind to look to the fairest side of things, and to extract some advantage from every situation in which she was placed, that pensive and thoughtful as was her disposition, the discriminating only perceived her deep dejection, while all admired her benevolence of manner and unaffected desire to please.

By degrees Alicia found that in some points she had been inaccurate in her idea of the style of living of those who form the best society of Edinburgh. The circle is so confined that its members are almost universally known to each other; and those various gradations of gentility, from the cit's snug party to the duchess's most crowded assembly, all totally distinct and separate, which are to be met with in London, have no prototype in Edinburgh. There the ranks and fortunes being more on an equality, no one is able greatly to exceed his neighbour in luxury and extravagance. Great magnificence, and the consequent gratification produced by the envy of others being out of the question, the object for which a reunion of individuals was originally invented becomes less of a secondary consideration. Private parties for the actual purpose of society and conversation are frequent, and answer the destined end; and in the societies of professed amusement are to be met the learned, the studious, and the rational; not presented as shows to the company by the host and hostess, but professedly seeking their own gratification.

Still the lack of beauty, fashion, and elegance disappoint the stranger accustomed to their brilliant combination in a London world. But Alicia had long since sickened in the metropolis at the frivolity of beauty, the heartlessness of fashion, and the insipidity of elegance; and it was a relief to her to turn to the variety of character she found beneath the cloak of simple, eccentric, and sometimes coarse manners.

We are never long so totally abstracted by our own feelings as to be unconscious of the attempts of others to please us. In Alicia, to be conscious of it and to be grateful was the same movement. Yet she was sensible that so many persons could not in that short period have become seriously interested in her. The observation did not escape her how much an English stranger is looked up to for fashion and taste in Edinburgh, though possessing little merit save that of being English; yet she felt gratified and thankful for the kindness and attention that greeted her appearance on all sides.

Amongst the many who expressed goodwill towards Alicia there were a few whose kindness and real affection failed not to meet with a return from her; and others whose rich and varied powers of mind for the first time afforded her a true specimen of the exalting enjoyment produced by a communion of intellect. She felt the powers of her understanding enlarge in proportion; and, with this mental activity, she sought to solace the languor of her heart and save it from the listlessness of despair.

Alicia had been about six weeks in Edinburgh when she received a letter from Lady Audley. No allusions were made to the past; she wrote upon general topics, in the cold manner that might be used to a common acquaintance; and slightly named her son as having set out upon a tour to the Continent.

Alicia's heart was heavy as she read the heartless letter of the woman whose cruelty had not been able to eradicate wholly from her breast the strong durable affection of early habit.

Sir Duncan and Alicia spent two months in Edinburgh, at the end of which time they went to his country seat in ——shire. The adjacent country was picturesque; and Sir Duncan's residence, though bearing marks of the absence of taste and comfort in its arrangements, possessed much natural beauty.

Two years of tranquil seclusion had passed over her head when her dormant feelings were all aroused by a letter from Sir Edmund. It informed her that he was now of age; that his affection remained unalterable; that he was newly arrived from abroad; and that, notwithstanding the death-blow she had given to his hopes, he could not refrain, on returning to his native land, from assuring her that he was resolved never to pay his addresses to any other woman. He concluded by declaring his intention of presenting himself at once to Sir Duncan, and soliciting his permission to claim her hand: when all scruples relating to Lady Audley must, from her change of abode, be at an end.

Alicia read the letter with grateful affection and poignant regret. Again she shed the bitter tears of disappointment, at the hard task of refusing for a second time so noble and affectionate a heart. But conscience whispered that to hold a passive line of conduct would be, in some measure, to deceive Lady Audley's expectations; and she felt, with exquisite anguish, that she had no means to put a final stop to Sir Edmund's pursuits, and to her own trials, but by bestowing her hand on another. The first dawning of this idea was accompanied by the most violent burst of anguish; but, far from driving away the painful subject, she strove to render it less appalling by dwelling upon it, and labouring to reconcile herself to what seemed her only plan of conduct. She acknowledged to herself that, to remain still single, a prey to Sir Edmund's importunities and the continual temptations of her own heart, was, for the sake of present indulgence, submitting to a fiery ordeal, from which she could not escape unblamable without the most repeated and agonising conflicts.

Three months still remained for her of peace and liberty, after which Sir Duncan would go to Edinburgh. There she would be sure of meeting with the loved companion of her youthful days; and the lurking weakness of her own breast would then be seconded by the passionate eloquence of the being she most loved and admired upon earth.

She wrote to him, repeating her former arguments; declaring that she could never feel herself absolved from the promise she had given Lady Audley but by that lady herself, and imploring him to abandon a pursuit which would be productive only of lasting pain to both.

Her arguments, her representations, all failed in
their effect on Sir Edmund's impetuous character.
His answer was short and decided; the purport of it,
that he should see her in Edinburgh the moment she
arrived there.

"My fate then is fixed," thought Alicia, as she read
this letter; "I must finish the sacrifice."

The more severe had been the struggle between
love and victorious duty, the more firmly was she
determined to maintain this dear-bought victory.

Alicia's resolution of marrying was now decided,
and the opportunity was not wanting. She had
become acquainted, during the preceding winter in
Edinburgh, with Major Douglas, eldest son of Mr.
Douglas of Glenfern. He had then paid her the most
marked attention; and, since her return to the country,
had been a frequent visitor at Sir Duncan's. At length
he avowed his partiality, which was heard by Sir
Duncan with pleasure, by Alicia with dread and submission. Yet she felt less repugnance towards him
than to any other of her suitors. He was pleasing in
his person; quiet and simple in his manners; and his
character stood high for integrity, good temper, and
plain sense. The sequel requires little further detail.
Alicia Malcolm became the wife of Archibald Douglas.

An eternal constancy is a thing so rare to be met
with, that persons who desire that sort of reputation
strive to obtain it by nourishing the ideas that recall
the passion, even though guilt and sorrow should go
hand in hand with it. But Alicia, far from piquing

herself in the lovelorn pensiveness she might have assumed, had she yielded to the impulse of her feelings, diligently strove not only to make up her mind to the lot which had devolved to her, but to bring it to such a frame of cheerfulness as should enable her to contribute to her husband's happiness.

When the soul is no longer buffeted by the storms of hope or fear, when all is fixed unchangeably for life, sorrow for the past will never long prey on a pious and well-regulated mind. If Alicia lost the buoyant spirit of youth, the bright and quick play of fancy, yet a placid contentment crowned her days; and at the end of two years she would have been astonished had any one marked her as an object of compassion.

She scarcely ever heard from Lady Audley; and in the few letters her aunt had favoured her with, she gave favourable, though vague accounts of her son. Alicia did not court a more unreserved communication, and had long since taught herself to hope that he was now happy. Soon after their marriage Major Douglas quitted the army, upon succeeding to a small estate on the banks of Lochmarlie by the death of an uncle; and there, in the calm seclusion of domestic life, Mrs. Douglas found that peace which might have been denied her amid gayer scenes.

CHAPTER XIV.

"And joyous was the scene in early summer."
MADOC.

ON Henry's return from his solitary ramble Mrs.
Douglas learnt from him the cause of the misunder-
standing that had taken place; and judging that, in
the present state of affairs, a temporary separation
might be of use to both parties, as they were now
about to return home she proposed to her husband
to invite his brother and Lady Juliana to follow and
spend a few weeks with them at Lochmarlie Cottage.

The invitation was eagerly accepted; for though
Lady Juliana did not anticipate any positive pleasure
from the change, still she thought that every place
must be more agreeable than her present abode,
especially as she stipulated for the utter exclusion of
the aunts from the party. To atone for this mortification Miss Becky was invited to fill the vacant seat
in the carriage; and, accordingly, with a cargo of
strong shoes, greatcoats, and a large work-bag well
stuffed with white-seam, she took her place at the
appointed hour.

The day they had chosen for their expedition was
one that "sent a summer feeling to the heart."

The air was soft and genial; not a cloud stained the bright azure of the heavens; and the sun shone out in all his splendour, shedding life and beauty even over all the desolate heath-clad hills of Glenfern. But, after they had journeyed a few miles, suddenly emerging from the valley, a scene of matchless beauty burst at once upon the eye. Before them lay the dark-blue waters of Lochmarlie, reflecting, as in a mirror, every surrounding object, and bearing on its placid transparent bosom a fleet of herring-boats, the drapery of whose black suspended nets contrasted with picturesque effect the white sails of the larger vessels, which were vainly spread to catch a breeze. All around, rocks, meadows, woods, and hills, mingled in wild and lovely irregularity.

On a projecting point of land stood a little fishing village, its white cottages reflected in the glassy waters that almost surrounded it. On the opposite side of the lake, or rather estuary, embosomed in wood, rose the lofty turrets of Lochmarlie Castle; while here and there, perched on some mountain's brow, were to be seen the shepherd's lonely hut, and the heath-covered summer shealing.

Not a breath was stirring, not a sound was heard save the rushing of a waterfall, the tinkling of some silver rivulet, or the calm rippling of the tranquil lake: now and then, at intervals, the fisherman's Gaelic ditty chanted, as he lay stretched on the sand in some sunny nook; or the shrill distant sound of childish glee. How delicious to the feeling heart to mans, and pictures; only what a pity you haven't a larger mirror."

Mrs. Douglas now rang for refreshments, and apologised for the absence of her husband, who, she said, was so much interested in his ploughing that he seldom made his appearance till sent for.

Henry then proposed that they should all go out and surprise his brother; and though walking in the country formed no part of Lady Juliana's amusements, yet, as Mrs. Douglas assured her the walks were perfectly dry, and her husband was so pressing, she consented. The way lay through a shrubbery, by the side of a brawling brook, whose banks retained all the wildness of unadorned nature. Moss and ivy and fern clothed the ground; and under the banks the young primroses and violets began to raise their heads; while the red wintry berry still hung thick on the hollies.

"This is really very pleasant," said Henry, stopping to contemplate a view of the lake through the branches of a weeping birch; "the sound of the stream, and the singing of the birds, and all those wild flowers make it appear as if it was summer in this spot; and only look, Julia, how pretty that wherry looks lying at anchor." Then whispering to her, "What would you think of such a desert as this, with the man of your heart?"

Lady Juliana made no reply but by complaining of the heat of the sun, the hardness of the gravel, and the damp from the water.

Henry, who now began to look upon the condition of a Highland farmer with more complacency than formerly, was confirmed in his favourable sentiments at sight of his brother, following the primitive occupation of the plough, his fine face glowing with health, and lighted up with good humour and happiness. He hastily advanced towards the party, and shaking his brother and sister-in-law most warmly by the hand, expressed, with all the warmth of a good heart, the pleasure he had in receiving them at his house. Then observing Lady Juliana's languid air, and imputing to fatigue of body what, in fact, was the consequence of mental vacuity, he proposed returning home by a shorter road than that by which they had come. Henry was again in raptures at the new beauties this walk presented, and at the high order and neatness in which the grounds were kept.

"This must be a very expensive place of yours, though," said he, addressing his sister-in-law; "there is so much garden and shrubbery, and such a number of rustic bridges, bowers, and so forth: it must require half a dozen men to keep it in any order."

"Such an establishment would very ill accord with our moderate means," replied she; "we do not pretend to one regular gardener; and had our little embellishments been productive of much expense, or tending solely to my gratification, I should never have suggested them. When we first took possession of this spot it was a perfect wilderness, with a dirty farm-house on it; nothing but mud about the doors;

never saw such roads. I suppose Glenfern means to bury you all in the highway; there are holes enough to make you graves, and stones big enough for coffins. You must all come and spend Tuesday here—not all, but some of you—you, dear child, and your brother, and a sister, and your pretty niece, and handsome nephew—I love handsome people. Miss M'Kraken has bounced away with her father's footman—I hope he will clean his knives on her. Come early, and come dressed, to your loving friend,

" ISABELLA MACLAUGHLAN."

The letter ended, a volley of applause ensued, which at length gave place to consultation. "Of course we all go—at least as many as the carriage will hold: we have no engagements, and there can be no objections."

Lady Juliana had already frowned a contemptuous refusal, but in due time it was changed to a sullen assent, at the pressing entreaties of her husband, to whom any place was now preferable to home. In truth, the mention of a party had more weight with her than either her husband's wishes or her aunts' remonstrances; and they had assured her that she should meet with a large assemblage of the very first company at Lochmarlie Castle.

The day appointed for the important visit arrived; and it was arranged that two of the elder ladies and one of the young ones should accompany Lady Juliana in her barouche, which Henry was to drive.

At peep of dawn the ladies were astir, and at eight
o'clock breakfast was hurried over that they might
begin the preparations necessary for appearing with
dignity at the shrine of this their patron saint. At
eleven they reappeared in all the majesty of sweeping
silk trains and well-powdered toupees. In outward
show Miss Becky was not less elaborate; the united
strength and skill of her three aunts and four sisters
had evidently been exerted in forcing her hair into
every position but that for which nature had intended
it; curls stood on end around her forehead, and tresses
were dragged up from the roots, and formed into a
club on the crown; her arms had been strapped back
till her elbows met, by means of a pink ribbon of no
ordinary strength or doubtful hue.

Three hours were past in all the anguish of full-
dressed impatience; an anguish in which every female
breast must be ready to sympathise. But Lady
Juliana sympathised in no one's distresses but her
own, and the difference of waiting in high dress or in
deshabille was a distinction to her inconceivable. But
those to whom *to be dressed* is an event will readily
enter into the feelings of the ladies in question as
they sat, walked, wondered, exclaimed, opened windows, wrung their hands, adjusted their dress, etc.
etc., during the three tedious hours they were doomed
to wait the appearance of their niece.

Two o'clock came, and with it Lady Juliana, as if
purposely to testify her contempt, in a loose morning
dress and mob cap. The sisters looked blank with

disappointment; for having made themselves mistresses of the contents of her ladyship's wardrobe, they had settled amongst themselves that the most suitable dress for the occasion would be black velvet, and accordingly many hints had been given the preceding evening on the virtues of black velvet gowns. They were warm, and not too warm; they were dressy, and not too dressy; Lady Maclaughlan was a great admirer of black velvet gowns; she had one herself with long sleeves, and that buttoned behind; black velvet gowns were very much wore; they knew several ladies who had them; and they were certain there would be nothing else wore amongst the matrons at Lady Maclaughlan's, etc. etc.

Time was, however, too precious to be given either to remonstrance or lamentation. Miss Jacky could only give an angry look, and Miss Grizzy a sorrowful one, as they hurried away to the carriage, uttering exclamations of despair at the lateness of the hour, and the impossibility that anybody could have time to dress after getting to Lochmarlie Castle.

The consequence of the delay was that it was dark by the time they reached the place of destination. The carriage drove up to the grand entrance; but neither lights nor servants greeted their arrival; and no answer was returned to the ringing of the bell.

"This is most alarming, I declare!" cried Miss Grizzy.

"It is quite incomprehensible!" observed Miss

Jacky. "We had best get out and try the back door."

The party alighted, and another attack being made upon the rear, it met with better success; for a little boy now presented himself at a narrow opening of the door, and in a strong Highland accent demanded "wha ta war seekin'?"

"Lady Maclaughlan, to be sure, Colin," was the reply.

"Weel, weel," still refusing admittance; "but te leddie's no to be spoken wi' to-night."

"Not to be spoken with!" exclaimed Miss Grizzy, almost sinking to the ground with apprehension. "Good gracious!—I hope!—I declare!—Sir Sampson!——"

"Oo ay, hur may see Lochmarlie hursel." Then opening the door, he led the way, and ushered them into the presence of Sir Sampson, who was reclining in an easy chair, arrayed in a *robe de chambre* and night-cap. The opening of the door seemed to have broken his slumber; for, gazing around with a look of stupefaction, he demanded in a sleepy peevish tone, "Who was there?"

"Bless me, Sir Sampson!" exclaimed both spinsters at once, darting forward and seizing a hand; "bless me, don't you know us? And here is our niece, Lady Juliana."

"My Lady Juliana Douglas!" cried he, with a shriek of horror, sinking again upon his cushions. "I am betrayed—I—Where is my Lady Maclaughlan?—

by yourself; and we have been received in a manner,
I must say, we did not expect, considering this is the
first visit of our niece Lady Juliana Douglas."

"I'll tell you what, girls," replied their friend, as
she still stood with her back to the fire, and her hands
behind her; "I'll tell you what,—you are not yourselves—you are all lost—quite mad—that's all—
humph!"

"If that's the case, we cannot be fit company for
your ladyship," retorted Miss Jacky warmly; "and
therefore the best thing we can do is to return the
way we came. Come, Lady Juliana—come, sister."

"I declare, Jacky, the impetuosity of your temper
is—I really cannot stand it——" and the gentle
Grizzy gave way to a flood of tears.

"You used to be rational, intelligent creatures,"
resumed her ladyship; "but what has come over
you, I don't know. You come tumbling in here at the
middle of the night—and at the top of the house—
nobody knows how—when I never was thinking of
you; and because I don't tell a parcel of lies, and
pretend I expected you, you are for flying off again—
humph! Is this the behaviour of women in their
senses? But since you are here, you may as well sit
down and say what brought you. Get down, Gil
Blas—go along, Tom Jones," addressing two huge
cats, who occupied a three-cornered leather chair by
the fireside, and who relinquished it with much
reluctance.

"How do you do, pretty creature?" kissing Lady

Juliana, as she seated her in this cat's cradle. "Now, girls, sit down, and tell what brought you here to-day —humph!"

"Can your Ladyship ask such a question, after having formally invited us?" demanded the wrathful Jacky.

"I'll tell you what, girls; you were just as much invited by me to dine here to-day as you were appointed to sup with the Grand Seignior—humph!"

"What day of the week does your Ladyship call this?"

"I call it Tuesday; but I suppose the Glenfern calendar calls it Thursday: Thursday was the day I invited you to come."

"I'm sure—I'm thankful we're got to the bottom of it at last," cried Miss Grizzy; "I read it, because I'm sure you wrote it, Tuesday."

"How could you be such a fool, my love, as to read it any such thing? Even if it had been written Tuesday, you might have had the sense to know it meant Thursday. When did you know me invite anybody for a Tuesday?"

"I declare it's very true; I certainly ought to have known better. I am quite confounded at my own stupidity; for, as you observe, even though you had said Tuesday, I might have known that you must have meant Thursday."

"Well, well, no more about it. Since you are here you must stay here, and you must have something to eat, I suppose. Sir Sampson and I have

"Yesterday was married, by special license, at the house of Mrs. D——, his Grace the Duke of L——, to the beautiful and accomplished Miss D——. His Royal Highness the Duke of —— was gracious enough to act as father to the bride upon this occasion, and was present in person, as were their Royal Highnesses the Dukes of ——, and of ——. The bride looked most bewitchingly lovely, in a simple robe of the finest Mechlin lace, with a superb veil of the same costly material, which hung down to her feet. She wore a set of pearls estimated at thirty thousand pounds, whose chaste elegance corresponded with the rest of the dress. Immediately after the ceremony they partook of a sumptuous collation, and the happy pair set off in a chariot and four, attended by six outriders, and two coaches and four.

"After spending the honeymoon at his Grace's unique villa on the Thames, their Graces will receive company at their splendid mansion in Portman Square. The wedding paraphernalia is said to have cost ten thousand pounds; and her Grace's jewel-box is estimated at little less than half a million."

Wretched as Lady Juliana had long felt herself to be, her former state of mind was positive happiness compared to what she now endured. Envy, regret, self-reproach, and resentment, all struggled in the breast of the self-devoted beauty, while the paper dropped from her hand, and she cast a fearful glance around, as if to ascertain the reality of her fate. The dreadful certainty smote her with a sense of wretchedness too acute to be suppressed; and, darting a look of horror at her unconscious husband, she threw herself back in her chair, while the scalding tears of envy, anger, and repentance fell from her eyes.

Accustomed as Henry now was to these ebullitions of *feeling* from his beauteous partner, he was not yet so indifferent as to behold them unmoved; and he sought to soothe her by the kindest expressions and most tender epithets. These indeed had long since ceased to charm away the lady's ill-humour, but they sometimes succeeded in mollifying it. But now their only effect seemed to be increasing the irritation, as she turned from all her husband's inquiries, and impatiently withdrew her hands from his.

Astonished at a conduct so incomprehensible, Douglas earnestly besought an explanation.

"There!" cried she, at length, pushing the paper towards him, "see there what I might have been but for you; and then compare it with what you have made me!"

Confounded by this reproach, Henry eagerly snatched up the paper, and his eye instantly fell on the fatal paragraph—the poisoned dart that struck the death-blow to all that now remained to him of happiness—the fond idea that, even amidst childish folly and capricious estrangement, still in the main he was beloved! With a quivering lip, and cheek blanched with mortification and indignant contempt, he laid down the paper; and without casting a look upon, or uttering a word to, his once *adored and adoring*

Juliana, quitted the apartment in all that bitterness
of spirit which a generous nature must feel when it
first discovers the fallacy of a cherished affection.
Henry had indeed ceased to regard his wife with
the ardour of romantic passion; nor had the solid
feelings of affectionate esteem supplied its place; but
he loved her still, because he believed himself the
engrossing object of her tenderness; and in that
blest delusion he had hitherto found palliatives for
her folly and consolation for all his own distresses.

To indifference he might for a time have remained
insensible; because, though his feelings were strong,
his perceptions were not acute. But the veil of illu-
sion was now rudely withdrawn. He beheld himself
detested where he imagined himself adored; and the
anguish of disappointed affection was heightened by
the stings of wounded pride and deluded self-love.

CHAPTER XVII.

" What's done, cannot be undone ; to bed, to bed, to bed ! "
Exit Lady Macbeth.

THE distance at which the whist party had placed
themselves, and the deep interest in which their
senses were involved while the fate of the odd trick
was pending, had rendered them insensible to the
scene that was acting at the other extremity of the
apartment.   The task of administering succour to the
afflicted fair one therefore devolved upon Miss Becky,
whose sympathetic powers never had been called
into action before.   Slowly approaching the wretched
Lady Juliana as she lay back in her chair, the tears
coursing each other down her cheeks, she tendered
her a smelling-bottle, to which her own nose, and the
noses of her sisters, were wont to be applied whenever, as they choicely expressed it, they wanted a
" fine smell."   But upon this trying occasion she
went still farther.   She unscrewed the stopper, un-
folded a cotton handkerchief, upon which she poured
a few drops of lavender water, and offered it to her
ladyship, deeming that the most elegant and efficient
manner in which she could afford relief.   But the

well-meant offering was silently waved off; and poor Miss Becky, having done all that the light of reason suggested to her, retreated to her seat, wondering what it was her fine sister-in-law would be at.

By the time the rubber was ended her ladyship's fears of Lady Maclaughlan had enabled her to conquer her feelings so far that they had now sunk into a state of sullen dejection, which the good aunts eagerly interpreted into the fatigue of the journey, Miss Grizzy declaring that although the drive was most delightful—nobody could deny that—and they all enjoyed it excessively, as indeed everybody must who had eyes in their head; yet she must own, at the same time, that she really felt as if all her bones were broke.

A general rising therefore took place at an early hour, and Lady Juliana, attended by all the females of the party, was ushered into the chamber of state, which was fitted up in a style acknowledged to be truly magnificent, by all who had ever enjoyed the honour of being permitted to gaze on its white velvet bedcurtains, surmounted by the family arms, and gracefully tucked up by hands *sinister-couped* at the wrists, etc. But lest my fashionable readers should be of a different opinion, I shall refrain from giving an inventory of the various articles with which this favoured chamber was furnished. Misses Grizzy and Jacky occupied the green room which had been fitted up at Sir Sampson's birth. The curtains hung at a respectful distance from the ground; the chimney-

piece was far beyond the reach even of the majestic
Jacky's arm; and the painted tiffany toilet was
covered with a shoal of little tortoise-shell boxes of
all shapes and sizes. A grim visage, scowling from
under a Highland bonnet, graced by a single black
feather, hung on high. Miss Grizzy placed herself
before it, and, holding up the candle, contemplated
it for about the nine hundredth time, with an awe
bordering almost on adoration.

"Certainly Sir Eneas must have been a most
wonderful man—nobody can deny that; and there
can be no question but he had the second-sight to the
greatest degree—indeed, I never heard it disputed;
many of his prophecies, indeed, seem to have been
quite incomprehensible; but that is so much the more
extraordinary; you know—for instance, the one with
regard to our family," lowering her voice; "for my
part I declare I never could comprehend it; and yet
there must be something in it, too; but how any
branch from the Glenfern tree—of course, you know,
that can only mean the family tree—should help to
prop Lochmarlie's walls, is what I can't conceive. If
Sir Sampson had a son, to be sure, some of the girls
—for you know it can't be any of us; at least I declare for my own part—I'm sure even if anything—
which I trust, in goodness, there is not the least chance
of, should ever happen to dear Lady Maclaughlan,
and Sir Sampson should take it into his head—which,
of course, is a thing not to be thought about—and
indeed I'm quite convinced it would be very much

out of respect to dear Lady Maclaughlan, as well as friendship for us, if such a thing was ever to come into his head."

Here the tender Grizzy got so involved in her own ideas as to the possibility of Lady Maclaughlan's death, and the propriety of Sir Sampson's proposals, together with the fulfilling of Sir Eneas the seer's prophecy, that there is no saying how far she strayed in her self-created labyrinth. Such as choose to follow her may. For our part, we prefer accompanying the youthful Becky to her chamber, whither she was also attended by the lady of the mansion. Becky's destiny for the night lay at the top of one of those little straggling wooden stairs common in old houses, which creaked in all directions. The bed was placed in a recess dark as Erebus, and betwixt the bed and the wall was a depth profound, which Becky's eye dared not attempt to penetrate.

"You will find everything right here, child," said Lady Maclaughlan ; "and if anything should be wrong you must think it right. I never suffer anything to be wrong here—humph!" Becky, emboldened by despair, cast a look towards the recess ; and in a faint voice ventured to inquire, "Is there no fear that Tom Jones or Gil Blas may be in that place behind the bed ?"

"And if they should," answered her hostess in her most appalling tone, "what is that to you ? Are you a mouse, that you are afraid they will eat you ? Yes, I suppose you are. You are perhaps the princess in

the fairy tale, who was a woman by day and a mouse
by night. I believe you are bewitched! So I wish
your mouseship a good night." And she descended
the creaking stair, singing,

" Mrs. Mouse, are you within?"

till even her stentorian voice was lost in distance.
Poor Becky's heart died with the retreating sounds,
and only revived to beat time with the worm in the
wood. Long and eerie was the night, as she gave
herself up to all the horrors of a superstitious mind—
ghosts, gray, black, and white, flitted around her
couch; cats, half human, held her throat; the death-
watch ticked in her ears. At length the light of
morning shed its brightening influence on the dim
opaque of her understanding; and when all things
stood disclosed in light, she shut her eyes and oped
her mouth in all the blissfulness of security. The
light of day was indeed favourable for displaying to
advantage the beauties of Lochmarlie Castle, which
owed more to nature than art. It was beautifully
situated on a smooth green bank, that rose somewhat
abruptly from the lake, and commanded a view, which,
if not extensive, was yet full of variety and grandeur.

Its venerable turrets reared themselves above the
trees which seemed coeval with them; and the vast
magnificence of its wide-spreading lawns and extensive
forests seemed to appertain to some feudal prince's
lofty domain. But in vain were creation's charms
spread before Lady Juliana's eyes. Woods and

mountains and lakes and rivers were odious things;
and her heart panted for dusty squares and suffocating
drawing-rooms.

Something was said of departing by the sisters
when the party met at breakfast; but this was immediately negatived in the most decided manner by
their hostess.

"Since you have taken your own time to come, my
dears, you must take mine to go. Thursday was the
day I invited you for, or at least wanted you for, so
you must stay Thursday, and go away on Friday, and
my blessing go with you—humph!"

The sisters, charmed with what they termed the
hospitality and friendship of this invitation, delightedly
agreed to remain; and as things were at least conducted in better style there than at Glenfern, uncomfortable as it was, Lady Juliana found herself somewhat
nearer home there than at the family chateau. Lady
Maclaughlan, who *could* be commonly civil in her own
house, was at some pains to amuse her guest by showing her collection of china and cabinet of gems, both
of which were remarkably fine. There was also a
library, and a gallery, containing some good pictures,
and, what Lady Juliana prized still more, a billiard-
table. Thursday, the destined day, at length arrived,
and a large party assembled to dinner. Lady Juliana,
as she half reclined on a sofa, surveyed the company
with a supercilious stare, and without deigning to take
any part in the general conversation that went on.
It was enough that they spoke with a peculiar accent

—everything they said must be barbarous; but she was pleased once more to eat off plate, and to find herself in rooms which, though grotesque and comfortless, yet wore an air of state, and whose vastness enabled her to keep aloof from those with whom she never willingly came in contact. It was therefore with regret she saw the day of her departure arrive, and found herself once more an unwilling inmate of her only asylum; particularly as her situation now required comforts and indulgences which it was there impossible to procure.

CHAPTER XVIII.

" No mother's care
Shielded my infant innocence with prayer:
*   *   *   *   *

Mother, miscall'd, farewell ! "

SAVAGE.

THE happy period, so long and anxiously anticipated by the ladies of Glenfern, at length arrived, and Lady Juliana presented to the house of Douglas—not, alas ! the ardently-desired heir to its ancient consequence, but twin-daughters, who could only be regarded as additional burdens on its poverty.

The old gentleman's disappointment was excessive ; and, as he paced up and down the parlour, with his hands in his pockets, he muttered, "Twa lasses ! I ne'er heard tell o' the like o't. I wonder whar their tochers are to come frae?"

Miss Grizzy, in great perturbation, declared it certainly was a great pity it had so happened, but these things couldn't be helped ; she was sure Lady Maclaughlan would be greatly surprised.

Miss Jacky saw no cause for regret, and promised herself an endless source of delight in forming the minds and training the ideas of her infant nieces.

Miss Nicky wondered how they were to be nursed. She was afraid Lady Juliana would not be able for both, and wet-nurses had such stomachs!

Henry, meanwhile, whose love had all revived in anxiety for the safety, and anguish for the sufferings of his youthful partner, had hastened to her apartment, and, kneeling by her side, he pressed her hands to his lips with feelings of the deepest emotion.

"Dearer—a thousand times dearer to me than ever," whispered he, as he fondly embraced her, "and those sweet pledges of our love!"

"Ah, don't mention them," interrupted his lady in a languid tone. "How very provoking! I hate girls so—and two of them—oh!" and she sighed deeply. Her husband sighed too; but from a different cause. The nurse now appeared, and approached with her helpless charges; and both parents for the first time looked on their own offspring.

"What nice little creatures!" said the delighted father, as, taking them in his arms, he imprinted the first kiss on the innocent faces of his daughters, and then held them to their mother; who, turning from them with disgust, exclaimed, "How can you kiss them, Harry? They are so ugly, and they squall so! Oh do, for heaven's sake, take them away! And see, there is poor Psyche quite wretched at being so long away from me. Pray, put her on the bed."

"She will grow fond of her babies by-and-by," said poor Henry to himself, as he quitted the apartment, with feelings very different from those with which he entered it.

At the pressing solicitations of her husband, the fashionable mother was prevailed upon to attempt nursing one of her poor starving infants; but the first trial proved also the last, as she declared nothing upon earth should ever induce her to perform so odious an office; and as Henry's entreaties and her aunts' remonstrances served alike to irritate and agitate her, the contest was, by the advice of her medical attendant, completely given up. A wet-nurse was therefore procured; but as she refused to undertake both children, and the old gentleman would not hear of having two such encumbrances in his family, it was settled, to the unspeakable delight of the maiden sisters, that the youngest should be entrusted entirely to their management, and brought up by hand.

The consequence was such as might have been foreseen. The child, who was naturally weak and delicate at its birth, daily lost a portion of its little strength, while its continued cries declared the intensity of its sufferings, though they produced no other effect on its unfeeling mother than her having it removed to a more distant apartment, as she could not endure to hear the cross little thing scream so for nothing. On the other hand, the more favoured twin, who was from its birth a remarkably strong lively infant, and met with all justice from its nurse, throve apace, and was pronounced by her to be the very picture of the *bonnie leddie, its mamma;* and then, with all the low cunning of her kind, she would launch forth into panegyrics of its beauty, and prophecies of the great dignities and honours that would one day be showered upon it; until, by her fawning and flattery, she succeeded in exciting a degree of interest, which nature had not secured for it in the mother's breast.

Things were in this situation when, at the end of three weeks, Mr. and Mrs. Douglas arrived to offer their congratulations on the birth of the twins. Lady Juliana received her sister-in-law in her apartment, which she had not yet quitted, and replied to her congratulations only by querulous complaints and childish murmurs.

"I am sure you are very happy in not having children," continued she, as the cries of the little sufferer reached her ear; "I hope to goodness I shall never have any more. I wonder if anybody ever had twin daughters before, and I, too, who hate girls so!"

Mrs Douglas, disgusted with her unfeeling folly, knew not what to reply, and a pause ensued; but a fresh burst of cries from the unfortunate baby again called forth its mother's indignation.

"I wish to goodness that child was gagged," cried she, holding her hands to her ears. "It has done nothing but scream since the hour it was born, and it makes me quite sick to hear it."

"Poor little dear!" said Mrs. Douglas compassionately, "it appears to suffer a great deal."

"Suffer!" repeated her sister-in-law; "what can it suffer? I am sure it meets with a great deal more attention than any person in the house. These three old women do nothing but feed it from morning to night, with everything they can think of, and make such a fuss about it!"

"I suspect, my dear sister, you would be very sorry for yourself," said Mrs. Douglas, with a smile, "were you to endure the same treatment as your poor baby; stuffed with improper food and loathsome drugs, and bandied about from one person to another."

"You may say what you please," retorted Lady Juliana pettishly; "but I know it's nothing but ill temper: nurse says so too; and it is so ugly with constantly crying that I cannot bear to look at it;" and she turned away her head as Miss Jacky entered with the little culprit in her arms, which she was vainly endeavouring to *talk* into silence, while she dandled it in the most awkward *maiden-like* manner imaginable.

"Good heavens! what a fright!" exclaimed the tender parent, as her child was held up to her. "Why, it is much less than when it was born, and its skin is as yellow as saffron, and it squints! Only look what a difference," as the nurse advanced and ostentatiously displayed her charge, who had just waked out of a long sleep; its cheeks flushed with heat; its skin completely filled up; and its large eyes rolling under its already dark eyelashes.

"The bonny wean's just her mamma's pickter,"

drawled out the nurse, "but the wee missy's unco like her aunties."

"Take her away," cried Lady Juliana in a tone of despair; "I wish I could send her out of my hearing altogether, for her noise will be the death of me."

"Alas! what would I give to hear the blessed sound of a living child!" exclaimed Mrs. Douglas, taking the infant in her arms. "And how great would be my happiness could I call the poor rejected one mine!"

"I'm sure you are welcome to my share of the little plague," said her sister-in-law, with a laugh, "if you can prevail upon Harry to give up his."

"I would give up a great deal could my poor child find a mother," replied her husband, who just then entered.

"My dear brother!" cried Mrs. Douglas, her eyes beaming with delight, "do you then confirm Lady Juliana's kind promise? Indeed I will be a mother to your dear baby, and love her as if she were my own; and in a month—oh! in much less time— you shall see her as stout as her sister."

Henry sighed, as he thought, "Why has not my poor babe such a mother of its own?" Then thanking his sister-in-law for her generous intentions, he reminded her that she must consult her husband, as few men liked to be troubled with any children but their own.

"You are in the right," said Mrs. Douglas, blushing at the impetuosity of feeling which had made her forget for an instant the deference due to her hus-

band; "I shall instantly ask his permission, and he is
so indulgent to all my wishes that I have little doubt
of obtaining his consent;" and, with the child in her
arms, she hastened to her husband, and made known
her request.

Mr. Douglas received the proposal with considerable coolness; wondering what his wife could see in
such an ugly squalling thing to plague herself about
it. If it had been a boy, old enough to speak and
run about, there might be some amusement in it; but
he could not see the use of a squalling sickly infant—
and a girl too!

His wife sighed deeply, and the tears stole down
her cheeks as she looked on the wan visage and closed
eyes of the little sufferer. "God help thee, poor
baby!" said she mournfully; "you are rejected on
all hands, but your misery will soon be at an end;"
and she was slowly leaving the room with her helpless charge when her husband, touched at the sight
of her distress, though the feeling that caused it he
did not comprehend, called to her, "I am sure, Alicia,
if you really wish to take charge of the infant I have
no objections; only I think you will find it a great
plague, and the mother is such a fool."

"Worse than a fool," said Mrs. Douglas indignantly,
"for she hates and abjures this her poor unoffending
babe."

"Does she so?" cried Mr. Douglas, every kindling
feeling roused within him at the idea of his blood
being hated and abjured; "then, hang me! if she

shall have any child of Harry's to hate as long as I have a house to shelter it and a sixpence to bestow upon it," taking the infant in his arms, and kindly kissing it.

Mrs. Douglas smiled through her tears as she em braced her husband, and praised his goodness and generosity; then, full of exultation and delight, she flew to impart the success of her mission to the parents of her *protégée*.

Great was the surprise of the maiden nurses at finding they were to be bereft of their little charge.

"I declare, I think the child is doing as well as possible," said Miss Grizzy. "To be sure it does yammer constantly—that can't be denied; and it is uncommonly small—nobody can dispute that. At the same time, I am sure, I can't tell what makes it cry, for I've given it two colic powders every day, and a tea-spoonful of Lady Maclaughlan's carminative every three hours."

"And I've done nothing but make water-gruel and chop rusks for it," quoth Miss Nicky, "and yet it is never satisfied; I wonder what it would be at."

"I know perfectly well what it would be at," said Miss Jacky, with an air of importance. "All this crying and screaming is for nothing else but a nurse; but it ought not to be indulged. There is no end of indulging the desires, and 'tis amazing how cunning children are, and how soon they know how to take advantage of people's weakness," glancing an eye of fire at Mrs. Douglas. "Were that my child, I would

feed her on bread and water before I would humour
her fancies.   A pretty lesson, indeed! if she's to have
her own way before she's a month old."

Mrs. Douglas knew that it was in vain to attempt
arguing with her aunts.   She therefore allowed them
to wonder and declaim over their sucking pots, colic
powders, and other instruments of torture, while she
sent to the wife of one of her tenants who had lately
lain-in, and who wished for the situation of nurse,
appointing her to be at Lochmarlie the following day.
Having made her arrangements, and collected the
scanty portion of clothing Mrs. Nurse chose to allow,
Mrs. Douglas repaired to her sister-in-law's apartment,
with her little charge in her arms.   She found her
still in bed, and surrounded with her favourites.

"So you really are going to torment yourself with
that little screech-owl?" said she.   "Well, I must
say it's very good of you; but I am afraid you will
soon tire of her.   Children are such plagues!   Are
they not, my darling?" added she, kissing her pug.

"You will not say so when you have seen my
little girl a month hence," said Mrs. Douglas, trying
to conceal her disgust for Henry's sake, who had just
then entered the room.   "She has promised me never
to cry any more; so give her a kiss, and let us be
gone."

The high-bred mother slightly touched the cheek
of her sleeping babe, extended her finger to her sister-
in-law, and carelessly bidding them good-bye, returned
to her pillow and her pugs.

Henry accompanied Mrs. Douglas to the carriage, and before they parted he promised his brother to ride over to Lochmarlie in a few days. He said nothing of his child, but his glistening eye and the warm pressure of his hand spoke volumes to the kind heart of his brother, who assured him that Alicia would be very good to his little girl, and that he was sure she would get quite well when she got a nurse. The carriage drove off, and Henry, with a heavy spirit, returned to the house to listen to his father's lectures, his aunts' ejaculations, and his wife's murmurs.

CHAPTER XIX.

" We may boldly spend upon the hope of what
Is to come in."

Henry IV.

THE birth of twin daughters awakened the young
father to a still stronger sense of the total dependence
and extreme helplessness of his condition. Yet how
to remedy it he knew not. To accept of his father's
proposal was out of the question, and it was equally
impossible for him, were he ever so inclined, to remain
much longer a burden on the narrow income of the
Laird of Glenfern. One alternative only remained,
which was to address the friend and patron of his
youth, General Cameron; and to him he therefore
wrote, describing all the misery of his situation, and
imploring his forgiveness and assistance. "The old
General's passion must have cooled by this time,"
thought he to himself, as he sealed the letter, "and
as he has often overlooked former scrapes, I think,
after all, he will help me out of this greatest one of
all."

For once Henry was not mistaken. He received
an answer to his letter, in which the General, after
execrating his folly in marrying a lady of quality,

swearing at the birth of his twin daughters, and giving him some wholesome counsel as to his future mode of life, concluded by informing him that he had got him reinstated in his former rank in the army; that he should settle seven hundred per annum on him till he saw how matters were conducted, and, in the meantime, enclosed a draught for four hundred pounds, to open the campaign.

Though this was not, according to Henry's notions, "coming down handsomely," still it was better than not coming down at all, and with a mixture of delight and disappointment he flew to communicate the tidings to Lady Juliana.

"Seven hundred pounds a year!" exclaimed she, in raptures: "Heavens! what a quantity of money! why, we shall be quite rich, and I shall have such a beautiful house, and such pretty carriages, and give such parties, and buy so many fine things. Oh dear, how happy I shall be!"

"You know little of money, Julia, if you think seven hundred pounds will do all that," replied her husband gravely. "I hardly think we can afford a house in town; but we may have a pretty cottage at Richmond or Twickenham, and I can keep a curricle, and drive you about, you know; and we may give famous good dinners."

A dispute here ensued; her ladyship hated cottages and curricles and good dinners as much as her husband despised fancy balls, opera boxes, and chariots.

The fact was that the one knew very nearly as
much of the real value of money as the other, and
Henry's *sober* scheme was just about as practicable as
his wife's extravagant one.

Brought up in the luxurious profusion of a great
house; accustomed to issue her orders and have them
obeyed, Lady Juliana, at the time she married, was
in the most blissful state of ignorance respecting the
value of pounds, shillings, and pence.   Her maid took
care to have her wardrobe supplied with all things
needful, and when she wanted a new dress or a
fashionable jewel, it was only driving to Madame D.'s,
or Mr. Y.'s, and desiring the article to be sent to
herself, while the bill went to her papa.

From never seeing money in its own vulgar form,
Lady Juliana had learned to consider it as a mere
nominal thing; while, on the other hand, her husband,
from seeing too much of it, had formed almost equally
erroneous ideas of its powers.   By the mistaken kindness of General Cameron he had been indulged in all
the fashionable follies of the day, and allowed to use
his patron's ample fortune as if it had already been
his own; nor was it until he found himself a prisoner
at Glenfern from want of money that he had ever
attached the smallest importance to it.   In short, both
the husband and wife had been accustomed to look
upon it in the same light as the air they breathed.
They knew it essential to life, and concluded that it
would come some way or other; either from the east
or west, north or south.   As for the vulgar concerns

of meat and drink, servants' wages, taxes, and so forth, they never found a place in the calculations of either. Birthday dresses, fêtes, operas, equipages, and state liveries whirled in rapid succession through Lady Juliana's brain, while clubs, curricles, horses, and claret, took possession of her husband's mind.

However much they differed in the proposed modes of showing off in London, both agreed perfectly in the necessity of going there, and Henry therefore hastened to inform his father of the change in his circumstances, and apprise him of his intention of immediately joining his regiment, the —— Guards.

"Seven hunder pound a year!" exclaimed the old gentleman; "Seven hunder pound! Oo what can ye mak' o' a' that siller? Ye'll surely lay by the half o't to tocher your bairns. Seven hunder pound a year for doing naething!"

Miss Jacky was afraid, unless they got some person of sense (which would not be an easy matter) to take the management of it, it would perhaps be found little enough in the long-run.

Miss Grizzy declared it was a very handsome income, nobody could dispute that; at the same time, everybody must allow that the money could not have been better bestowed.

Miss Nicky observed "there was a great deal of good eating and drinking in seven hundred a year, if people knew how to manage it."

All was bustle and preparation throughout Glenfern Castle, and the young ladies' good-natured activity and muscular powers were again in requisition to collect the wardrobe, and pack the trunks, imperial, etc., of their noble sister.

Glenfern remarked "that fules war fond o' flitting, for they seemed glad to leave the good quarters they were in."

Miss Grizzy declared there was a great excuse for their being glad, poor things! young people were always so fond of a change; at the same time, nobody could deny but that it would have been quite natural for them to feel sorry too.

Miss Jacky was astonished how any person's mind could be so callous as to think of leaving Glenfern without emotion.

Miss Nicky wondered what was to become of the christening cake she had ordered from Perth; it might be as old as the hills before there would be another child born amongst them.

The Misses were ready to weep at the disappointment of the dreaming-bread.

In the midst of all this agitation, mental and bodily, the long-looked-for moment arrived. The carriage drove round ready packed and loaded, and, absolutely screaming with delight, Lady Juliana sprang into it. As she nodded and kissed her hand to the assembled group, she impatiently called to Henry to follow. His adieus were, however, not quite so tonish as those of his high-bred lady, for he went duly and severally through all the evolutions of kissing, embracing, shaking of hands, and promises to write; then taking his station by the side of the nurse and child—the rest of the carriage being completely filled by the favourites—he bade a long farewell to his paternal halls and the land of his birth.

CHAPTER XX.

" For trifles, why should I displease
The man I love ? For trifles such as these
To serious mischiefs lead the man I love."

HORACE.

BRIGHT prospects of future happiness and endless plans of expense floated through Lady Juliana's brain, and kept her temper in some degree of serenity during the journey.

Arrived in London, she expressed herself enraptured at being once more in a civilised country, and restored to the society of human creatures. An elegant house and suitable establishment were immediately provided; and a thousand dear friends, who had completely forgotten her existence, were now eager to welcome her to her former haunts, and lead her thoughtless and willing steps in the paths of dissipation and extravagance.

Soon after their arrival they were visited by General Cameron. It was two o'clock, yet Lady Juliana had not appeared; and Henry, half-stretched upon a sofa, was dawdling over his breakfast with half-a-dozen newspapers scattered round.

The first salutations over, the General demanded,

"Am I not to be favoured with a sight of your lady? Is she afraid that I am one of your country relations, and taken her flight from the breakfast-table in consequence?"

"She has not yet made her appearance," replied Douglas; "but I will let her know you are here. I am sure she will be happy to make acquaintance with one to whom I am so much indebted."

A message was despatched to Lady Juliana, who returned for answer that she would be down immediately. Three quarters of an hour, however, elapsed; and the General, provoked with this inattention and affectation, was preparing to depart when the Lady made her appearance.

"Juliana, my love," said her husband, "let me present you to General Cameron—the generous friend who has acted the part of a father towards me, and to whom you owe all the comforts you enjoy."

Lady Juliana slightly bowed with careless ease, and half uttered a "How d'ye do?—very happy indeed," as she glided on to pull the bell for breakfast. "Cupid, Cupid!" cried she to the dog, who had flown upon the General, and was barking most vehemently. "Poor darling Cupid! are you almost starved to death? Harry, do give him that muffin on your plate."

"You are very late to-day, my love," cried the mortified husband.

"I have been pestered for the last hour with Duval and the court dresses, and I could not fix on what I should like."

" I think you might have deferred the ceremony of choosing to another opportunity. General Cameron has been here above an hour."

"Dear! I hope you did not wait for me. I shall be quite shocked!" drawled out her ladyship in a tone denoting how very indifferent the answer would be to her.

"I beg your ladyship would be under no uneasiness on that account," replied the General in an ironical tone, which, though lost upon her, was obvious enough to Henry.

"Have you breakfasted?" asked Lady Juliana, exerting herself to be polite.

"Absurd, my love!" cried her husband. "Do you suppose I should have allowed the General to wait for that too all this time, if he had not breakfasted many hours ago?"

"How cross you are this morning, my Harry! I protest my Cupidon is quite ashamed of your *grossièreté !* "

A servant now entered to say Mr. Shagg was come to know her ladyship's final decision about the hammer-cloths; and the new footman was come to be engaged; and the china merchant was below.

"Send up one of them at a time; and as to the footman, you may say I'll have him at once," said Lady Juliana.

"I thought you had engaged Mrs. D.'s footman last week. She gave him the best character, did she not?" asked her husband.

"Oh yes! his character was good enough ; but he was a horrid cheat for all that. He called himself five feet nine, and when he was measured he turned out to be only five feet seven and a half."

"Pshaw !" exclaimed Henry angrily. " What the devil did that signify if the man had a good character ?"

"How absurdly you talk, Harry, as if a man's character signified who has nothing to do but to stand behind my carriage ! A pretty figure he'd made there beside Thomas, who is at least five feet ten !"

The entrance of Mr. Shagg, bowing and scraping, and laden with cloths, lace, and fringes, interrupted the conversation.

"Well, Mr. Shagg," cried Lady Juliana, "what's to be done with that odious leopard's skin ? You must positively take it off my hands. I would rather never go in a carriage again as show myself in the Park with that frightful thing."

"Certainly, my Lady," replied the obsequious Mr. Shagg, "anything your Ladyship pleases ; your Ladyship can have any hammer-cloth you like ; and I have accordingly brought patterns of the very newest fashions for your Ladyship to make choice. Here are some uncommon elegant articles. At the same time, my Lady, your Ladyship must be sensible that it is impossible that we can take back the leopard's skin. It was not only cut out to fit your Ladyship's coach-box—and consequently your Ladyship understands it would not fit any other—but the silver feet and crests have also been affixed quite ready for use, so that the article is quite lost to us. I am confident, therefore, that your Ladyship will consider of this, and allow it to be put down in your bill."

"Put it anywhere but on my coach-box, and don't bore me!" answered Lady Juliana, tossing over the patterns, and humming a tune.

"What," said her husband, "is that the leopard's skin you were raving about last week, and are you tired of it before it has been used?"

"And no wonder. Who do you think I saw in the Park yesterday but that old quiz Lady Denham, just come from the country, with her frightful old coach set off with a hammer-cloth precisely like the one I had ordered. Only fancy people saying, Lady Denham sets the fashion for Lady Juliana Douglas! Oh, there's confusion and despair in the thought!"

Confusion, at least, if not despair, was painted in Henry's face as he saw the General's glance directed alternately with contempt at Lady Juliana, and at himself, mingled with pity. He continued to fidget about in all directions, while Lady Juliana talked nonsense to Mr. Shagg, and wondered if the General never meant to go away. But he calmly kept his ground till the man was dismissed, and another introduced, loaded with china jars, monsters, and distorted teapots, for the capricious fair one's choice and approbation.

"Beg ten thousand pardons, my Lady, for not

calling yesterday, according to appointment—quite an unforeseen impediment. The Countess of Godolphin had somehow got private intelligence that I had a set of fresh commodities just cleared from the custom-house, and well knowing such things are not long in hand, her La'ship came up from the country on purpose—the Countess has so much taste!—she drove straight to my warehouse, and kept me a close prisoner till after your La'ship's hour; but I hope it may not be taken amiss, seeing that it is not a customary thing with us to be calling on customers, not to mention that this line of goods is not easily transported about. However, I flatter myself the articles now brought for your Ladyship's inspection will not be found beneath your notice. Please to observe this choice piece —it represents a Chinese cripple squat on the ground, with his legs crossed. Your Ladyship may observe the head and chin advanced forwards, as in the act of begging. The tea pours from the open mouth; and, till your Ladyship tries, you can have no idea of the elegant effect it produces."

"That is really droll," cried Lady Juliana, with a laugh of delight; "and I must have the dear sick beggar; he is so deliciously hideous."

"And here," continued Mr. Brittle, "is an amazing delicate article, in the way of a jewel—a frog of Turkish agate for burning pastiles in, my Lady; just such as they use in the seraglio; and indeed this one I may call invaluable, for it was the favourite toy of one of the widowed Sultanas till she grew devout and

gave up perfumes. One of her slaves disposed of it
to my foreign partner. Here it opens at the tail,
where you put in the pastiles, and closing it up, the
vapour issues beautifully through the nostrils, eyes,
ears, and mouth, all at once. Here, sir," turning to
Douglas, "if you are curious in new workmanship, I
would have you examine this. I defy any jeweller in
London to come up to the fineness of these hinges,
and delicacy of the carving——"

"Pshaw, damn it!" said Douglas, turning away,
and addressing some remark to the General, who was
provokingly attentive to everything that went on.

"Here," continued Mr. Brittle, "are a set of jars,
teapots, mandarins, sea-monsters, and pug-dogs, all of
superior beauty, but such as your Ladyship may have
seen before."

"Oh, the dear, dear little puggies! I must have
them to amuse my own darlings. I protest here is
one the image of Psyche; positively I must kiss it!"

"Oh dear! I am sure," cried Mr. Brittle, simpering,
and making a conceited bow, "your Ladyship does it
and me too much honour. But here, as I was going
to say, is the phœnix of all porcelain ware—the *ne
plus ultra* of perfection—what I have kept in my back
room, concealed from all eyes, until your Ladyship
shall pronounce upon it. Somehow one of my shop-
men got word of it, and told her Grace of L—— (who
has a pretty taste in these things for a young lady)
that I had some particular choice article that I was
keeping for a lady that was a favourite of mine. Her

Grace was in the shop the matter of a full hour and a half, trying to wheedle me out of a sight of this rare piece; and I, pretending not to know what her Grace would be after, but showing her thing after thing, to put it out of her head. But she was not so easily bubbled, and at last went away ill enough pleased. Now, my Lady, prepare all your eyes." He then went to the door, and returned, carrying with difficulty a large basket, which till then had been kept by one of his satellites. After removing coverings of all descriptions, an uncouth group of monstrous size was displayed, which, on investigation, appeared to be a serpent coiled in regular folds round the body of a tiger placed on end; and the whole structure, which was intended for a vessel of some kind, was formed of the celebrated green mottled china, invaluable to connoisseurs.

"View that well," exclaimed Mr. Brittle, in a transport of enthusiasm, "for such a specimen not one of half the size has ever been imported to Europe. There is a long story about this my phœnix, as I call it; but, to be brief, it was secretly procured from one of the temples, where, gigantic as it may seem, and uncouth for the purpose, it was the idol's principal teapot!"

"Oh delicious!" cried Lady Juliana, clasping her hands in ecstasy. "I will give a party for the sole purpose of drinking tea out of this machine; and I will have the whole room fitted up like an Indian temple. Oh! it will be so new! I die to send out my cards. The Duchess of B—— told me the other day, with such a triumphant air, when I was looking at her two little green jars, not a quarter the size of this, that there was not a bit more of that china to be had for love or money. Oh, she will be so provoked!" And she absolutely skipped for joy.

A loud rap at the door now announcing a visitor, Lady Juliana ran to the balcony, crying, "Oh, it must be Lady Gerard, for she promised to call early in the morning, that we might go together to a wonderful sale in some far-off place in the city—at Wapping, for aught I know. Mr. Brittle, Mr. Brittle, for the love of heaven, carry the dragon into the back drawing-room—I purchase it, remember!—make haste!—Lady Gerard is not to get a glimpse of it for the world."

The servant now entered with a message from Lady Gerard, who would not alight, begging that Lady Juliana would make haste down to her, as they had not a moment to lose. She was flying away, without further ceremony than a "Pray, excuse me," to the General, when her husband called after her to know whether the child was gone out, as he wished to show her to the General.

"I don't know, indeed," replied the fashionable mother; "I haven't had time to see her to-day;" and, before Douglas could reply she was downstairs.

A pause ensued—the General whistled a quick step, and Douglas walked up and down the room in a pitiable state of mind, guessing pretty much what was passing in the mind of his friend, and fully sensible that it must be of a severer nature than anything he could yet allow himself to think of his Juliana.

"Douglas," said the General, "have you made any step towards a reconciliation with your father-in-law? I believe it will become shortly necessary for your support."

"Juliana wrote twice after her marriage," replied he; "but the reception which her letters met with was not such as to encourage perseverance on our part. With regard to myself, it is not an affair in which delicacy will permit me to be very active, as I might be accused of mercenary motives, which I am far from having."

"Oh, of that I acquit you; but surely it ought to be a matter of moment, even to a—Lady Juliana. The case is now altered. Time must have accustomed him to the idea of this imaginary affront; and, on my honour, if he thought like a gentleman and a man of sense, I know where he would think the misfortune lay. Nay, don't interrupt me. The old Earl must now, I say, have cooled in his resentment; perhaps, too, his grandchildren may soften his heart; this must have occurred to you. Has her Ladyship taken any further steps since her arrival in town?"

"I—I believe she has not; but I will put her in mind."

"A daughter who requires to have her memory refreshed on such a subject is likely to make a valuable wife!" said the General drily.

Douglas felt as if it was incumbent on him to be angry, but remained silent.

"Hark ye, Douglas," continued the General, "I

speak this for your interest. You cannot go on without the Earl's help. You know I am not on ceremony with you; and if I refrain from saying what you see I think about your present ruinous mode of life, it is not to spare your feelings, but from a sense of the uselessness of any such remonstrance. What I do give you is with goodwill; but all my fortune would not suffice to furnish pug-dogs and deformed teapots for such a vitiated taste; and if it would, hang me if it should! But enough on this head. The Earl has been in bad health, and is lately come to town. His son, too, and his lady are to come about the same time, and are to reside with him during the season. I have heard Lord Lindore spoken of as a good-natured easy man, and he would probably enter willingly into any scheme to reinstate his sister into his father's good graces. Think of this, and make what you can of it; and my particular advice to you personally is, try to exchange into a marching regiment; for a fellow like you, with such a wife, London is the very devil! and so good morning to you." He snatched up his hat, and was off in a moment.

CHAPTER XXI.

" To reckon up a thousand of her pranks,
    Her pride, her wasteful spending, her unkindness,
    Her scolding, pouting, . . .
    Were to reap an endless catalogue."

Old Play.

WHEN Lady Juliana returned from her expedition, it was so late that Douglas had not time to speak to her; and separate engagements carrying them different ways, he had no opportunity to do so until the following morning at breakfast. He then resolved no longer to defer what he had to say, and began by reproaching her with the cavalier manner in which she had behaved to his good friend the General.

"Upon my life, Harry, you are grown perfectly savage," cried his Lady. "I was most particularly civil; I wonder what you would have me to do? You know very well I cannot have anything to say to old men of that sort."

"I think," returned Henry, "you might have been gratified by making an acquaintance with my benefactor, and the man to whom you owe the enjoyment of your favourite pleasures. At any rate, you need not have made yourself ridiculous. May I perish

if I did not wish myself underground while you
were talking nonsense to those sneaking rascals who
wheedle you out of your money! S'death! I had a
good mind to throw them and their trumpery out
of the window when I saw you make such a fool of
yourself."

"A fool of myself! how foolishly you talk! and as
for that vulgar, awkward General, he ought to have
been too much flattered. Some of the monsters were
so like himself, I am sure he must have thought I
took them for the love of his round bare pate."

"Upon my soul, Julia, I am ashamed of you! Do
leave off this excessive folly, and try to be rational.
What I particularly wished to say to you is that your
father is in town, and it will be proper that you should
make another effort to be reconciled to him."

"I dare say it will," answered Lady Juliana, with
a yawn.

"And you must lose no time. When will you
write?"

"There's no use in writing, or indeed doing anything in the matter. I am sure he won't forgive me."

"And why not?"

"Oh, why should he do it now? He did not forgive me when I asked him before."

"And do you think, then, for a father's forgiveness
it is not worth while to have a little perseverance?"

"I am sure he won't do it; so 'tis in vain to try,"
repeated she, going to the glass, and singing, "*Papa
non dite di no*," etc.

"By heavens, Julia!" cried her husband passionately, "you are past all endurance! Can nothing touch you?—nothing fix your thoughts, and make you serious for a single moment? Can I not make you understand that you are ruining yourself and me; that we have nothing to depend upon but the bounty of that man whom you disgust by your caprice, extravagance, and impertinence; and that if you don't get reconciled to your father what is to become of you? You already know what you have to expect from my family, and how you like living with them."

"Heavens, Harry!" exclaimed her Ladyship, "what is all this tirade about? Is it because I said papa wouldn't forgive me? I'm sure I don't mind writing to him; I have no objection, the first leisure moment I have; but really, in town, one's time is so engrossed."

At this moment her maid entered in triumph, carrying on her arms a satin dress, embroidered with gold and flowers.

"See, my Lady," cried she, "your new robe, as Madame has sent home half a day sooner than her word; and she has disobliged several of the quality by not giving the pattern."

"Oh, lovely! charming! Spread it out, Gage; hold it to the light; all my own fancy. Only look, Harry; how exquisite! how divine!"

Harry had no time to express his contempt for embroidered robes; for just then one of his knowing friends came, by appointment, to accompany him to

Tattersal's, where he was to bid for a famous pair of curricle grays.

Days passed on without Lady Juliana's ever thinking it worth while to follow her husband's advice about applying to her father; until a week after, Douglas overheard the following conversation between his wife and one of her acquaintance.

"You are going to this grand *fête*, of course," said Mrs. G. "I'm told it is to eclipse everything that has been yet seen or heard of."

"Of what *fête* do you speak?" demanded Lady Juliana.

"Lord, my dear creature, how Gothic you are! Don't you know anything about this grand affair that everybody has been talking of for two days? Lady Lindore gives, at your father's house, an entertainment which is to be a concert, ball, and masquerade at once. All London is asked, of any distinction, *c'a s'entend.* But, bless me, I beg pardon, I totally forgot that you were not on the best terms possible in that quarter; but never mind, we must have you go; there is not a person of fashion that will stay away; I must get you asked; I shall petition Lady Lindore in your favour."

"Oh pray don't trouble yourself," cried Lady Juliana, in extreme pique. "I believe I can get this done without your obliging interference; but I don't know whether I shall be in town then."

From this moment Lady Juliana resolved to make a vigorous effort to regain a footing in her father's

house. Her first action the next morning was to
write to her brother, who had hitherto kept aloof,
because he could not be at the trouble of having a
difference with the Earl, entreating him to use his
influence in promoting a reconciliation between her
father and herself.

No answer was returned for four days, at the end
of which time Lady Juliana received the following
note from her brother :—

"DEAR JULIA—I quite agree with you in thinking
that you have been kept long enough in the corner,
and shall certainly tell Papa that you are ready to
become a good girl whenever he shall please to take
you out of it. I shall endeavour to see Douglas and
you soon.—Yours affectionately,   LINDORE."

"Lady Lindore desires me to say you can have
tickets for her ball, if you choose to come *en masque.*"

Lady Juliana was delighted with this billet, which
she protested was everything that was kind and
generous; but the postscript was the part on which
she dwelt with the greatest delight, as she repeatedly
declared it was a great deal more than she expected.
"You see, Harry," said she, as she tossed the note to
him, "I was in the right. Papa won't forgive me;
but Lindore says he will send me a ticket for the
fête; it is vastly attentive of him, for I did not ask
it. But I must go disguised, which is monstrous provoking, for I'm afraid nobody will know me."

A dispute here ensued. Henry swore she should not steal into her father's house as long as she was his wife. The lady insisted that she should go to her brother's *fête* when she was invited; and the altercation ended as altercations commonly do, leaving both parties more wedded to their own opinion than at first.

In the evening Lady Juliana went to a large party; and as she was passing from one room into another she was startled by a little paper pellet thrown at her. Turning round to look for the offender, she saw her brother standing at a little distance, smiling at her surprise. This was the first time she had seen him for two years, and she went up to him with an extended hand, while he gave her a familiar nod, and a "How d'ye do, Julia?" and one finger of his hand, while he turned round to speak to one of his companions. Nothing could be more characteristic of both parties than this fraternal meeting; and from this time they were the best friends imaginable.

CHAPTER XXII.

" Helas ! où donc chercher ou trouver le bonheur,
Nulle part tout entier, partout avec mesure !"

VOLTAIRE.

SOME days before the expected *fête* Lady Juliana, at
the instigation of her adviser, Lady Gerard, resolved
upon taking the field against the Duchess of L——.
Her Grace had issued cards for a concert; and after
mature deliberation it was decided that her rival
should strike out something new, and announce a
christening for the same night.

The first intimation Douglas had of the honour
intended him by this arrangement was through the
medium of the newspaper, for the husband and wife
were now much too fashionable to be at all *au fait* of
each other's schemes. His first emotion was to be
extremely surprised; the next to be exceedingly displeased; and the last to be highly gratified at the
éclat with which his child was to be made a Christian.
True, he had intended requesting the General to act
as godfather upon the occasion; but Lady Juliana
protested she would rather the child never should be
christened at all (which already seemed nearly to
have been the case) than have that cross vulgar-look-

ing man to stand sponsor. Her Ladyship, however,
so far conceded that the General was to have the
honour of giving his name to the next, if a boy, for
she was now near her second confinement; and, with
this promise Henry was satisfied to slight the only
being in the world to whom he looked for support to
himself and his children. In the utmost delight the
fond mother drove away to consult her confidants
upon the name and decorations of the child, whom
she had not even looked at for many days.

Everything succeeded to admiration. Amid crowds
of spectators, in all the pomp of lace and satin, surrounded by princes and peers, and handed from
duchesses to countesses, the twin daughter of Henry
Douglas, and the heroine of future story, became a
Christian by the names of Adelaide Julia.

Some months previous to this event Lady Juliana
had received a letter from Mrs. Douglas, informing
her of the rapid improvement that had taken place in
her little charge, and requesting to know by what
name she should have her christened; at the same
time gently insinuating her wish that, in compliance
with the custom of the country, and as a compliment
due to the family, it should be named after its paternal grandmother.

Lady Juliana glanced over the first line of the
letter, then looked at the signature, resolved to read
the rest as soon as she should have time to answer it;
and in the meantime tossed it into a drawer, amongst
old visiting cards and unpaid bills.

After vainly waiting for an answer, much beyond the accustomed time when children are baptized, Mrs. Douglas could no longer refuse to accede to the desires of the venerable inmates of Glenfern ; and about a month before her favoured sister received her more elegant appellations, the neglected twin was baptized by the name of Mary.

Mrs. Douglas's letter had been enclosed in the following one from Miss Grizzy, and as it had not the good fortune to be perused by the person to whom it was addressed, we deem it but justice to the writer to insert it here :—

"GLENFERN CASTLE, *July 30th*, 17—.

"MY DEAREST NIECE, LADY JULIANA — I am Certain, as indeed we all are, that it will Afford your Ladyship and our dear Nephew the greatest Pleasure to see this letter Franked by our Worthy and Respectable Friend Sir Sampson Maclaughlan, Bart., especially as it is the First he has ever franked ; out of compliment to you, as I assure you he admires you excessively, as indeed we all do. At the same Time, you will of course, I am sure, Sympathise with us all in the distress Occasioned by the melancholy Death of our late Most Obliging Member, Duncan M'Dunsmuir, Esquire, of Dhunacrag and Auchnagoil, who you never have had the Pleasure of seeing. What renders his death Particularly distressing, is, that Lady Maclaughlan is of opinion it was entirely owing to eating

Raw oysters, and damp feet. This ought to be a warning to all Young people to take care of Wet feet, and Especially eating Raw oysters, which are certainly Highly dangerous, particularly where there is any Tendency to Gout. I hope, my dear Niece, you have got a pair of Stout walking shoes, and that both Henry and you remember to Change your feet after Walking. I am told Raw Oysters are much the fashion in London at present; but when this Fatal Event comes to be Known, it will of course Alarm people very much, and put them upon their guard both as to Damp Feet and Raw oysters. Lady Maclaughlan is in High spirits at Sir Sampson's Success, though, at the Same Time, I assure you, she Felt much for the Distress of poor Mr. M'Dunsmuir, and had sent him a Large Box of Pills, and a Bottle of Gout Tincture, only two days before he died. This will be a great Thing for you, and especially for Henry, my dear niece, as Sir Sampson and Lady Maclaughlan are going to London directly to take his Seat in Parliament; and she will make a point of Paying you every attention, and will Matronise you to the play, and any other Public places you may wish to go; as both my Sisters and I are of opinion you are rather Young to matronise yourself yet, and you could not get a more Respectable Matron than Lady Maclaughlan. I hope Harry wont take it amiss if Sir Sampson does not pay him so much Attention as he might expect; but he says that he will not be master of a moment of his own Time in London. He

will be so much taken up with the King and the Duke
of York, that he is afraid he will Disoblige a great
Number of the Nobility by it, besides injuring his
own health by such Constant application to business.
He is to make a very fine Speech in Parliament, but
it is not yet Fixed what his First Motion is to be upon.
He himself wishes to move for a New Subsidy to the
Emperor of Germany; but Lady Maclaughlan is of
opinion that it would be better to Bring in a Bill for
Building a bridge over the Water of Dlin; which, to
be sure, is very much wanted, as a Horse and Cart
were drowned at the Ford last Speat.   We are All, I
am happy to Say, in excellent Health.   Becky is re-
covering from the Measles as well as could be Wished,
and the Rose[1] is quite gone out of Bella's Face.
Beennie has been prevented from Finishing a most
Beautiful Pair of bottle Sliders for your Ladyship by
a whitlow, but it is now Mending, and I hope will be
done in Time to go with Babby's Vase Carpet, which
is extremely elegant, by Sir S. and Lady Maclaughlan.
This Place is in great Beauty at present, and the new
Byre is completely finished.   My Sisters and I regret
Excessively that Henry and you should have seen
Glenfern to such disadvantage; but when next you
favour us with a visit, I hope it will be in Summer,
and the New Byre you will think a Prodigious Improvement.   Our dear Little Grand-niece is in great
health, and much improved.   We reckon her Extremely
like our Family, Particularly Becky; though she has

---

[1] Erysipelas.

a great Look of Bella, at the Same Time, when she Laughs. Excuse the Shortness of this Letter, my dear Niece, as I shall Write a much Longer one by Lady Maclaughlan.

"Meantime, I remain, my
    "Dear Lady Juliana, yours and
        "Henry's most affect. aunt,
            "GRIZZEL DOUGLAS."

In spite of her husband's remonstrance Lady Juliana persisted in her resolution of attending her sister-in-law's masked ball, from which she returned, worn out with amusement and surfeited with pleasure ; protesting all the while she dawdled over her evening breakfast the following day that there was nobody in the world so much to be envied as Lady Lindore. Such jewels ! such dresses ! such a house ! such a husband ! so easy and good-natured, and rich and generous ! She was sure Lindore did not care what his wife did. She might give what parties she pleased, go where she liked, spend as much money as she chose, and he would never trouble his head about the matter. She was quite certain Lady Lindore had not a single thing to wish for : *ergo*, she must be the happiest woman in the world ! All this was addressed to Henry, who had, however, attained the happy art of not hearing above one word out of a hundred that happened to fall from the "angel lips of his adored Julia ;" and, having finished the newspapers, and made himself acquainted with all the blood-horses, thorough-bred *fillies*, and brood mares therein set forth, with a yawn and whistle sauntered away to G——'s, to look at the last regulation epaulettes.

Not long after, as Lady Juliana was stepping into the carriage that was to whirl her to Bond Street she was met by her husband, who, with a solemnity of manner that would have startled any one but his volatile lady, requested she would return with him into the house, as he wished to converse with her upon a subject of some importance. He prevailed on her to return, upon condition that he would not detain her above five minutes. When, shutting the drawing-room doors, he said, with earnestness, "I think, Julia, you were talking of Lady Lindore this morning: oblige me by repeating what you said, as I was reading the papers, and really did not attend much to what passed."

Her Ladyship, in extreme surprise, wondered how Harry could be so tiresome and absurd as to stop her airing for any such purpose. She really did not know what she said. How could she? It was more than an hour ago.

"Well, then, say what you think of her now," cried Douglas impatiently.

"Think of her! why, what all the world must think—that she is the happiest woman in it. She looked so uncommonly well last night, and was in such spirits, in her fancy dress, before she masked. After that, I quite lost sight of her."

"As every one else has done. She has not been

seen since.   Her favourite St. Leger is missing too,
and there is hardly a doubt but that they are gone off
together."

Even Lady Juliana was shocked at this intelligence,
though the folly, more than the wickedness, of the
thing, seemed to strike her mind; but Henry was no
nice observer, and was therefore completely satisfied
with the disapprobation she expressed for her sister-
in-law's conduct.

"I am so sorry for poor dear Lindore," said Lady
Juliana after having exhausted herself in invectives
against his wife.   "Such a generous creature as he
to be used in such a manner—it is quite shocking
to think of it!   If he had been an ill-natured stingy
wretch it would have been nothing; but Frederick is
such a noble-hearted fellow—I dare say he would give
me a thousand pounds if I were to ask him, for he
don't care about money."

"Lord Lindore takes the matter very coolly, I
understand," replied her husband; "but—don't be
alarmed, dear Julia—your father has suffered a little
from the violence of his feelings.   He has had a sort
of apoplectic fit, but is not considered in immediate
danger."

Lady Juliana burst into tears, desired the carriage
might be put up, as she should not go out, and even
declared her intention of abstaining from Mrs. D——'s
assembly that evening.   Henry warmly commended
the extreme propriety of these measures; and, not to
be outdone in greatness of mind, most heroically sent

an apology to a grand military dinner at the Duke of Y——'s; observing, at the same time, that, in the present state of the family, one or two friends to a quiet family dinner was as much as they should be up to.

CHAPTER XXIII.

" I but purpose to embark with thee
On the smooth surface of a summer sea,
While gentle zephyrs play in prosp'rous gales,
And Fortune's favour fills the swelling sails."

Henry and Emma.

How long these voluntary sacrifices to duty and propriety might have been made it would not be difficult
to guess ; but Lady Juliana's approaching confinement
rendered her seclusion more and more a matter of
necessity; and shortly after these events took place
she presented her delighted husband with a son.
Henry lost no time in announcing the birth of his
child to General Cameron, and at the same time
requesting he would stand godfather, and give his
name to the child. The answer was as follows :—

"HORT LODGE, BERKS.

"DEAR HENRY—By this time twelvemonth I hope
it will be my turn to communicate to you a similar
event in my family to that which your letter an-
nounces to me. As a preliminary step, I am just
about to march into quarters for life with a young
woman, daughter to my steward. She is healthy,

good-humoured, and of course vulgar, since she is no connoisseur in china, and never spoke to a pug-dog in her life.

"Your allowance will be remitted regularly from my Banker until the day of my death; you will then succeed to ten thousand pounds, secured to your children, which is all you have to expect from me. If, after this, you think it worth your while, you are very welcome to give your son the name of yours faithfully,   WILLIAM CAMERON."

Henry's consternation at the contents of this epistle was almost equalled by Juliana's indignation. "The daughter of a steward!—Heavens! it made her sick to think of it. It was too shocking! The man ought to be shut up. Henry ought to prevent him from disgracing his connexions in such a manner. There ought to be a law against old men marrying—— "

"And young ones too," groaned Douglas, as he thought of the debts he had contracted on the faith and credit of being the General's heir; for with all the sanguine presumption of thoughtless youth and buoyant spirits, Henry had no sooner found his fault forgiven than he immediately fancied it forgotten, and himself completely restored to favour. His friends and the world were of the same opinion; and, as the future possessor of immense wealth, he found nothing so easy as to borrow money and contract debts, which he now saw the impossibility of ever discharging. Still he flattered himself the General

might only mean to frighten him; or he might relent; or the marriage might go off; or he might not
have any children; and, with these *mighty* hopes,
things went on as usual for some time longer. Lady
Juliana, who, to do her justice, was not of a more
desponding character than her husband, had also her
stock of hopes and expectations always ready to act
upon. She was quite sure that if papa ever came to
his senses (for he had remained in a state of stupefaction since the apoplectic stroke) he would forgive
her, and take her to live with him, now that that vile
Lady Lindore was gone, or, if he should never recover,
she was equally sure of benefiting by his death; for
though he had said he was not to leave her a shilling,
she did not believe it. She was sure papa would
never do anything so cruel; and at any rate, if he
did, Lindore was so generous, he would do something
very handsome for her; and so forth.

At length the bubbles burst. The same paper that
stated the marriage of General William Cameron to
Judith Broadcast, Spinster, announced, in all the
dignity of woe, the death of that most revered nobleman and eminent statesman, Augustus, Earl of Courtland.

In weak minds it has generally been remarked
that no medium can be maintained. Where hope
holds her dominion she is too buoyant to be accompanied by her anchor; and between her and despair
there are no gradations. Desperate indeed now
became the condition of the misjudging pair. Lady

Juliana's name was not even mentioned in her father's will, and the General's marriage rendered his settlements no longer a secret. In all the horrors of desperation, Henry now found himself daily beset by creditors of every description. At length the fatal blow came. Horses, carriages, everything they could call their own, were seized. The term for which they held the house was expired, and they found themselves on the point of being turned into the street, when Lady Juliana, who had been for two days, as her woman expressed it, *out of one fit into another*, suddenly recovered strength to signify her desire of being conveyed to her brother's house. A hackney coach was procured, into which the hapless victim of her own follies was carried. Shuddering with disgust, and accompanied by her children and their attendants, she was set down at the noble mansion from which she had fled two years before.

Her brother, whom she fortunately found at home, lolling upon a sofa with a new novel in his hand, received her without any marks of surprise; said those things happened every day; hoped Captain Douglas would contrive to get himself extricated from this slight embarrassment; and informed his sister that she was welcome to occupy her old apartments, which had been lately fitted up for Lady Lindore. Then ringing the bell, he desired the housekeeper might show Lady Juliana upstairs, and put the children in the nursery; mentioned that he generally dined at eight o'clock; and, nodding to his sister as she quitted the room, returned to his book, as if nothing had occurred to disturb him from it.

In ten minutes after her entrance into Courtland house Lady Juliana had made greater advances in *religion* and *philosophy* than she had done in the whole nineteen years of her life ; for she not only perceived that "out of evil cometh good," but was perfectly ready to admit that "all is for the best," and that " whatever is, is right."

" How lucky is it for me," exclaimed she to herself, as she surveyed the splendid suite of apartments that were destined for her accommodation—" how very fortunate that things have turned out as they have done ; that Lady Lindore should have run off, and that the General's marriage should have taken place just at the time of poor papa's death "—and, in short, Lady Juliana set no bounds to her self-gratulations on the happy turn of affairs which had brought about this change in her situation.

To a heart not wholly devoid of feeling, and a mind capable of anything like reflection, the desolate appearance of this magnificent mansion would have excited emotions of a very different nature. The apartments of the late Earl, with their wide extended doors and windows, sheeted furniture, and air of dreary order, exhibited that waste and chilling aspect which marks the chambers of death ; and even Lady Juliana shuddered, she knew not why, as she passed through them.

Those of Lady Lindore presented a picture not less

striking, could her thoughtless successor have profited by the lesson they offered. Here was all that the most capricious fancy, the most boundless extravagance, the most refined luxury, could wish for or suggest. The bedchamber, dressing-room, and boudoir were each fitted up in a style that seemed rather suited for the pleasures of an Eastern sultana or Grecian courtesan than for the domestic comfort of a British matron.

"I wonder how Lady Lindore could find in her heart to leave this delicious boudoir," observed Lady Juliana to the old housekeeper.

"I rather wonder, my Lady, how she could find in her heart to leave these pretty babies," returned the good woman, as a little boy came running into the room, calling, "Mamma, mamma!" Lady Juliana had nothing to say to children beyond a "How d'ye do, love?" and the child, after regarding her for a moment, with a look of disappointment, ran away back to his nursery.

When Lady Juliana had fairly settled herself in her new apartments, and the tumult of delight began to subside, it occurred to her that something must be done for poor Harry, whom she had left in the hands of a brother officer, in a state little short of distraction. She accordingly went in search of her brother, to request his advice and assistance, and found him, it being nearly dark, preparing to set out on his morning's ride. Upon hearing the situation of his brother-in-law he declared himself ready to assist Mr. Douglas as far

as he was able; but he had just learned from his
people of business that his own affairs were somewhat
involved. The late Earl had expended enormous
sums on political purposes; Lady Lindore had run
through a prodigious deal of money, he believed; and
he himself had some debts, amounting, he was told,
to seventy thousand pounds. Lady Juliana was all
aghast at this information, which was delivered with
the most perfect *nonchalance* by the Earl, while he
amused himself with his Newfoundland dog. Unable
to conceal her disappointment at these effects of her
brother's "liberality and generosity," Lady Juliana
burst into tears.

The Earl's sensibility was akin to his generosity;
he gave money (or rather allowed it to be taken)
freely when he had it, from indolence and easiness of
temper; he hated the sight of distress in any individual, because it occasioned trouble, and was, in
short, a *bore*. He therefore made haste to relieve his
sister's alarm by assuring her that these were mere
trifles; that, as for Douglas's affairs, he would order
his agent to arrange everything in his name; hoped
to have the pleasure of seeing him at dinner; recommended to his sister to have some pheasant pies for
luncheon; and, calling Carlo, set out upon his ride.

However much Lady Juliana had felt mortified
and disappointed at learning the state of her brother's
finances, she began, by degrees, to extract the greatest
consolation from the comparative insignificance of her
own debts to those of the Earl; and accordingly, in

high spirits at this newly discovered and judicious source of comfort, she despatched the following note to her husband :—

"DEAREST HENRY—I have been received in the kindest manner imaginable by Frederick, and have been put in possession of my old apartments, which are so much altered, I should never have known them. They were furnished by Lady Lindore, who really has a divine taste. I long to show you all the delights of this abode. Frederick desired me to say that he expects to see you here at dinner, and that he will take charge of paying all our bills whenever he gets money. Only think of his owing a hundred thousand pounds, besides all papa's and Lady Lindore's debts! I assure you I was almost ashamed to tell him of ours, they sounded so trifling; but it is quite a relief to find other people so much worse. Indeed, I always thought it quite natural for us to run in debt, considering that we had no money to pay anything, while Courtland, who is as rich as a Jew, is so hampered. I shall expect you at eight, until when, adieu, *mio caro*,

"Your JULIE.

"I am quite wretched about you."

This tender and consolatory billet Henry had not the satisfaction of receiving, having been arrested, shortly after his wife's departure, at the suit of Mr. Shagg, for the sum of two thousand some odd hundreds, for carriages jobbed, bought, exchanged, repaired, returned, etc.

Lady Juliana's horror and dismay at the news of her husband's arrest were excessive. Her only ideas of confinement were taken from those pictures of the Bastile and Inquisition that she had read so much of in French and German novels; and the idea of a prison was indissolubly united in her mind with bread and water, chains and straw, dungeons and darkness. Callous and selfish, therefore, as she might be, she was not yet so wholly void of all natural feeling as to think with indifference of the man she had once fondly loved reduced to such a pitiable condition.

Almost frantic at the phantom of her own creation, she flew to her brother's apartment, and, in the wildest and most incoherent manner, besought him to rescue her poor Henry from chains and a dungeon.

With some difficulty Lord Courtland at length apprehended the extent of his brother-in-law's misfortune; and, with his usual *sang froid*, smiled at his sister's simplicity, assured her the King's Bench was the pleasantest place in the world; that some of his own most particular friends were there, who gave capital dinners, and led the most desirable lives imaginable.

"And will he really not be fed on bread and water, and wear chains, and sleep upon straw?" asked the tender wife in the utmost surprise and delight. "Oh, then, he is not so much to be pitied, though I daresay he would rather get out of prison too."

The Earl promised to obtain his release the following day, and Lady Juliana returned to her toilet with a much higher opinion of prisons than she had ever entertained before.

Lord Courtland, for once in his life, was punctual to his promise; and even interested himself so thoroughly in Douglas's affairs, though without inquiring into any particulars, as to take upon himself the discharge of his debts, and to procure leave for him to exchange into a regiment of the line, then under orders for India.

Upon hearing of this arrangement Lady Juliana's grief and despair, as usual, set all reason at defiance. She would not suffer her dear, dear Harry to leave her. She knew she could not live without him; she was sure she should die; and Harry would be sea-sick, and grow so yellow and so ugly that when he came back she should never have any comfort in him again.

Henry, who had never doubted her readiness to accompany him, immediately hastened to assuage her anguish by assuring her that it had always been his intention to take her along with him.

That was worse and worse : she wondered how he could be so barbarous and absurd as to think of her leaving all her friends and going to live amongst savages. She had done a great deal in living so long contentedly with him in Scotland; but she never could nor would make such another sacrifice. Besides, she was sure poor Courtland could not do without her; she knew he never would marry again ; and who would take care of his dear children, and educate them properly, if she did not? It would be too ungrateful to desert Frederick, after all he had done for them.

The pride of the man, as much as the affection of the husband, was irritated by this resistance to his will; and a violent scene of reproach and recrimination terminated in an eternal farewell.

CHAPTER XXIV.

" In age, in infancy, from others' aid
  Is all our hope ; to teach us to be kind,
  That nature's first, last lesson."

YOUNG.

THE neglected daughter of Lady Juliana Douglas experienced all the advantages naturally to be expected from her change of situation. Her watchful aunt superintended the years of her infancy, and all that a tender and judicious mother *could* do—all that most mothers *think* they do—she performed. Mrs. Douglas, though not a woman either of words or systems, possessed a reflecting mind, and a heart warm with benevolence towards everything that had a being ; and all the best feelings of her nature were excited by the little outcast thus abandoned by her unnatural parent. As she pressed the unconscious babe to her bosom she thought how blest she should have been had a child of her own thus filled her arms ; but the reflection called forth no selfish murmurs from her chastened spirit. While the tear of soft regret trembled in her eye, that eye was yet raised in gratitude to Heaven for having called forth those delightful affections which might otherwise have slumbered in her heart.

Mrs. Douglas had read much, and reflected more, and many faultless theories of education had floated in her mind. But her good sense soon discovered how unavailing all theories were whose foundations rested upon the inferred wisdom of the teacher, and how intricate and unwieldy must be the machinery for the human mind where the human hand alone is to guide and uphold it. To engraft into her infant soul the purest principles of religion was therefore the chief aim of Mary's preceptress. The fear of God was the only restraint imposed upon her dawning intellect; and from the Bible alone was she taught the duties of morality—not in the form of a dry code of laws, to be read with a solemn face on Sundays, or learned with weeping eyes as a week-day task—but adapted to her youthful capacity by judicious illustration, and familiarised to her taste by hearing its stories and precepts from the lips she best loved. Mrs. Douglas was the friend and confidant of her pupil: to her all her hopes and fears, wishes and dreads were confided; and the first effort of her reason was the discovery that to please her aunt she must study to please her Maker.

"L'inutilité de la vie des femmes est la premier source de leurs désordres."

Mrs. Douglas was fully convinced of the truth of this observation, and that the mere selfish cares and vulgar bustle of life are not sufficient to satisfy the immortal soul, however they may serve to engross it.

A portion of Mary's time was therefore devoted to

the daily practice of the great duties of life ; in administering in some shape or other to the wants and misfortunes of her fellow-creatures, without requiring from them that their virtue should have been immaculate, or expecting that their gratitude should be everlasting.

"It is better," thought Mrs. Douglas, "that we should sometimes be deceived by others than that we should learn to deceive ourselves; and the charity and goodwill that is suffered to lie dormant, or feed itself on speculative acts of beneficence, for want of proper objects to call it into use, will soon become the corroding rust that will destroy the best feelings of our nature."

But although Mary strenuously applied herself to the uses of life, its embellishments were by no means neglected. She was happily endowed by nature ; and, under the judicious management of her aunt, made rapid though unostentatious progress in the improvement of the talents committed to her care. Without having been blessed with the advantages of a dancing-master, her step was light, and her motions free and graceful ; and if her aunt had not been able to impart to her the favourite graces of the most fashionable singer of the day, neither had she thwarted the efforts of her own natural taste in forming a style full of simplicity and feeling. In the modern languages she was perfectly skilled ; and if her drawings wanted the enlivening touches of the master to give them effect, as an atonement they displayed a perfect knowledge of the rules of perspective and the study of the bust.

All this was, however, mere leather and prunella to the ladies of Glenfern; and many were the cogitations and consultations that took place on the subject of Mary's mismanagement. According to their ideas there could be but one good system of education; and that was the one that had been pursued with them, and through them transmitted to their nieces.

To attend the parish church and remember the text; to observe who was there and who was *not* there; and to wind up the evening with a sermon stuttered and stammered through by one of the girls (the worst reader always piously selected, for the purpose of improving their reading), and particularly addressed to the Laird, openly and avowedly snoring in his arm-chair, though at every pause starting up with a peevish "Weel?"—this was the sum total of their religious duties. Their moral virtues were much upon the same scale; to knit stockings, scold servants, cement china, trim bonnets, lecture the poor, and look up to Lady Maclaughlan, comprised nearly their whole code. But these were the virtues of ripened years and enlarged understandings—what their pupils might hope to arrive at, but could not presume to meddle with. *Their* merits consisted in being compelled to sew certain large portions of white-work; learning to read and write in the worst manner; occasionally *wearing* a *collar*, and learning the notes on the spinnet. These acquirements, accompanied with

a great deal of lecturing and fault-finding, sufficed for
the first fifteen years; when the two next, passed at
a provincial boarding-school, were supposed to impart
every graceful accomplishment to which women could
attain.

Mrs. Douglas's method of conveying instruction, it
may easily be imagined, did not square with their
ideas on that subject. They did nothing themselves
without a bustle, and to do a thing quietly was to
them the same as not doing it at all—it could not be
done, for nobody had ever heard of it. In short, like
many other worthy people, their ears were their only
organs of intelligence. They believed everything they
were told; but unless they were told, they believed
nothing. They had never heard Mrs. Douglas expatiate on the importance of the trust reposed in her, or
enlarge on the difficulties of female education; *ergo*,
Mrs. Douglas could have no idea of the nature of the
duties she had undertaken.

Their visits to Lochmarlie only served to confirm
the fact. Miss Jacky deponed that during the month
she was there she never could discover when or how
it was that Mary got her lessons; luckily the child
was quick, and had contrived, poor thing, to pick up
things wonderfully, nobody knew how, for it was really
astonishing to see how little pains were bestowed upon
her; and the worst of it was, that she seemed to do
just as she liked, for nobody ever heard her reproved,
and everybody knew that young people never could
have enough said to them. All this differed widely

from the éclat of their system, and could not fail of
causing great disquiet to the sisters.

"I declare I'm quite confounded at all this!" said
Miss Grizzy, at the conclusion of Miss Jacky's communication. "It really appears as if Mary, poor
thing, was getting no education at all; and yet she
can do things, too. I can't understand it; and it's
very odd in Mrs. Douglas to allow her to be so much
neglected, for certainly Mary's constantly with herself;
which, to be sure, shows that she is very much spoilt;
for although our girls are as fond of us as I am sure
any creatures can be, yet, at the same time, they are
always very glad—which is quite natural—to run
away from us."

"I think it's high time Mary had done something
fit to be seen," said Miss Nicky; "she is now sixteen
past."

"Most girls of Mary's time of life that ever *I* had
anything to do with," replied Jacky, with a certain
wave of the head, peculiar to sensible women, "had
something to show before her age. Bella had worked
the globe long before she was sixteen; and Baby did
her filigree tea-caddy the first quarter she was at
Miss Macgowk's," glancing with triumph from the one
which hung over the mantelpiece, to the other which
stood on the tea-table, shrouded in a green bag.

"And, to be sure," rejoined Grizzy, "although
Betsy's screen did cost a great deal of money—that
can't be denied; and her father certainly grudged it
very much at the time—there's no doubt of that; yet

certainly it does her the greatest credit, and it is a great satisfaction to us all to have these things to show. I am sure nobody would ever think that ass was made of crape, and how naturally it seems to be eating the beautiful chenille thistle! I declare, I think the ass is as like an ass as anything can be!"

"And as to Mary's drawing," continued the narrator of her deficiencies, "there is not one of them fit for framing: mere scratches with a chalk pencil— what any child might do."

"And to think," said Nicky, with indignation, "how little Mrs. Douglas seemed to think of the handsome coloured views the girls did at Miss Macgowk's."

"All our girls have the greatest genius for drawing," observed Grizzy; "there can be no doubt of that; but it's a thousand pities, I'm sure, that none of them seem to like it. To be sure they say—what I dare say is very true—that they can't get such good paper as they got at Miss Macgowk's; but they have showed that they *can* do, for their drawings are quite astonishing. Somebody lately took them to be Mr. Touchup's own doing; and I'm sure there couldn't be a greater compliment than that! I represented all that to Mrs. Douglas, and urged her very strongly to give Mary the benefit of at least a quarter of Miss Macgowk's, were it only for the sake of her carriage; or, at least, to make her wear our collar."

This was the tenderest of all themes, and bursts of sorrowful exclamations ensued. The collar had long

been a galling yoke upon their minds; its iron had
entered into their very souls; for it was a collar
presented to the family of Glenfern by the wisest,
virtuousest, best of women and of grandmothers, the
the good Lady Girnachgowl; and had been worn in
regular rotation by every female of the family till
now that Mrs. Douglas positively refused to subject
Mary's pliant form to its thraldom. Even the Laird,
albeit no connoisseur in any shapes save those of his
kine, was of opinion that since the thing was in the
house it was a pity it should be lost. Not Venus's
girdle even was supposed to confer greater charms
than the Girnachgowl collar.

"It's really most distressing!" said Miss Grizzy to
her friend Lady Maclaughlan.

"Mary's back won't be worth a farthing; and we
have always been quite famous for our backs."

"Humph!—that's the reason people are always so
glad to see them, child."

With regard to Mary's looks, opinions were not so
decided. Mrs. Douglas thought her, what she was,
an elegant, interesting-looking girl. The Laird, as he
peered at her over his spectacles, pronounced her to
be but a shilpit thing, though weel eneugh, considering the ne'er-do-weels that were aught her. Miss
Jacky opined that she would have been quite a
different creature had she been brought up like any
other girl. Miss Grizzy did not know what to think;
she certainly was pretty—nobody could dispute that.
At the same time, many people would prefer Bella's

looks; and Baby was certainly uncommonly comely.
Miss Nicky thought it was no wonder she looked pale
sometimes. She never supped her broth in a wise-
like way at dinner; and it was a shame to hear of a
girl of Mary's age being set up with tea to her breakfast, and wearing white petticoats in winter—and
such roads, too!

Lady Maclaughlan pronounced (and that was next
to a special revelation) that the girl would be handsome when she was forty, not a day sooner; and she
would be clever, for her mother was a fool; and
foolish mothers had always wise children, and *vice
versa,* "and your mother was a very clever woman,
girls—humph!"

Thus passed the early years of the almost forgotten
twin; blest in the warm affection and mild authority
of her more than mother. Sometimes Mrs. Douglas
half formed the wish that her beloved pupil should
mix in society and become known to the world; but
when she reflected on the dangers of that world, and
on the little solid happiness its pleasures afford, she
repressed the wish, and only prayed she might be
allowed to rest secure in the simple pleasures she
then enjoyed. "Happiness is not a plant of this
earth," said she to herself with a sigh; "but God
gives peace and tranquillity to the virtuous in all
situations, and under every trial. Let me then strive
to make Mary virtuous, and leave the rest to Him
who alone knoweth what is good for us!"

CHAPTER XXV.

" Th' immortal line in sure succession reigns,
    The fortune of the family remains,
    And grandsires' grandsons the long list contains."
                                        DRYDEN's *Virgil.*

    " We are such stuff
As dreams are made on ; and our little life
Is rounded with a sleep."
                                        Tempest.

BUT Mary's back and Mary's complexion now ceased
to be the first objects of interest at Glenfern ; for, to
the inexpressible delight and amazement of the sisters,
Mrs. Douglas, after due warning, became the mother
of a son. How this event had been brought about
without the intervention of Lady Maclaughlan was
past the powers of Miss Grizzy's comprehension. To
the last moment they had been sceptical, for Lady
Maclaughlan had shook her head and humphed whenever the subject was mentioned. For several months
they had therefore vibrated between their own sanguine hopes and their oracle's disheartening doubts ;
and even when the truth was manifest, a sort of vague
tremor took possession of their mind as to what Lady
Maclaughlan would think of it.

    " I declare I don't very well know how to announce

this happy event to Lady Maclaughlan," said Miss
Grizzy, as she sat in a ruminating posture, with her
pen in her hand; "it will give her the greatest pleasure, I know that; she has such a regard for our
family, she would go any lengths for us. At the
same time, everybody must be sensible it is a delicate
matter to tell a person of Lady Maclaughlan's skill
they have been mistaken. I'm sure I don't know how
she may take it: and yet she can't suppose it will
make any difference in our sentiments for her. She
must be sensible we have all the greatest respect for
her opinion."

"The wisest people are sometimes mistaken," observed Miss Jacky.

"I'm sure, Jacky, that's very true," said Grizzy,
brightening up at the brilliancy of this remark.

"And it's better she should have been mistaken
than Mrs. Douglas," followed up Miss Nicky.

"I declare, Nicky, you are perfectly right; and I
shall just say so at once to Lady Maclaughlan."

The epistle was forthwith commenced by the enlightened Grizelda. Miss Joan applied herself to the
study of "The Whole Duty of Man," which she was
determined to make herself mistress of for the benefit
of her grand-nephew; and Miss Nicholas fell to
reckoning all who could, would, or should be at the
christening, that she might calculate upon the quantity of *dreaming-bread* that would be required. The
younger ladies were busily engaged in divers and
sundry disputes regarding the right to succession to a

once-white lutestring negligée of their mother's, which
three of them had laid their accounts with figuring
in at the approaching celebration. The old gentleman
was the only one in the family who took the least of
the general happiness. He had got into a habit of
being fretted about everything that happened, and he
could not entirely divest himself of it even upon this
occasion. His parsimonious turns, too, had considerably increased; and his only criterion of judging of
anything was according to what it would bring.

"Sorra tak me if ane wadnae think, to hear ye,
this was the first bairn that e'er was born! What's
a' the fraize aboot, ye gowks?" (to his daughters)—
"a whingin get! that'll tak mair oot o' fowk's pockets
than e'er it'll pit into them! Mony a guid profitable
beast's been brought into the warld and ne'er a word
in in'ts heed."

All went on smoothly. Lady Maclaughlan testified
no resentment. Miss Jacky had the "The Whole
Duty of Man" at her finger-ends; and Miss Nicky
was not more severe than could have been expected,
considering, as she did, how the servants at Lochmarlie must be living at hack and manger. It had
been decided at Glenfern that the infant heir to its
consequence could not with propriety be christened
anywhere but at the seat of his forefathers. Mr. and
Mrs. Douglas had good-humouredly yielded the point;
and, as soon as she was able for the change, the whole
family took up their residence for a season under the
paternal roof.

Blissful visions floated around the pillows of the happy spinsters the night preceding the christening, which were duly detailed at the breakfast-table the following morning.

"I declare I don't know what to think of my dream," began Miss Grizzy. "I dreamt that Lady Maclaughlan was upon her knees to you, brother, to get you to take an emetic ; and just as she had mixed it up so nicely in some of our black-currant jelly, little Norman snatched it out of your hand and ran away with it."

"You're eneugh to turn onybody's stamick wi' your nonsense," returned the Laird gruffly.

"And I," said Miss Jacky, "thought I saw you standing in your shirt, brother, as straight as a rash, and good Lady Girnachgowl buckling her collar upon you with her own hands."

"I wish ye wadna deive me wi' your havers !" still more indignantly, and turning his shoulder to the fair dreamer, as he continued to con over the newspaper.

"And I," cried Miss Nicky, eager to get her mystic tale disclosed, "I thought, brother, I saw you take and throw all the good dreaming-bread into the ash-hole."

"By my troth, an' ye deserve to be thrown after't !" exclaimed the exasperated Laird, as he quitted the room in high wrath, muttering to himself, "Hard case —canna get peace—eat my vittals—fules—tawpies— clavers !" etc. etc.

"I declare I can't conceive why Glenfern should

be so ill pleased at our dreams," said Miss Grizzy. "Everybody knows dreams are always contrary; and even were it otherwise, I'm sure I should think no shame to take an emetic, especially when Lady Mac- laughlan was at the trouble of mixing it up so nicely."

"And we have all worn good Lady Girnachgowl's collar before now," said Miss Jacky.

"I think I had the worst of it, that had all my good dreaming-bread destroyed," added Miss Nicky.

"Nothing could be more natural than your dreams," said Mrs. Douglas, "considering how all these subjects have engrossed you for some time past. You, Aunt Grizzy, may remember how desirous you were of administering one of Lady Maclaughlan's powders to my little boy yesterday; and you, Aunt Jacky, made a point of trying Lady Girnachgowl's collar upon Mary, to convince her how pleasant it was; while you, Aunt Nicky, had experienced a great alarm in supposing your cake had been burned in the oven. And these being the most vivid impressions you had received during the day, it was perfectly natural that they should have retained their influence during a portion of the night."

The interpretations were received with high dis- dain. One and all declared they never dreamed of anything that *had* occurred; and therefore the visions of the night portended some extraordinary good for- tune to the family in general, and to little Norman in particular.

"The best fortune I can wish for him, and all of

us, for this day is, that he should remain quiet during the ceremony," said his mother, who was not so elated as Lady Macbeth at the predictions of the sisters.

The christening party mustered strong; and the rites of baptism were duly performed by the Rev. Duncan M'Drone. The little Christian had been kissed by every lady in company, and pronounced by the matrons to be "a dainty little *doug!*" and by the misses to be "the sweetest lamb they had ever seen!" The cake and wine was in its progress round the company; when, upon its being tendered to the old gentleman, who was sitting silent in his arm-chair, he abruptly exclaimed, in a most discordant voice, "Hey! what's a' this wastery for?"— and ere an answer could be returned his jaw dropped, his eyes fixed, and the Laird of Glenfern ceased to breathe!

CHAPTER XXVI.

"They say miracles are past; and we have our philosophical persons to make modern and familiar things supernatural and causeless. Hence it is that we make trifles of terrors; ensconcing ourselves into seeming knowledge, when we should submit ourselves to an unknown fear."—*All's Well that Ends Well.*

ALL attempts to reanimate the lifeless form proved unavailing; and the horror and consternation that reigned in the castle of Glenfern may be imagined, but cannot be described. There is perhaps no feeling of our nature so vague, so complicated, so mysterious, as that with which we look upon the cold remains of our fellow-mortals. The dignity with which death invests even the meanest of his victims inspires us with an awe no living thing can create. The monarch on his throne is less awful than the beggar in his shroud. The marble features—the powerless hand—the stiffened limbs—oh! who can contemplate these with feelings that can be defined? These are the mockery of all our hopes and fears, our fondest love, our fellest hate. Can it be that we now shrink with horror from the touch of that hand which but yesterday was fondly clasped in our own? Is that tongue, whose accents even now dwell in our ear, for ever

chained in the silence of death? These black and
heavy eyelids, are they for ever to seal up in darkness
the eyes whose glance no earthly power could restrain?
And the spirit which animated the clay, where is
it now? Is it wrapt in bliss, or dissolved in woe?
Does it witness our grief, and share our sorrows? or
is the mysterious tie that linked it with mortality for
ever broken? And the remembrance of earthly scenes,
are they indeed to the enfranchised spirit as the morning dream, or the dew upon the early flower? Reflections such as these naturally arise in every breast.
Their influence is felt, though their import cannot
always be expressed. The principle is in all the same,
however it may differ in its operations.

In the family assembled round the lifeless form
that had so long been the centre of their domestic
circle, grief showed itself under various forms. The
calm and manly sorrow of the son; the saint-like feelings of his wife; the youthful agitation of Mary; the
weak superstitious wailings of the sisters; and the
loud uncontrolled lamentations of the daughters; all
betokened an intensity of suffering that arose from
the same source, varied according to the different
channels in which it flowed. Even the stern Lady
Maclaughlan was subdued to something of kindred
feeling; and though no tears dropped from her eyes,
she sat by her friends, and sought, in her own way,
to soften their affliction.

The assembled guests, who had not yet been able
to take their departure, remained in the drawing-room

in a sort of restless solemnity peculiar to seasons of
collateral affliction, where all seek to heighten the
effect upon others, and shift the lesson from themselves. Various were the surmises and speculations
as to the cause of the awful transition that had just
taken place.

"Glenfern was nae like a man that wad hae gaen
aff in this gate," said one.

"I dinna ken," said another; "I've notic'd a
chainge on Glenfern for a gey while noo."

"I agree wi' you, sir," said a third. "In my mind
Glenfern's been droopin' very sair ever since the last
tryst."

"At Glenfern's time o' life it's no surprisin',"
remarked a fourth, who felt perfectly secure of being
fifteen years his junior.

"Glenfern was na that auld neither," retorted a
fifth, whose conscience smote him with being several
years his senior.

"But he had a deal o' vexation frae his faemily,"
said an elderly bachelor.

"Ye offen see a hale stoot man, like oor puir
freend, gang like the snuff o' a cannel," coughed up
a pthisicky gentleman.

"He was aye a tume, boss-looking man ever since
I mind him," wheezed out a swollen asthmatic figure.

"An' he took nae care o' himsel'," said the Laird
of Pettlechass. "His diet was nae what it should
hae been at his time o' life. An' he was oot an' in,
up an' doon, in a' wathers, wat an' dry."

"Glenfern's doings had naething to du wi' his death," said an ancient gentlewoman with solemnity. "They maun ken little wha ne'er heard the bod-word of the family." And she repeated in Gaelic words to the following effect :—

> " When Lochdow shall turn to a lin,[1]
> In Glenfern ye'll hear the din ;
> When frae Benenck they shool the sna',
> O'er Glenfern the leaves will fa' ;
> When foreign geer grows on Benenck tap,
> Then the fir tree will be Glenfern's hap."

"An' noo, ma'am, will ye be sae gude as point oot the meanin' o' this freet," said an incredulous-looking member of the company ; "for when I passed Lochdow this mornin' I neither saw nor heard o' a lin ; an' frae this window we can a' see Benenck wi' his white night-cap on ; an' he wad hae little to do that wad try to shool it aff."

"It's neither o' the still water nor the stay brae that the word was spoke," replied the dame, with a disdainful frown ; "they tak' nae part in our doings : but kent ye nae that Lochdow himsel' had tined his sight in a cataract ; an' is nae there dule an' din eneuch in Glenfern the day ? An' kent ye nae that Benenck had his auld white pow shaven, an' that he's gettin' a jeezy frae Edinburgh ?—an' I'se warran' he'll be in his braw wig the very day that Glenfern'll be laid in his deal coffin."

The company admitted the application was too

---

[1] Cataract.

close to be resisted; but the same sceptic (who, by-
the-bye, was only a low country merchant, elevated
by purchase to the dignity of a Highland laird) was
seen to shrug his shoulders, and heard to make some
sneering remarks on the days of second-sights and
such superstitious nonsense being past. This was
instantly laid hold of; and amongst many others of
the same sort, the truth of the following story was
attested by one of the party, as having actually
occurred in his family within his own remembrance.

"As Duncan M'Crae was one evening descending
Benvoilloich, he perceived a funeral procession in the
vale beneath. He was greatly surprised, not having
heard of any death in the country; and this appeared
to be the burial of some person of consequence, from
the number of the attendants. He made all the
haste he could to get down; and as he drew near
he counted all the lairds of the country except my
father, Sir Murdoch. He was astonished at this, till
he recollected that he was away to the low country
to his cousin's marriage; but he felt curious to know
who it was, though some unaccountable feeling prevented him from mixing with the followers. He
therefore kept on the ridge of the hill, right over
their heads, and near enough to hear them speak:
but although he saw them move their lips, no sound
reached his ear. He kept along with the procession
in this way till it reached the Castle Dochart burying-
ground, and there it stopped. The evening was close
and warm, and a thick mist had gathered in the glen,

while the tops of the hills shone like gold. Not a breath of air was stirring, but the trees that grew round the burying-ground waved and soughed, and some withered leaves were swirled round and round, as if by the wind. The company stood a while to rest, and then they proceeded to open the iron gates of the burying-ground; but the lock was rusted and would not open. Then they began to pull down part of the wall, and Duncan thought how angry his master would be at this, and he raised his voice and shouted and hallooed to them, but to no purpose. Nobody seemed to hear him. At last the wall was taken down, and the coffin was lifted over, and just then the sun broke out, and glinted on a new-made grave; and as they were laying the coffin in it, it gave way, and disclosed Sir Murdoch himself in his dead clothes; and then the mist grew so thick, Duncan could see no more, and how to get home he knew not; but when he entered his own door he was bathed in sweat, and white as any corpse; and all that he could say was, that he had seen Castle Dochart's burying.

"The following day," continued the narrator, "he was more composed, and gave the account you have now heard; and three days after came the intelligence of my father's death. He had dropped down in a fit that very evening, when entertaining a large company in honour of his cousin's marriage; and that day week his funeral passed through Glenvalloch exactly as described by Duncan M'Crae, with all the particulars:

The gates of the burying-ground could not be opened; part of the wall was taken down to admit the coffin, which received some injury, and gave way as they were placing it in the grave."

Even the low-country infidel was silenced by the solemnity of this story; and soon after the company dispersed, every one panting to be the first to circulate the intelligence of Glenfern's death.

But soon—oh, how soon! "dies in human hearts the thought of death!" Even the paltry detail which death creates serves to detach our minds from the cause itself. So it was with the family of Glenfern. Their light did not "shine inward;" and after the first burst of sorrow their ideas fastened with avidity on all the paraphernalia of affliction. Mr. Douglas, indeed, found much to do and to direct to be done. The elder ladies began to calculate how many yards of broad hemming would be required, and to form a muster-roll of the company; with this improvement, that it was to be ten times as numerous as the one that had assembled at the christening; while the young ones busied their imaginations as to the effect of new mournings—a luxury to them hitherto unknown. Mrs. Douglas and Mary were differently affected. Religion and reflection had taught the former the enviable lesson of possessing her soul in patience under every trial; and while she inwardly mourned the fate of the poor old man who had been thus suddenly snatched from the only world that ever had engaged his thoughts, her outward aspect was calm and serene. The impression made upon Mary's feelings was of a more powerful nature. She had witnessed suffering, and watched by sick-beds; but death, and death in so terrific a form, was new to her. She had been standing by her grandfather's chair— her head was bent to his—her hand rested upon his, when, by a momentary convulsion, she beheld the last dread change—the living man transformed into the lifeless corpse. The countenance but now fraught with life and human thoughts, in the twinkling of an eye was covered with the shades of death! It was in vain that Mary prayed and reasoned and strove against the feelings that had been thus powerfully excited. One object alone possessed her imagination —the image of her grandfather dying—dead; his grim features, his ghastly visage, his convulsive grasp, were ever present, by day and by night. Her nervous system had received a shock too powerful for all the strength of her understanding to contend with. Mrs. Douglas sought by every means to soothe her feelings and divert her attention; and flattered herself that a short time would allay the perturbation of her youthful emotions.

Five hundred persons, horse and foot, high and low, male and female, graced the obsequies of the Laird of Glenfern. Benenck was there in his new wig, and the autumnal leaves dropped on the coffin as it was borne slowly along the vale !

CHAPTER XXVII.

"It is no diminution, but a recommendation of human nature, that, in some instances, passion gets the better of reason, and all that we can think is impotent against half what we feel."—*Spectator*.

"Life is a mingled yarn;" few of its afflictions but are accompanied with some alleviation—none of its blessings that do not bring some alloy. Like most other events that long have formed the object of yearning and almost hopeless wishes, and on which have been built the fairest structure of human felicity, the arrival of the young heir of Glenfern produced a less extraordinary degree of happiness than had been anticipated. The melancholy event which had marked the first ceremonial of his life had cast its gloom alike on all nearly connected with him; and when time had dispelled the clouds of recent mourning, and restored the mourners to their habitual train of thought and action, somewhat of the novelty which had given him such lively interest in the hearts of the sisters had subsided. The distressing conviction, too, more and more forced itself upon them, that their advice and assistance were likely to be wholly overlooked in the nurture of the infant mind and manage-

ment of the thriving frame of their little nephew.
Their active energies, therefore, driven back to the
accustomed channels, after many murmurs and severe
struggles, again revolved in the same sphere as before.
True, they sighed and mourned for a time, but soon
found occupation congenial to their nature in the little
departments of life—dressing crape ; reviving black
silk ; converting narrow hems into broad hems ; and
in short, who so busy, who so important, as the ladies
of Glenfern ? As Madame de Staël, or de Something
says, "they fulfilled their destinies." Their walk lay
amongst threads and pickles ; their sphere extended
from the garret to the pantry ; and often as they
sought to diverge from it, their instinct always led
them to return to it, as the tract in which they were
destined to move. There are creatures of the same
sort in the male part of the creation, but it is foreign
to my purpose to describe them at present. Neither
are the trifling and insignificant of either sex to be
treated with contempt, or looked upon as useless by
those whom God has gifted with higher powers. In
the arrangements of an all-wise Providence there is
nothing created in vain. Every link of the vast chain
that embraces creation helps to hold together the
various relations of life ; and all is beautiful gradation,
from the human vegetable to the glorious archangel.

If patient hope, if unexulting joy, and chastened
anticipation, sanctifying a mother's love, could have
secured her happiness, Mrs. Douglas would have found,
in the smiles of her infant, all the comfort her virtue

deserved. But she still had to drink of that cup of sweet and bitter, which must bathe the lips of all who breathe the breath of life.

While the instinct of a parent's love warmed her heart, as she pressed her infant to her bosom, the sadness of affectionate and rational solicitude stifled every sentiment of pleasure as she gazed on the altered and drooping form of her adopted daughter— of the child who had already repaid the cares that had been lavished on her, and in whom she descried the promise of a plenteous harvest from the good seed she had sown. Though Mary had been healthy in childhood, her constitution was naturally delicate, and she had latterly outgrown her strength. The shock she had sustained by her grandfather's death, thus operating on a weakened frame, had produced an effect apparently most alarming; and the efforts she made to exert herself only served to exhaust her. She felt all the watchful solicitude, the tender anxieties of her aunt, and bitterly reproached herself with not better repaying these exertions for her happiness. A thousand times she tried to analyse and extirpate the saddening impression that weighed upon her heart.

"It is not sorrow," reasoned she with herself, " that thus oppresses me ; for though I reverenced my grandfather, yet the loss of his society has scarcely been felt by me. It cannot be fear—the fear of death ; for my soul is not so abject as to confine its desires to this sublunary scene. What, then, is this mysterious

dread that has taken possession of me? Why do I
suffer my mind to suggest to me images of horror,
instead of visions of bliss? Why can I not, as
formerly, picture to myself the beauty and the bright-
ness of a soul casting off mortality? Why must the
convulsed grasp, the stifled groan, the glaring eye,
for ever come betwixt heaven and me?"

Alas! Mary was unskilled to answer. Hers was
the season for feeling, not for reasoning. She knew
not that hers was the struggle of imagination striving
to maintain its ascendency over reality. She had heard
and read, and thought and talked of death; but it was
of death in its fairest form, in its softest transition :
and the veil had been abruptly torn from her eyes ; the
gloomy pass had suddenly disclosed itself before her,
not strewed with flowers but shrouded in horrors.
Like all persons of sensibility, Mary had a disposition
to view everything in a *beau ideal :* whether that is a
boon most fraught with good or ill it were difficult to
ascertain. While the delusion lasts it is productive
of pleasure to its possessor ; but oh ! the thousand
aches that heart is destined to endure which clings to
the stability and relies on the permanency of earthly
happiness ! But the youthful heart must ever remain
a stranger to this saddening truth. Experience only
can convince us that happiness is not a plant of this
world ; and that, though many an eye hath beheld its
blossoms no mortal hand hath ever gathered its fruits.
This, then, was Mary's first lesson in what is called
the knowledge of life, as opposed to the *beau ideal* of

a young and ardent imagination in love with life,
and luxuriating in its own happiness. And, upon such
a mind it could not fail of producing a powerful
impression.

The anguish Mrs. Douglas experienced as she witnessed the changing colour, lifeless step, and forced
smile of her darling *élève* was not mitigated by the
good sense or sympathy of those around her. While
Mary had prospered under her management, in the
consciousness that she was fulfilling her duty to the
best of her abilities, she could listen with placid cheerfulness to the broken hints of disapprobation, or forced
good wishes for the success of her new-fangled schemes,
that were levelled at her by the sisters. But now,
when her cares seemed defeated, it was an additional
thorn in her heart to have to endure the commonplace
wisdom and self-gratulations of the almost exult-
ing aunts; not that they had the slightest intention
of wounding the feelings of their niece, whom they
really loved, but the temptation was irresistible of
proving that they had been in the right and she in
the wrong, especially as no such acknowledgment had
yet been extorted from her.

"It is nonsense to ascribe Mary's dwining to her
grandfather's death," said Miss Jacky. "We were all
nearer to him in propinquity than she was, and none
of our healths have suffered."

"And there's his own daughters," added Miss
Grizzy, "who, of course, must have felt a great deal
more than anybody else—there can be no doubt of

that—such sensible creatures as them must feel a
great deal; but yet you see how they have got up
their spirits—I'm sure it's wonderful!"

"It shows their sense and the effects of education,"
said Miss Jacky.

"Girls that sup their porridge will always cut a
good figure," quoth Nicky.

"With their fine feelings I'm sure we have all
reason to be thankful that they have been blest with
such hearty stomachs," observed Miss Grizzy; "if
they had been delicate, like poor Mary's, I'm sure I
declare I don't know what we would have done; for
certainly they were all most dreadfully affected at their
excellent father's death; which was quite natural, poor
things! I'm sure there's no pacifying poor Baby, and
even yet, neither Bella nor Betsey can bear to be left
alone in a dark room. Tibby has to sleep with them
still every night; and a lighted candle too—which is
much to their credit—and yet I'm sure it's not with
reading. I'm certain—indeed, I think there's no doubt
of it—that reading does young people much harm. It
puts things into their heads that never would have
been there but for books. I declare, I think reading's
a very dangerous thing; I'm certain all Mary's bad
health is entirely owing to reading. You know we
always thought she read a great deal too much for
her good."

"Much depends upon the choice of books," said
Jacky, with an air of the most profound wisdom.
"Fordyce's Sermons and the History of Scotland are

two of the very few books *I* would put into the hands
of a young woman. Our girls have read little else,"
—casting a look at Mrs. Douglas, who was calmly
pursuing her work in the midst of this shower of
darts all levelled at her.

"To be sure," returned Grizzy, "it is a thousand
pities that Mary has been allowed to go on so long ;
not, I'm sure, that any of us mean to reflect upon you,
my dear Mrs. Douglas ; for of course it was all owing
to your ignorance and inexperience ; and that, you
know, you could not help ; for it was not your fault ;
nobody can blame you. I'm certain you would have
done what is right if you had only known better ;
but of course we must all know much better than
you ; because, you know, we are all a great deal older,
and especially Lady Maclaughlan, who has the greatest
experience in the diseases of old men especially, and
infants. Indeed it has been the study of her life
almost ; for, you know, poor Sir Sampson is never
well ; and I dare say, if Mary had taken some of her
nice worm-lozenges, which certainly cured Duncan
M'Nab's wife's daughter's little girl of the jaundice,
and used that valuable growing embrocation, which
we are all sensible made Baby a great deal fatter, I
dare say there would have been nothing the matter
with her to-day."

"Mary has been too much accustomed to spend
both her time and money amongst idle vagrants,"
said Nicky.

"Economy of both," subjoined Jacky, with an air

of humility, "I confess *I* have ever been accustomed to consider as virtues. These handsome respectable new bonnets"—looking *from* Mrs. Douglas—"that our girls got just before their poor father's death, were entirely the fruits of their own savings."

"And I declare," said Grizzy, who did not excel in inuendos, "I declare, for my part—although at the same time, my dear niece, I'm certain you are far from intending it—I really think it's very disrespectful to Sir Sampson and Lady Maclaughlan, in anybody, and especially such near neighbours, to give more in charity than they do; for you may be sure they give as much as they think proper, and they must be the best judges, and can afford to give what they please; for Sir Sampson could buy and sell all of us a hundred times over if he liked. It's long since the Lochmarlie estate was called seven thousand a year; and besides that there's the Birkendale property and the Glenmavis estate, and I'm sure I can't tell you all what; but there's no doubt he's a man of immense fortune."

Well it was known and frequently was it discussed, the iniquity of Mary being allowed to waste her time and squander her money amongst the poor, instead of being taught the practical virtues of making her own gowns, and of hoarding up her pocket-money for some selfish gratification.

In colloquies such as these day after day passed on without any visible improvement taking place in her health. Only one remedy suggested itself to Mrs. Douglas, and that was to remove her to the south of England for the winter. Milder air and change of scene she had no doubt would prove efficacious; and her opinion was confirmed by that of the celebrated Dr. ——, who, having been summoned to the Laird of Pettlechass, had paid a visit at Glenfern *en passant*. How so desirable an event was to be accomplished was the difficulty. By the death of his father a variety of business and an extent of farming had devolved upon Mr. Douglas which obliged him to fix his residence at Glenfern, and rendered it impossible for him to be long absent from it. Mrs. Douglas had engaged in the duties of a nurse to her little boy, and to take him or leave him was equally out of the question.

In this dilemma the only resource that offered was that of sending Mary for a few months to her mother. True, it was a painful necessity; for Mrs. Douglas seldom heard from her sister-in-law, and when she did, her letters were short and cold. She sometimes desired "a kiss to her (Mrs. Douglas's) little girl," and once, in an extraordinary fit of good humour, had actually sent a locket with her hair in a letter by post, for which Mrs. Douglas had to pay something more than the value of the present. This was all that Mary knew of her mother, and the rest of her family were still greater strangers to her. Her father remained in a distant station in India, and was seldom heard of. Her brother was gone to sea; and though she had written repeatedly to her sister, her letters remained unnoticed. Under these circumstances there was something revolting in the idea of obtruding Mary upon the notice of her relations, and trusting to their kindness even for a few months; yet her health, perhaps her life, was at stake, and Mrs. Douglas felt she had scarcely a right to hesitate.

"Mary has perhaps been too long an alien from her own family," said she to herself; "this will be a means of her becoming acquainted with them, and of introducing her to that sphere in which she is probably destined to walk. Under her uncle's roof she will surely be safe, and in the society of her mother and sister she cannot be unhappy. New scenes will give a stimulus to her mind; the necessity of exertion will brace the languid faculties of her soul, and a few short months, I trust, will restore her to me such and even superior to what she was. Why, then, should I hesitate to do what my conscience tells me ought to be done? Alas! it is because I selfishly shrink from the pain of separation, and am unwilling to relinquish, even for a season, one of the many blessings Heaven has bestowed upon me." And Mrs. Douglas, noble and disinterested as ever, rose superior to the weakness that she felt was besetting her. Mary listened to her communication with a throbbing heart and eyes suffused with tears; to part from her aunt was agony; but to behold her mother—she to whom she owed her existence, to embrace a sister too—and one for whom she felt all those mysterious yearnings which twins are said to entertain towards each other —oh, there was rapture in the thought, and Mary's buoyant heart fluctuated between the extremes of anguish and delight.

The venerable sisters received the intelligence with much surprise : they did not know very well what to say about it; there was much to be said both for and against it. Lady Maclaughlan had a high opinion of English air; but then they had heard the morals of the people were not so good, and there were a great many dissipated young men in England; though, to be sure, there was no denying but the mineral waters were excellent; and, in short, it ended in Miss Grizzy's sitting down to concoct an epistle to Lady Maclaughlan; in Miss Jacky's beginning to draw up a code of instructions for a young woman upon her entrance into life; and Miss Nicky hoping that if Mary did go, she would take care not to bring back any extravagant English notions with her. The younger set debated amongst themselves how many of them would be invited to accompany Mary to England, and from thence fell to disputing the possession of a brown hair trunk, with a flourished D in brass letters on the top.

Mrs. Douglas, with repressed feelings, set about offering the sacrifice she had planned, and in a letter to Lady Juliana, descriptive of her daughter's situation, she sought to excite her tenderness without creating an alarm. How far she succeeded will be seen hereafter. In the meantime we must take a retrospective glance at the last seventeen years of her Ladyship's life.

CHAPTER XXVIII.

Her "only labour was to kill the time;
And labour dire it is, and weary woe."
Castle of Indolence.

YEARS had rolled on amidst heartless pleasures and joyless amusements, but Lady Juliana was made neither the wiser nor the better by added years and increased experience. Time had in vain turned his glass before eyes still dazzled with the gaudy allurements of the world, for she took "no note of time" but as the thing that was to take her to the Opera and the Park, and that sometimes hurried her excessively, and sometimes bored her to death. At length she was compelled to abandon her chase after happiness in the only sphere where she believed it was to be found. Lord Courtland's declining health unfitted him for the dissipation of a London life; and, by the advice of his physician, he resolved upon retiring to a country seat which he possessed in the vicinity of Bath. Lady Juliana was in despair at the thoughts of this sudden wrench from what she termed "life;" but she had no resource; for though her good-natured husband gave her the whole of General Cameron's allowance, that scarcely served to keep her in clothes; and though

her brother was perfectly willing that she and her
children should occupy apartments in his house, yet
he would have been equally acquiescent had she proposed to remove from it. Lady Juliana had a sort of
instinctive knowledge of this, which prevented her
from breaking out into open remonstrance. She
therefore contented herself with being more than
usually peevish and irascible to her servants and
children, and talking to her friends of the prodigious
sacrifice she was about to make for her brother and
his family, as if it had been the cutting off of a hand
or the plucking out of an eye. To have heard her,
any one unaccustomed to the hyperbole of fashionable
language would have deemed Botany Bay the nearest
possible point of destination. Parting from her
fashionable acquaintances was tearing herself from
all she loved; quitting London was bidding adieu to
the world. Of course there could be no society where
she was going, but still she would do her duty; she
would not desert dear Frederick and his poor children!
In short, no martyr was ever led to the stake with
half the notions of heroism and self-devotion as those
with which Lady Juliana stepped into the barouche
that was to conduct her to Beech Park. In the society
of piping bullfinches, pink canaries, gray parrots, gold
fish, green squirrels, Italian greyhounds, and French
poodles, she sought a refuge from despair. But even
these varied charms, after a while, failed to please.
The bullfinches grew hoarse; the canaries turned
brown; the parrots became stupid; the gold fish

would not eat; the squirrels were cross; the dogs fought; even a shell grotto that was constructing fell down; and by the time the aviary and conservatory were filled, they had lost their interest. The children were the next subjects for her Ladyship's ennui to discharge itself upon. Lord Courtland had a son some years older, and a daughter nearly of the same age as her own. It suddenly occurred to her that they must be educated, and that she would educate the girls herself. As the first step she engaged two governesses, French and Italian; modern treatises on the subject of education were ordered from London, looked at, admired, and arranged on gilded shelves and sofa tables; and could their contents have exhaled with the odours of their Russia leather bindings, Lady Juliana's dressing-room would have been what Sir Joshua Reynolds says every seminary of learning *is*, "an atmosphere of floating knowledge." But amidst this splendid display of human lore, THE BOOK found no place. She *had* heard of the Bible, however, and even knew it was a book appointed to be read in churches, and given to poor people, along with Rumford soup and flannel shirts; but as the rule of life, as the book that alone could make wise unto salvation, this Christian parent was ignorant as the Hottentot or Hindoo.

Three days beheld the rise, progress, and decline of Lady Juliana's whole system of education; and it would have been well for the children had the trust been delegated to those better qualified to discharge it. But neither of the preceptresses was better skilled in the only true knowledge. Signora Cicianai was a bigoted Catholic, whose faith hung upon her beads, and Madame Grignon was an *esprit forte*, who had no faith in anything but *le plaisir*. But the Signora's singing was heavenly, and Madame's dancing was divine, and what lacked there more?

So passed the first years of beings training for immortality. The children insensibly ceased to be children, and Lady Juliana would have beheld the increasing height and beauty of her daughter with extreme disapprobation, had not that beauty, by awakening her ambition, also excited her affection, if the term affection could be applied to that heterogeneous mass of feelings and propensities that "shape had none distinguishable." Lady Juliana had fallen into an error very common with wiser heads than hers—that of mistaking the *effect* for the *cause*. She looked no farther than to her union with Henry Douglas for the foundation of all her unhappiness; it never once occurred to her that her marriage was only the *consequence* of something previously wrong; she saw not the headstrong passions that had impelled her to please herself—no matter at what price. She thought not of the want of principle, she blushed not at the want of delicacy, that had led her to deceive a parent and elope with a man to whose character she was a total stranger. She therefore considered herself as having fallen a victim to love; and could she only save her daughter from a similar error she might yet

by her means retrieve her fallen fortune. To implant
principles of religion and virtue in her mind was not
within the compass of her own ; but she could scoff at
every pure and generous affection ; she could ridicule
every disinterested attachment ; and she could expatiate on the never-fading joys that attend on wealth
and titles, jewels and equipages ; and all this she did
in the belief that she was acting the part of a most
wise and tender parent ! The seed, thus carefully
sown, promised to bring forth an abundant harvest.
At eighteen Adelaide Douglas was as heartless and
ambitious as she was beautiful and accomplished ; but
the surface was covered with flowers, and who would
have thought of analysing the soil ?

It sometimes happens that the very means used
with success in the formation of one character produce a totally opposite effect upon another. The
mind of Lady Emily Lindore had undergone exactly
the same process in its formation as that of her cousin ;
yet in all things they differed. Whether it were the
independence of high birth, or the pride of a mind
conscious of its own powers, she had hitherto resisted
the sophistry of her governesses and the solecisms of
her aunt. But her notions of right and wrong were
too crude to influence the general tenor of her life, or
operate as restraints upon a naturally high spirit and
impetuous temper. Not all the united efforts of her
preceptresses had been able to form a manner for
their pupil ; nor could their authority restrain her
from saying what she thought, and doing what she

pleased; and, in spite of both precept and example,
Lady Emily remained as insupportably natural and
sincere as she was beautiful and *piquante*. At six
years old she had declared her intention of marrying
her cousin Edward Douglas, and at eighteen her words
were little less equivocal. Lord Courtland, who never
disturbed himself about anything, was rather diverted
with this juvenile attachment; and Lady Juliana, who
cared little for her son, and still less for her niece,
only wondered how people could be such fools as to
think of marrying for love, after she had told them
how miserable it would make them.

CHAPTER XXIX.

" Unthought of frailties cheat us in the wise ;
The fool lies hid in inconsistencies."

POPE.

SUCH were the female members of the family to whom
Mary was about to be introduced. In her mother's
heart she had no place, for of her absent husband and
neglected daughter she seldom thought; and their
letters were scarcely read, and rarely answered. Even
good Miss Grizzy's elaborate epistle, in which were
curiously entwined the death of her brother and the
birth and christening of her grand-nephew, in a truly
Gordian manner, remained disentangled. Had her
Ladyship only read to the middle of the seventh page
she would have learned the indisposition of her
daughter, with the various opinions thereupon; but
poor Miss Grizzy's labours were vain, for her letter
remains a dead letter to this day. Mrs. Douglas was
therefore the first to convey the unwelcome intelligence,
and to suggest to the mind of the mother that her
alienated daughter still retained some claims upon her
care and affection ; and although this was done with
all the tenderness and delicacy of a gentle and enlight-

ened mind, it called forth the most bitter indignation
from Lady Juliana.

She almost raved at what she termed the base
ingratitude and hypocrisy of her sister-in-law. After
the sacrifice she had made in giving up her child to
her when she had none of her own, it was a pretty
return to send her back only to die. But she saw
through it. She did not believe a word of the girl's
illness; that was a trick to get rid of her. Now they
had a child of their own, they had no use for hers;
but she was not to be made a fool of in such a way,
and by such people, etc. etc.

"If Mrs. Douglas is so vile a woman," said the
provoking Lady Emily, "the sooner my cousin is
taken from her the better."

"You don't understand these things, Emily," returned her aunt impatiently.

"What things?"

"The trouble and annoyance it will occasion me
to take charge of the girl at this time."

"Why at this time more than at any other?"

"Absurd, my dear! how can you ask so foolish a
question? Don't you know that you and Adelaide are
both to bring out this winter, and how can I possibly
do you justice with a dying girl upon my hands?"

"I thought you suspected it was all a trick," continued the persecuting Lady Emily.

"So I do; I haven't the least doubt of it. The
whole story is the most improbable stuff I ever
heard."

"Then you will have less trouble than you expect."

"But I hate to be made a dupe of, and imposed upon by low cunning. If Mrs. Douglas had told me candidly she wished me to take the girl, I would have thought nothing of it; but I can't bear to be treated like a fool."

"I don't see anything at all unbecoming in Mrs. Douglas's treatment."

"Then what can I do with a girl who has been educated in Scotland? She must be vulgar—all Scotchwomen are so. They have red hands and rough voices; they yawn, and blow their noses, and talk, and laugh loud, and do a thousand shocking things. Then, to hear the Scotch brogue—oh, heavens! I should expire every time she opened her mouth!"

"Perhaps my sister may not speak so *very* broad," kindly suggested Adelaide in her sweetest accents.

"You are very good, my love, to think so; but nobody can live in that odious country without being infected with its *patois*. I really thought I should have caught it myself; and Mr. Douglas" (no longer Henry) "became quite gross in his language after living amongst his relations."

"This is really too bad," cried Lady Emily indignantly. "If a person speaks sense and truth, what does it signify how it is spoken? And whether your Ladyship chooses to receive your daughter here or not, I shall at any rate invite my cousin to my father's house." And, snatching up a pen, she instantly began a letter to Mary.

Lady Juliana was highly incensed at this freedom of her niece; but she was a little afraid of her, and therefore, after some sharp altercation, and with infinite violence done to her feelings, she was prevailed upon to write a decently civil sort of a letter to Mrs. Douglas, consenting to receive her daughter for a *few months;* firmly resolving in her own mind to conceal her from all eyes and ears while she remained, and to return her to her Scotch relations early in the summer.

This worthy resolution formed, she became more serene and awaited the arrival of her daughter with as much firmness as could reasonably have been expected.

CHAPTER XXX.

" And for unfelt imaginations
    They often feel a world of restless cares."
                                    SHAKESPEARE.

LITTLE weened the good ladies of Glenfern the ungracious reception their *protégée* was likely to experience from her mother; for, in spite of the defects of
her education, Mary was a general favourite in the
family; and however they might solace themselves
by depreciating her to Mrs. Douglas, to the world in
general, and their young female acquaintances in particular, she was upheld as an epitome of every perfection above and below the sun.   Had it been possible
for them to conceive that Mary could have been received with anything short of rapture, Lady Juliana's
letter might in some measure have opened the eyes
of their understanding; but to the guileless sisters it
seemed everything that was proper.   Sorry for the
necessity Mrs. Douglas felt under of parting with her
adopted daughter, was "prettily expressed;" had no
doubt it was merely a slight nervous affection, "was
kind and soothing;" and the assurance, more than
once repeated, that her friends might rely upon her
being returned to them in the course of a very few

months, "showed a great deal of feeling and consideration." But as their minds never maintained a
just equilibrium long upon any subject, but, like falsely-
adjusted scales, were ever hovering and vibrating at
either extreme, so they could not rest satisfied in the
belief that Mary was to be happy; there must be
something to counteract that stilling sentiment; and
that was the apprehension that Mary would be spoilt.
This, for the present, was the pendulum of their
imaginations.

"I declare, Mary, my sisters and I could get no
sleep last night for thinking of you," said Miss Grizzy;
"we are all certain that Lady Juliana especially, but
indeed all your English relations, will think so much
of you—from not knowing you, you know—which
will be quite natural. I'm sure that my sisters and I
have taken it into our heads—but I hope it won't be
the case, as you have a great deal of good sense of
your own—that they will quite turn your head."

"Mary's head is on her shoulders to little purpose,"
followed up Miss Jacky, "if she can't stand being
made of when she goes amongst strangers; and she
ought to know by this time that a mother's partiality
is no proof of a child's merit."

"You hear that, Mary," rejoined Miss Grizzy; "so
I'm sure I hope you won't mind a word that your
mother says to you, I mean about yourself; for of
course you know she can't be such a good judge of
you as us, who have known you all your life. As to
other things, I daresay she is very well informed

about the country, and politics, and these sort of things—I'm certain Lady Juliana knows a great deal."

"And I hope, Mary, you will take care and not get into the daadlin' handless ways of the English women," said Miss Nicky; "I wouldn't give a pin for an Englishwoman."

"And I hope you will never look at an Englishman, Mary," said Miss Grizzy, with equal earnestness; "take my word for it they are a very dissipated, unprincipled set. They all drink, and game, and keep race-horses; and many of them, I'm told, even keep play-actresses; so you may think what it would be for all of us if you were to marry any of them,"—and tears streamed from the good spinster's eyes at the bare supposition of such a calamity.

"Don't be afraid, my dear aunt," said Mary, with a kind caress; "I shall come back to you your own 'Highland Mary.' No Englishman with his round face and trim meadows shall ever captivate me. Heath-covered hills and high cheek-bones are the charms that must win my heart."

"I'm delighted to hear you say so, my dear Mary," said the literal-minded Grizzy. "Certainly nothing can be prettier than the heather when it's in flower; and there is something very manly—nobody can dispute that—in high cheek-bones; and besides, to tell you a secret, Lady Maclaughlan has a husband in her eye for you. We none of us can conceive who it is, but of course he must be suitable in every respect; for you know Lady Maclaughlan has had three husbands herself; so of course she must be an excellent judge of a good husband."

"Or a bad one," said Mary, "which is the same thing. Warning is as good as example."

Mrs. Douglas's ideas and those of her aunts did not coincide upon this occasion more than upon most others. In her sister-in-law's letter she flattered herself she saw only fashionable indifference; and she fondly hoped that would soon give way to a tenderer sentiment, as her daughter became known to her. At any rate it was proper that Mary should make the trial, and whichever way it ended, it must be for her advantage.

"Mary has already lived too long in these mountain solitudes," thought she; "her ideas will become romantic, and her taste fastidious. If it is dangerous to be too early initiated into the ways of the world, it is perhaps equally so to live too long secluded from it. Should she make herself a place in the heart of her mother and sister it will be so much happiness gained; and should it prove otherwise, it will be a lesson learnt—a hard one indeed! but hard are the lessons we must all learn in the school of life!" Yet Mrs. Douglas's fortitude almost failed her as the period of separation approached.

It had been arranged by Lady Emily that a carriage and servants should meet Mary at Edinburgh, whither Mr. Douglas was to convey her. The cruel moment came; and mother, sister, relations, friends,—all the bright visions which Mary's sanguine spirit had conjured up to soften the parting pang, all were absorbed

in one agonising feeling, one overwhelming thought.
Oh, who that for the first time has parted from the
parent whose tenderness and love were entwined with
our earliest recollections, whose sympathy had soothed
our infant sufferings, whose fondness had brightened
our infant felicity;—who that has a heart, but must
have felt it sink beneath the anguish of a first farewell! Yet bitterer still must be the feelings of the
parent upon committing the cherished object of their
cares and affections to the stormy ocean of life.
When experience points to the gathering cloud and
rising surge which soon may assail their defenceless
child, what can support the mother's heart but trust
in Him whose eye slumbereth not, and whose power
extendeth over all? It was this pious hope, this holy
confidence, that enabled this more than mother to
part from her adopted child with a resignation which
no earthly motive could have imparted to her mind.
It seems almost profanation to mingle with her elevated feelings the coarse yet simple sorrows of the
aunts, old and young, as they clung around the nearly
lifeless Mary, each tendering the parting gift they had
kept as a solace for the last.

Poor Miss Grizzy was more than usually incoherent,
as she displayed " a nice new umbrella that could be
turned into a nice walking-stick, or anything;" and a
dressing-box, with a little of everything in it; and,
with a fresh burst of tears, Mary was directed where
she would *not* find eye-ointment, and where she was
not to look for sticking-plaister.

Miss Jacky was more composed as she presented a flaming copy of Fordyce's Sermons to Young Women, with a few suitable observations; but Miss Nicky could scarcely find voice to tell that the *housewife* she now tendered had once been Lady Girnachgowl's, and that it contained Whitechapel needles of every size and number. The younger ladies had clubbed for the purchase of a large locket, in which was enshrined a lock from each subscriber, tastefully arranged by the —— jeweller, in the form of a wheat sheaf upon a blue ground. Even old Donald had his offering, and, as he stood tottering at the chaise door, he contrived to get a "bit snishin mull" laid on Mary's lap, with a "God bless her bonny face, an' may she ne'er want a good sneesh!"

The carriage drove off, and for a while Mary's eyes were closed in despair.

CHAPTER XXXI.

" Farewell to the mountains, high covered with snow ;
  Farewell to the straths, and green valleys below ;
  Farewell to the forests, and wild hanging woods,
  Farewell to the torrents, and loud roaring floods ! "

Scotch Song.

HAPPILY in the moral world as in the material one the
warring elements have their prescribed bounds, and
" the flood of grief decreaseth when it can swell no
higher ;" but it is only by retrospection we can bring
ourselves to believe in this obvious truth. The young
and untried heart hugs itself in the bitterness of its
emotions, and takes a pride in believing that its
anguish can end but with its existence ; and it is not
till time hath almost steeped our senses in forgetful-
ness that we discover the mutability of all human
passions.

But Mary left it not to the slow hand of time to
subdue in some measure the grief that swelled her
heart. Had she given way to selfishness, she would
have sought the free indulgence of her sorrow as the
only mitigation of it ; but she felt also for her uncle.
He was depressed at parting with his wife and child,
and he was taking a long and dreary journey entirely

upon her account. Could she therefore be so selfish
as to add to his uneasiness by a display of her sufferings? No—she would strive to conceal it from his
observation, though to overcome it was impossible.
Her feelings must ever remain the same, but she would
confine them to her own breast; and she began to
converse with and even strove to amuse, her kind-
hearted companion. Ever and anon indeed a rush of
tender recollections came across her mind, and the
soft voice and the bland countenance of her maternal
friend seemed for a moment present to her senses;
and then the dreariness and desolation that succeeded
as the delusion vanished, and all was stillness and
vacuity! Even self-reproach shot its piercing sting
into her ingenuous heart; levities on which, in her
usual gaiety of spirit, she had never bestowed a
thought, now appeared to her as crimes of the deepest
dye. She thought how often she had slighted the
counsels and neglected the wishes of her gentle moni-
tress; how she had wearied of her good old aunts,
their cracked voices, and the everlasting *tic-a-tic* of
their knitting needles; how coarse and vulgar she
had sometimes deemed the younger ones; how she
had mimicked Lady Maclaughlan, and caricatured
Sir Sampson, and "even poor dear old Donald," said
she, as she summed up the catalogue of her crimes,
"could not escape my insolence and ill-nature. How
clever I thought it to sing ' Haud awa frae me, Donald,'
and how affectedly I shuddered at everything he
touched;" and the "sneeshin mull" was bedewed

with tears of affectionate contrition. But every painful sentiment was for a while suspended in admiration of the magnificent scenery that was spread around them. Though summer had fled, and few even of autumn's graces remained, yet over the august features of mountain scenery the seasons have little control. Their charms depend not upon richness of verdure, or luxuriance of foliage, or any of the mere prettinesses of nature; but whether wrapped in snow, or veiled in mist, or glowing in sunshine, their lonely grandeur remains the same; and the same feelings fill and elevate the soul in contemplating these mighty works of an Almighty hand. The eye is never weary in watching the thousand varieties of light and shade, as they flit over the mountain and gleam upon the lake; and the ear is satisfied with the awful stillness of nature in her solitude.

Others besides Mary seemed to have taken a fanciful pleasure in combining the ideas of the mental and elemental world, for in the dreary dwelling where they were destined to pass the night she found inscribed the following lines :—

" The busy winds war mid the waving boughs,
    And darkly rolls the heaving surge to land ;
  Among the flying clouds the moonbeam glows
    With colours foreign to its softness bland.

" Here, one dark shadow melts, in gloom profound,
    The towering Alps—the guardians of the Lake;
  There, one bright gleam sheds silver light around,
    And shows the threat'ning strife that tempests wake.

" Thus o'er my mind a busy memory plays,
    That shakes the feelings to their inmost core ;
Thus beams the light of Hope's fallacious rays,
    When simple confidence can trust no more.

" So one dark shadow shrouds each bygone hour,
    So one bright gleam the coming tempest shows ;
That tells of sorrows, which, though past, still lower,
    And *this* reveals th' approach of future woes."

While Mary was trying to decipher these somewhat
mystic lines, her uncle was carrying on a colloquy in
Gaelic with their hostess. The consequences of the
consultation were not of the choicest description, con-
sisting of braxy [1] mutton, raw potatoes, wet bannocks,
hard cheese, and whisky. Very differently would the
travellers have fared had the good Nicky's intentions
been fulfilled. She had prepared with her own hands
a moorfowl pie and potted nowt's head, besides a profusion of what she termed "trifles, just for Mary,
poor thing, to divert herself with upon the road."
But alas ! in the anguish of separation, the covered
basket had been forgot, and the labour of Miss Nicky's
hands fell to be consumed by the family, though Miss
Grizzy protested, with tears in her eyes, " that it went
to her heart like a knife to eat poor Mary's puffs and
snaps."

Change of air and variety of scene failed not to
produce the happiest effects upon Mary's languid
frame and drooping spirits. Her cheek already
glowed with health, and was sometimes dimpled with
smiles. She still wept, indeed, as she thought of

---

[1] Sheep that have died a natural death and been salted.

those she had left ; but often, while the tear trembled in her eye, its course was arrested by wonder, or admiration, or delight ; for every object had its charms for her. Her cultivated taste and unsophisticated mind could descry beauty in the form of a hill, and grandeur in the foam of the wave, and elegance in the weeping birch, as it dipped its now almost leafless boughs in the mountain stream. These simple pleasures, unknown alike to the sordid mind and vitiated taste, are ever exquisitely enjoyed by the refined yet unsophisticated child of nature.

CHAPTER XXXII.

" Her native sense improved by reading,
Her native sweetness by good breeding."

DURING their progress through the Highlands the travellers were hospitably entertained at the mansions of the country gentlemen, where old-fashioned courtesy and modern comfort combined to cheer the stranger guest. But upon *coming out*, as it is significantly expressed by the natives of these mountain regions, viz. entering the low country, they found they had only made a change of difficulties. In the Highlands they were always sure that wherever there was a house that house would be to them a home; but on a fair-day in the little town of G—— they found themselves in the midst of houses, and surrounded by people, yet unable to procure rest or shelter.

At the only inn the place afforded they were informed "the horses were baith oot, an' the ludgin' a' tane up, an' mair tu;" while the driver asserted, what indeed was apparent, "that his beasts war nae fit to gang the length o' their tae farrer—no for the king himsel'."

At this moment a stout, florid, good-humoured-looking man passed, whistling "Roy's Wife" with all his heart; and just as Mr. Douglas was stepping out of the carriage to try what could be done, the same person, evidently attracted by curiosity, repassed, changing his tune to "There's cauld kail in Aberdeen."

He started at sight of Mr. Douglas; then eagerly grasping his hand, "Ah! Archie Douglas, is this you?" exclaimed he with a loud laugh and hearty shake. "What! you haven't forgot your old schoolfellow Bob Gawffaw?"

A mutual recognition now took place, and much pleasure was manifested on both sides at this unexpected rencontre. No time was allowed to explain their embarrassments, for Mr. Gawffaw had already tipped the post-boy the wink (which he seemed easily to comprehend); and forcing Mr. Douglas to resume his seat in the carriage, he jumped in himself.

"Now for Howffend and Mrs. Gawffaw! ha, ha, ha! This will be a surprise upon her. She thinks I'm in my barn all this time—ha, ha, ha!"

Mr. Douglas here began to express his astonishment at his friend's precipitation, and his apprehensions as to the trouble they might occasion Mrs. Gawffaw; but bursts of laughter and broken expressions of delight were the only replies he could procure from his friend.

After jolting over half a mile of very bad road, the carriage stopped at a mean vulgar-looking mansion, with dirty windows, ruinous thatched offices, and broken fences.

Such was the picture of still life. That of animated nature was not less picturesque. Cows bellowed, and

cart-horses neighed, and pigs grunted, and geese
gabbled, and ducks quacked, and cocks and hens
flapped and fluttered promiscuously, as they mingled
in a sort of yard divided from the house by a low
dyke, possessing the accommodation of a crazy gate,
which was bestrode by a parcel of bare-legged boys.

"What are you about, you confounded rascals?"
called Mr. Gawffaw to them.

"Naething," answered one.

"We're just takin' a heize on the yett," answered
another.

"I'll heize ye, ye scoundrels!" exclaimed the incensed Mr. Gawffaw, as he burst from the carriage;
and, snatching the driver's whip from his hand, flew
after the more nimble-footed culprits.

Finding his efforts to overtake them in vain, he
returned to the door of his mansion, where stood his
guests, waiting to be ushered in. He opened the door
himself, and led the way to a parlour which was quite
of a piece with the exterior of the dwelling. A dim
dusty table stood in the middle of the floor, heaped
with a variety of heterogeneous articles of dress; an
exceeding dirty volume of a novel lay open amongst
them. The floor was littered with shapings of flannel,
and shreds of gauzes, ribbons, etc. The fire was
almost out, and the hearth was covered with ashes.

After insisting upon his guests being seated, Mr.
Gawffaw walked to the door of the apartment, and
hallooed out, "Mrs. Gawffaw,—ho! May, my dear!
—I say, Mrs. Gawffaw!"

A low, croaking, querulous voice was now heard in reply, "For heaven's sake, Mr. Gawffaw, make less noise! For God's sake, have mercy on the walls of your house, if you've none on my poor head!" And thereupon entered Mrs. Gawffaw, a cap in one hand, which she appeared to have been tying on—a smelling-bottle in the other.

She possessed a considerable share of insipid and somewhat faded beauty, but disguised by a tawdry trumpery style of dress, and rendered almost disgusting by the air of affectation, folly, and peevishness that overspread her whole person and deportment. She testified the utmost surprise and coldness at sight of her guests; and, as she entered, Mr. Gawffaw rushed out, having descried something passing in the yard that called for his interposition. Mr. Douglas was therefore under the necessity of introducing himself and Mary to their ungracious hostess; briefly stating the circumstances that had led them to be her guests, and dwelling, with much warmth, on the kindness and hospitality of her husband in having relieved them from their embarrassment. A gracious smile, or what was intended as such, beamed over Mrs. Gawffaw's face at first mention of their names.

"Excuse me, Mr. Douglas," said she, making a profound reverence to him, and another to Mary, while she waved her hand for them to be seated. "Excuse me, Miss Douglas; but situated as I am, I find it necessary to be very distant to Mr. Gawffaw's friends sometimes. He is a thoughtless man, Mr.

Douglas—a very thoughtless man. He makes a perfect inn of his house. He never lies out of the town, trying who he can pick up and bring home with him. It is seldom I am so fortunate as to see such guests as Mr. and Miss Douglas of Glenfern Castle in my house," with an elegant bow to each, which of course was duly returned. "But Mr. Gawffaw would have shown more consideration, both for you and me, had he apprised me of the honour of your visit, instead of bringing you here in this ill-bred, unceremonious manner. As for me, I am too well accustomed to him to be hurt at these things now. He has kept me in hot water, I may say, since the day I married him!"

In spite of the conciliatory manner in which this agreeable address was made, Mr. Douglas felt considerably disconcerted, and again renewed his apologies, adding something about hopes of being able to proceed.

"Make no apologies, my dear sir," said the lady, with what she deemed a most bewitching manner; "it affords me the greatest pleasure to see any of your family under my roof. I meant no reflection on you; it is entirely Mr. Gawffaw that is to blame, in not having apprised me of the honour of this visit, that I might not have been caught in this deshabille; but I was really so engaged by my studies—" pointing to the dirty novel—"that I was quite unconscious of the lapse of time." The guests felt more and more at a loss what to say; but the lady was at none.

Seeing Mr. Douglas still standing with his hat in his hand, and his eye directed towards the door, she resumed her discourse.

"Pray be seated, Mr. Douglas; I beg you will sit off the door. Miss Douglas, I entreat you will walk into the fire; I hope you will consider yourself as quite at home"—another elegant bend to each. "I only regret that Mr. Gawffaw's folly and ill-breeding should have brought you into this disagreeable situation, Mr. Douglas. He is a well-meaning man, Mr. Douglas, and a good-hearted man; but he is very deficient in other respects, Mr. Douglas."

Mr. Douglas, happy to find anything to which he could assent, warmly joined in the eulogium on the excellence of his friend's heart. It did not appear, however, to give the satisfaction he expected. The lady resumed with a sigh, "Noboby can know Mr. Gawffaw's heart better than I do, Mr. Douglas. It *is* a good one, but it is far from being an elegant one; it is one in which I find no congeniality of sentiment with my own. Indeed, Mr. Gawffaw is no companion for me, nor I for him, Mr. Douglas; he is never happy in my society, and I really believe he would rather sit down with the tinklers on the roadside as spend a day in my company."

A deep sigh followed; but its pathos was drowned in the obstreperous ha, ha, ha! of her joyous helpmate, as he bounced into the room, wiping his forehead.

"Why, May, my dear, what have you been about

to-day? Things have been all going to the deuce. Why didn't you hinder these boys from sweein' the gate off its hinges, and——"

"Me hinder boys from sweein' gates, Mr. Gawffaw! Do I look like as if I was capable of hindering boys from sweein' gates, Miss Douglas?"

"Well, my dear, you ought to look after your pigs a little better. That jade, black Jess, has trod a parcel of them to death, ha, ha, ha! and——"

"Me look after pigs, Mr. Gawffaw! I am really astonished at you!" again interrupted the lady, turning pale with vexation. Then, with an affected giggle, appealing to Mary, "I leave you to judge, Miss Douglas, if I look like a person made for running after pigs!"

"Indeed," thought Mary, "you don't look like as if you could do anything half so useful."

"Well, never mind the pigs, my dear; only don't give us any of them for dinner—ha, ha, ha!—and, May, when will you let us have it?"

"Me let you have it, Mr. Gawffaw! I'm sure I don't hinder you from having it when you please, only you know I prefer late hours myself. I was always accustomed to them in my poor father's lifetime. He never dined before four o'clock; and I seldom knew what it was to be in my bed before twelve o'clock at night, Miss Douglas, till I married Mr. Gawffaw!"

Mary tried to look sorrowful, to hide the smile that was dimpling her cheek.

"Come, let us have something to eat in the mean-time, my dear."

"I'm sure you may eat the house, if you please, for me, Mr. Gawffaw! What would you take, Miss Douglas? But pull the bell—softly, Mr. Gawffaw! You do everything so violently."

A dirty maid-servant, with bare feet, answered the summons.

"Where's Tom?" demanded the lady, well knowing that Tom was afar off at some of the farm operations.

"I ken nae whar he's. He'll be aether at the patatees, or the horses, I'se warran. Div ye want him?"

"Bring some glasses," said her mistress, with an air of great dignity. "Mr. Gawffaw, you must see about the wine yourself since you have sent Tom out of the way."

Mr. Gawffaw and his handmaid were soon heard in an adjoining closet; the one wondering where the screw was, the other vociferating for a knife to cut the bread; while the mistress of this well-regulated mansion sought to divert her guests' attention from what was passing by entertaining them with com-plaints of Mr. Gawffaw's noise and her maid's inso-lence till the parties appeared to speak for themselves.

After being refreshed with some very bad wine and old baked bread, the gentlemen set off on a survey of the farm, and the ladies repaired to their toilets. Mary's simple dress was quickly adjusted; and upon descending she found her uncle alone in what Mrs. Gawffaw had shown to her as the drawing-room.   He guessed her curiosity to know something of her hosts, and therefore briefly informed her that Mrs. Gawffaw was the daughter of a trader in some manufacturing town, who had lived in opulence and died insolvent.   During his life his daughter had eloped with Bob Gawffaw, then a gay lieutenant in a marching regiment, who had been esteemed a very lucky fellow in getting the pretty Miss Croaker, with the prospect of ten thousand pounds.   None thought more highly of her husband's good fortune than the lady herself; and though *her* fortune never was realised, she gave herself all the airs of having been the making of his.   At this time Mr. Gawffaw was a reduced lieutenant, living upon a small paternal property, which he pretended to farm; but the habits of a military life, joined to a naturally social disposi-tion, were rather inimical to the pursuits of agri-culture, and most of his time was spent in loitering about the village of G——, where he generally con-tinued either to pick up a guest or procure a dinner.

Mrs. Gawffaw despised her husband; had weak nerves and headaches—was above managing her house—read novels—dyed ribbons—and altered her gowns according to every pattern she could see or hear of.

Such were Mr. and Mrs. Gawffaw—one of the many ill-assorted couples in this world—joined, not matched.   A sensible man would have curbed her folly and peevishness; a good-tempered woman would

have made his home comfortable, and rendered him
more domestic.

The dinner was such as might have been expected
from the previous specimens—bad of its kind, cold,
ill-dressed, and slovenly set down ; but Mrs. Gawffaw
seemed satisfied with herself and it.

"This is very fine mutton, Mr. Douglas, and not
underdone to most people's tastes ; and this fowl, I
have no doubt will eat well, Miss Douglas, though it
is not so white as some I have seen."

"The fowl, my dear, looks as if it had been the
great-grandmother of this sheep, ha, ha, ha !"

"For heaven's sake, Mr. Gawffaw, make less noise,
or my head will split in a thousand pieces !" putting
her hands to it, as if to hold. the frail tenement
together.   This was always her refuge when at a loss
for a reply.

A very ill-concocted pudding next called forth her
approbation.

"This pudding should be good ; for it is the same
I used to be so partial to in my poor father's lifetime,
when I was used to every delicacy, Miss Douglas, that
money could purchase."

"But you thought me the greatest delicacy of all,
my dear, ha, ha, ha ! for you left all your other deli-
cacies for me, ha, ha, ha !—what do you say to that,
May ? ha, ha, ha !"

May's reply consisted in putting her hands to her
head, with an air of inexpressible vexation ; and finding all her endeavours to be elegant frustrated by the

overpowering vulgarity of her husband, she remained
silent during the remainder of the repast; solacing
herself with complacent glances at her yellow silk
gown, and adjusting the gold chains and necklaces
that adorned her bosom.

Poor Mary was doomed to a *tête-à-tête* with her
during the whole evening; for Mr. Gawffaw was too
happy *with* his friend, and *without* his wife, to quit
the dining-room till a late hour; and then he was so
much exhilarated, that she could almost have joined
Mrs. Gawffaw in her exclamation of "For heaven's
sake, Mr. Gawffaw, have mercy on my head!"

The night, however, like all other nights, had a
close; and Mrs. Gawffaw, having once more enjoyed
the felicity of finding herself in company at twelve
o'clock at night, at length withdrew; and having
apologised, and hoped, and feared, for another hour
in Mary's apartment, she finally left her to the blessings of solitude and repose.

As Mr. Douglas was desirous of reaching Edinburgh the following day, he had, in spite of the urgent
remonstrances of his friendly host and the elegant
importunities of his lady, ordered the carriage at an
early hour; and Mary was too eager to quit Howffend
to keep it waiting. Mr. Gawffaw was in readiness to
hand her in, but fortunately Mrs. Gawffaw's head did
not permit of her rising. With much the same hearty
laugh that had welcomed their meeting, honest Gawffaw now saluted the departure of his friend; and as
he went whistling over his gate, he ruminated sweet

and bitter thoughts as to the destinies of the day—
whether he should solace himself with a good dinner
and the company of Bailie Merrythought at the Cross
Keys in G——, or put up with cold mutton, and May,
at home.

CHAPTER XXXIII.

" Edina ! Scotia's darling seat !
  All hail thy palaces and tow'rs,
  Where once, beneath a monarch's feet,
  Sat legislation's sov'reign pow'rs !"

BURNS.

ALL Mary's sensations of admiration were faint
compared to those she experienced as she viewed the
Scottish metropolis. It was associated in her mind
with all the local prepossessions to which youth and
enthusiasm love to give "a local habitation and a
name;" and visions of older times floated o'er her
mind as she gazed on its rocky battlements, and traversed the lonely arcades of its deserted palace.

"And this was once a gay court !" thought she, as
she listened to the dreary echo of her own footsteps;
"and this very ground on which I now stand was
trod by the hapless Mary Stuart ! Her eye beheld
the same objects that mine now rests upon ; her hand
has touched the draperies I now hold in mine. These
frail memorials remain ; but what remains of Scotland's Queen but a blighted name !"

Even the blood-stained chamber possessed a
nameless charm for Mary's vivid imagination. She

had not entirely escaped the superstitions of the
country in which she had lived; and she readily
yielded her assent to the asseverations of her guide
as to its being the *bona fide* blood of *David Rizzio*,
which for nearly three hundred years had resisted
all human efforts to efface.

"My credulity is so harmless," said she in answer
to her uncle's attempt to laugh her out of her belief,
"that I surely may be permitted to indulge it —
especially since I confess I feel a sort of indescribable
pleasure in it."

"You take a pleasure in the sight of blood!" exclaimed Mr. Douglas in astonishment, "you who turn
pale at sight of a cut finger, and shudder at a leg of
mutton with the juice in it!"

"Oh! mere modern vulgar blood is very shocking,"
answered Mary, with a smile; "but observe how this
is mellowed by time into a tint that could not offend
the most fastidious fine lady; besides," added she in
a graver tone, "I own I love to believe in things
supernatural; it seems to connect us more with another
world than when everything is seen to proceed in the
mere ordinary course of nature, as it is called. I
cannot bear to imagine a dreary chasm betwixt the
inhabitants of this world and beings of a higher
sphere; I love to fancy myself surrounded by——"

"I wish to heaven you would remember you are
surrounded by rational beings, and not fall into such
rhapsodies," said her uncle, glancing at a party who
stood near them, jesting upon all the objects which

Mary had been regarding with so much veneration.
"But come, you have been long enough here. Let
us try whether a breeze on the Calton Hill will not
dispel these cobwebs from your brain."

The day, though cold, was clear and sunny; and
the lovely spectacle before them shone forth in all its
gay magnificence. The blue waters lay calm and
motionless. The opposite shores glowed in a thousand
varied tints of wood and plain, rock and mountain,
cultured field and purple moor. Beneath, the old
town reared its dark brow, and the new one stretched
its golden lines; while all around the varied charms
of nature lay scattered in that profusion which nature's
hand alone can bestow.

"Oh! this is exquisite!" exclaimed Mary after a
long pause, in which she had been riveted in admiration of the scene before her. "And you are in the
right, my dear uncle. The ideas which are inspired
by the contemplation of such a spectacle as this are
far—oh, how far!—superior to those excited by the
mere works of art. There I can, at best, think but
of the inferior agents of Providence; here the soul
rises from nature up to nature's God."

"Upon my soul, you will be taken for a Methodist,
Mary, if you talk in this manner," said Mr. Douglas,
with some marks of disquiet, as he turned round at
the salutation of a fat elderly gentleman, whom he
presently recognised as Bailie Broadfoot.

The first salutations over, Mr. Douglas's fears of
Mary having been overheard recurred, and he felt

anxious to remove any unfavourable impression with regard to his own principles, at least, from the mind of the enlightened magistrate.

"Your fine views here have set my niece absolutely raving," said he, with a smile ; "but I tell her it is only in romantic minds that fine scenery inspires romantic ideas. I daresay many of the worthy inhabitants of Edinburgh walk here with no other idea than that of sharpening their appetites for dinner."

"Nae doot," said the Bailie, "it's a most capital place for that. Were it no' for that I ken nae muckle use it would be of."

"You speak from experience of its virtues in that respect, I suppose?" said Mr. Douglas gravely.

"'Deed, as to that I canna compleen. At times, to be sure, I am troubled with a little kind of a squeamishness after our public interteenments ; but three rounds o' the hill sets a' to rights."

Then observing Mary's eyes exploring, as he supposed, the town of Leith, "You see that prospeck to nae advantage the day, miss," said he. "If the glass-houses had been workin', it would have looked as weel again. Ye hae nae glass-houses in the Highlands ; na, na."

The Bailie had a share in the concern ; and the volcanic clouds of smoke that issued from thence were far more interesting subjects of speculation to him than all the eruptions of Vesuvius or Etna. But there was nothing to charm the lingering view to-day ; and he therefore proposed their taking a look at Bridewell, which, next to the smoke from the glass-houses, he reckoned the object most worthy of notice. It was indeed deserving of the praises bestowed upon it; and Mary was giving her whole attention to the details of it when she was suddenly startled by hearing her own name wailed in piteous accents from one of the lower cells, and, upon turning round, she discovered in the prisoner the son of one of the tenants of Glenfern. Duncan M'Free had been always looked upon as a very honest lad in the Highlands, but he had left home to push his fortune as a pedlar; and the temptations of the low country having proved too much for his virtue, poor Duncan was now expiating his offence in durance vile.

"I shall have a pretty account of you to carry to Glenfern," said Mr. Douglas, regarding the culprit with his sternest look.

"Oh 'deed, sir, it's no' my faut!" answered Duncan, blubbering bitterly; "but there's nae freedom at a' in this country. Lord, an' I war oot o't! Ane canna ca' their head their ain in't; for ye canna lift the bouk o' a prin but they're a' upon ye." And a fresh burst of sorrow ensued.

Finding the *peccadillo* was of a venial nature, Mr. Douglas besought the Bailie to use his interest to procure the enfranchisement of this his vassal, which Mr. Broadfoot, happy to oblige a good customer, promised should be obtained on the following day; and Duncan's emotions being rather clamorous, the party found it necessary to withdraw.

"And noo," said the Bailie, as they emerged from this place of dole and durance, "will ye step up to the monument, and tak a rest and some refreshment?"

"Rest and refreshment in a monument!" exclaimed Mr. Douglas. "Excuse me, my good friend, but we are not inclined to bait there yet a while."

The Bailie did not comprehend the joke; and he proceeded in his own drawling humdrum accent to assure them that the monument was a most convenient place.

"It was erected in honour of Lord Neilson's memory," said he, "and is let aff to a pastrycook and confectioner, where you can always find some trifles to treat the ladies, such as pies and custards, and berries, and these sort of things; but we passed an order in the cooneil that there should be naething of a spirituous nature introduced; for if ance spirits got admittance there's no saying what might happen."

This was a fact which none of the party were disposed to dispute; and the Bailie, triumphing in his dominion over the spirits, shuffled on before to do the honours of this place, appropriated at one and the same time to the manes of a hero and the making of minced pies. The regale was admirable, and Mary could not help thinking times were improved, and that it was a better thing to eat tarts in Lord Nelson's Monument than to have been poisoned in Julius Cæsar's.

CHAPTER XXXIV.

"Having a tongue rough as a cat, and biting like an adder, and all their reproofs are direct scoldings, their common intercourse is open contumely."—JEREMY TAYLOR.

"THOUGH last, not least of nature's works, I must now introduce you to a friend of mine," said Mr. Douglas, as, the Bailie having made his bow, they bent their steps towards the Castle Hill. "Mrs. Violet Macshake is an aunt of my mother's, whom you must often have heard of, and the last remaining branch of the noble race of Girnachgowl."

"I am afraid she is rather a formidable person, then?" said Mary.

Her uncle hesitated. "No, not formidable—only rather particular, as all old people are; but she is very good-hearted."

"I understand, in other words, she is very disagreeable. All ill-tempered people, I observe, have the character of being good-hearted; or else all good people are ill-tempered, I can't tell which."

"It is more than reputation with her," said Mr. Douglas, somewhat angrily: "for she is, in reality, a very good-hearted woman, as I experienced when a boy at college. Many a crown piece and half-guinea

I used to get from her. Many a scold, to be sure,
went along with them; but that, I daresay, I deserved.
Besides, she is very rich, and I am her reputed heir;
therefore gratitude and self-interest combine to render
her extremely amiable in my estimation."

They had now reached the airy dwelling where
Mrs. Macshake resided, and having rung, the door
was at length most deliberately opened by an ancient,
sour-visaged, long-waisted female, who ushered them
into an apartment, the *coup d'œil* of which struck a
chill to Mary's heart. It was a good-sized room, with
a bare sufficiency of small-legged dining-tables, and
lank haircloth chairs, ranged in high order round the
walls. Although the season was advanced, and the
air piercing cold, the grate stood smiling in all the
charms of polished steel; and the mistress of the
mansion was seated by the side of it in an arm-chair,
still in its summer position. She appeared to have
no other occupation than what her own meditations
afforded; for a single glance sufficed to show that not a
vestige of book or work was harboured there. She was
a tall, large-boned woman, whom even Time's iron hand
scarcely bent, as she merely stooped at the shoulders.
She had a drooping snuffy nose, a long turned-up chin,
small quick gray eyes, and her face projected far
beyond her figure, with an expression of shrewd restless curiosity. She wore a mode (not *à-la-mode*)
bonnet, and cardinal of the same, a pair of clogs over
her shoes, and black silk mittens on her arms.

As soon as she recognised Mr. Douglas she wel-

comed him with much cordiality, shook him long and
heartily by the hand, patted him on the back, looked
into his face with much seeming satisfaction; and, in
short, gave all the demonstrations of gladness usual
with gentlewomen of a certain age. Her pleasure,
however, appeared to be rather an *impromptu* than
an habitual feeling; for as the surprise wore off her
visage resumed its harsh and sarcastic expression, and
she seemed eager to efface any agreeable impression
her reception might have excited.

"An' wha thought o' seein ye enow?" said she, in
a quick gabbling voice. "What's brought you to the
toon? Are ye come to spend your honest faither's
siller ere he's weel cauld in his grave, puir man?"

Mr. Douglas explained that it was upon account of
his niece's health.

"Health!" repeated she, with a sardonic smile;
"it wad mak' an ool laugh to hear the wark that's
made aboot young fowk's health noo-a-days. I wonder
what ye're aw made o'"—grasping Mary's arm in her
great bony hand—"a wheen puir feckless windlestraes;
ye maun awa' to Ingland for ye're healths. Set ye up!
I wonder what cam' o' the lasses i' my time, that bute
to bide at hame? And whilk o' ye, I sude like to
ken, 'll ere leive to see ninety-sax, like me? Health!
—he, he!"

Mary, glad of a pretence to indulge the mirth the
old lady's manner and appearance had excited, joined
most heartily in the laugh.

"Tak aff ye're bannet, bairn, an' let me see ye're

face. Wha can tell what like ye are wi' that snule o'
a thing on ye're head?" Then after taking an accurate
survey of her face, she pushed aside her pelisse.
"Weel, it's ae mercy, I see ye hae neither the red
heed nor the muckle cuits o' the Douglases. I ken
nae whuther ye're faither had them or no. I ne'er set
een on him; neither him nor his braw leddie thought
it worth their while to speer after me; but I was at
nae loss, by aw accounts."

"You have not asked after any of your Glenfern
friends," said Mr. Douglas, hoping to touch a more
sympathetic chord.

"Time eneugh. Wull ye let me draw my breath,
man? Fowk canna say awthing at ance. An' ye
bute to hae an Inglish wife tu; a Scotch lass wad nae
serr ye. An' ye're wean, I'se warran', it's ane o' the
warld's wonders; it's been unco lang o' cummin—he,
he!"

"He has begun life under very melancholy auspices,
poor fellow!" said Mr. Douglas, in allusion to his
father's death.

"An' wha's faut was that? I ne'er heard tell the
like o't; to hae the bairn kirsened an' its grandfather
decin! But fowk are naither born, nor kirsened, nor
do they wad or dee as they used to du—awthing's
changed."

"You must, indeed, have witnessed many changes,"
observed Mr. Douglas, rather at a loss how to utter
anything of a conciliatory nature.

"Changes!—weel a wat, I sometimes wonder if

it's the same warld, an' if it's my ain heed that's
upon my shoothers."

"But with these changes you must also have
seen many improvements?" said Mary, in a tone of
diffidence.

"Impruvements!" turning sharply round upon her;
"what ken ye about impruvements, bairn? A bony
impruvement or ens no, to see tyleyors and sclaters
leavin whar I mind jewks an yerls. An' that great
glowrin' new toon there"—pointing out of her windows
—"whar I used to sit an' luck oot at bonny green parks,
and see the coos milket, and the bits o' bairnies row-
in' an' tummlin,' an' the lasses trampin i' their tubs—
what see I noo, but stane an' lime, an' stoor an' dirt,
an' idle cheels, an' dinket-oot madams prancin'. Impruvements, indeed!"

Mary found she was not likely to advance her
uncle's fortune by the judiciousness of her remarks,
therefore prudently resolved to hazard no more. Mr.
Douglas, who was more *au fait* to the prejudices of
old age, and who was always amused with her bitter
remarks when they did not touch himself, encouraged
her to continue the conversation by some observation
on the prevailing manners.

"Mainers!" repeated she, with a contemptuous
laugh, "what caw ye mainers noo, for I dinna ken?
Ilk ane gangs bang in till their necbor's hoose, and
bang oot o't as it war a chynge-hoose; an' as for the
maister o't, he's no o' sae muckle vaalu as the flunky
ahynt his chyre. I' my grandfather's time, as I hae

heard him tell, ilka maister o' a faamily had his ain
sate in his ain hoose aye, an' sat wi' his hat on his
heed afore the best o' the land, an' had his ain dish,
an' was aye helpit first, an' keepit up his owthority as
a man sude du. Paurents war paurents then ; bairnes
dardna set up their gabs afore them than as they du
noo. They ne'er presumed to say their heeds war
their ain i' thae days—wife an' servants, reteeners an'
childer, aw trummelt i' the presence o' their heed."

Here a long pinch of snuff caused a pause in the
old lady's harangue ; but after having duly wiped her
nose with her coloured handkerchief, and shook off
all the particles that might be presumed to have
lodged upon her cardinal, she resumed—

"An' nae word o' ony o' your sisters gaun to get
husbands yet ? They tell me they're but coorse lasses :
an' wha'll tak ill-farred tocherless queans whan there's
walth o' bonny faces an' lang purses i' the market—
he, he !" Then resuming her scrutiny of Mary—
"An' I'se warran' ye'll be lucken for an Inglish sweet-
heart tu ; that'll be what's takin' ye awa' to Ingland."

"On the contrary," said Mr. Douglas, seeing Mary
was too much frightened to answer for herself—"on
the contrary, Mary declares she will never marry any
but a true Highlander—one who wears the dirk and
plaid, and has the second-sight. And the nuptials
are to be celebrated with all the pomp of feudal
times ; with bagpipes, and bonfires, and gatherings
of clans, and roasted sheep, and barrels of whisky,
and——"

"Weel a wat, an' she's i' the right there," interrupted Mrs. Macshake, with more complacency than she had yet shown. "They may caw them what they like, but there's nae waddins noo. Wha's the better o' them but innkeepers and chise-drivers? I wud nae count mysel' married i' the hiddlins way they gang aboot it noo."

"I daresay you remember these things done in a very different style?" said Mr. Douglas.

"I dinna mind them whan they war at the best; but I hae heard my mither tell what a bonny ploy was at her waddin. I canna tell ye hoo mony was at it; mair nor the room wad haud, ye may be sure, for every relation an' freend o' baith sides war there, as well they sude; an' aw in full dress: the leddies in their hoops round them, an' some o' them had sutten up aw night till hae their heeds drest; for they hadnae thae pooket-like taps ye hae noo," looking with contempt at Mary's Grecian contour. "An' the bride's goon was aw shewed ow'r wi' favours, frae the tap doon to the tail, an' aw roond the neck, an' aboot the sleeves; and, as soon as the ceremony was ow'r, ilk ane ran till her, an' rugget an' rave at her for the favours, till they hardly left the claise upon her back. Than they did nae run awa as they du noo, but sax an' thretty o' them sat doon till a graund denner, and there was a ball at night, an' ilka night till Sabbath cam' roond; an' than the bride an' the bridegroom, drest in their waddin suits, an' aw their freends in theirs, wi' their favours on their breests, walkit in procession till the kirk. An' was nae that something like a waddin? It was worth while to be married i' thae days—he, he!"

"The wedding seems to have been admirably conducted," said Mr. Douglas, with much solemnity. "The christening, I presume, would be the next distinguished event in the family?"

"Troth, Archie—an' ye sude keep your thoomb upon kirsnins as lang's ye leeve; yours was a bonnie kirsnin or ens no! I hae heard o' mony things, but a bairn kirsened whan its grandfaither was i' the deed-thraw, I ne'er heard tell o' before." Then observing the indignation that spread over Mr. Douglas's face, she quickly resumed, "An' so ye think the kirsnin was the neist ploy?—He, he! Na; the cryin was a ploy, for the leddies did nae keep themsels up than as they do noo; but the day after the bairn was born, the leddy sat up i' her bed, wi' her fan intill her hand; an' aw her freends cam' an' stud roond her, an' drank her health an' the bairn's. Than at the leddy's recovery there was a graund supper gien that they caw'd the *cummerfealls*, an' there was a great pyramid o' hens at the tap o' the table, an' anither pyramid o' ducks at the fit, an' a muckle stoup fu' o' posset i' the middle, an' aw kinds o' sweeties doon the sides; an' as sune as ilk ane had eatin their fill they aw flew till the sweeties, an' fought, an' strave, an' wrastled for them, leddies an' gentlemen an' aw; for the brag was wha could pocket maist; an' whiles they wad hae the claith aff the table, an' aw thing i' the middle i' the floor, an' the chyres upside doon. Oo! muckle gude diversion, I'se warran,' was at the *cummerfealls*. Than whan they had drank the stoup dry, that ended the ploy. As for the kirsnin, that was aye whar it sude be—i' the hoose o' God, an' aw the kith an' kin bye in full dress, an' a band o' maiden cimmers aw in white; an' a bonny sight it was, as I've heard my mither tell."

Mr. Douglas, who was now rather tired of the old lady's reminiscences, availed himself of the opportunity of a fresh pinch to rise and take leave.

"Oo, what's takin' ye awa, Archie, in sic a hurry? Sit doon there," laying her hand upon his arm, "an' rest ye, an' tak a glass o' wine, an' a bit breed; or may be," turning to Mary, "ye wad rather hae a drap broth to warm ye. What gars ye luck sae blae, bairn? I'm sure it's no cauld; but ye're juste like the lave; ye gang aw skiltin aboot the streets half naked, an' than ye maun sit an' birsle yoursels afore the fire at hame."

She had now shuffled along to the farther end of the room, and opening a press, took out wine, and a plateful of various-shaped articles of bread, which she handed to Mary.

"Hae, bairn—tak a cookie; tak it up—what are you fear'd for? It'll no bite ye. Here's t'ye, Glenfern, an' your wife, an' your wean, puir tead; it's no had a very chancy ootset, weel a wat."

The wine being drunk, and the cookies discussed, Mr. Douglas made another attempt to withdraw, but in vain.

"Canna ye sit still a wee, man, an' let me spear

after my auld freens at Glenfern? Hoo's Grizzy, an'
Jacky, and Nicky? Aye workin awa at the pills an'
the drogs?—he, he! I ne'er swallowed a pill, nor gied
a doit for drogs aw my days, an' see an ony of them'll
rin a race wi' me whan they're naur five score."

Mr. Douglas here paid her some compliments upon
her appearance, which were pretty graciously received;
and added that he was the bearer of a letter from his
Aunt Grizzy, which he would send along with a roebuck and brace of moor-game.

"Gin your roebuck's nae better than your last,
atweel it's no worth the sendin'—poor dry fisinless
dirt, no worth the chowing; weel a wat I begrudged
my teeth on't. Your muirfowl was na that ill, but
they're no worth the carryin; they're dong cheap i'
the market enoo, so it's nae great compliment. Gin
ye had brought me a leg o' gude mutton, or a cauler
sawmont, there would hae been some sense in't; but
ye're ane o' the fowk that'll ne'er harry yoursel' wi'
your presents; it's but the pickle poother they cost
you, an' I'se warran' ye're thinkin mair o' your ain
diversion than o' my stamick, when ye're at the
shootin' o' them, puir beasts."

Mr. Douglas had borne the various indignities
levelled against himself and his family with a philosophy that had no parallel in his life before; but to
this attack upon his game he was not proof. His
colour rose, his eyes flashed fire, and something resembling an oath burst from his lips as he strode
indignantly towards the door.

His friend, however, was too nimble for him. She
stepped before him, and, breaking into a discordant
laugh, as she patted him on the back, "So I see ye're
just the auld man, Archie,—aye ready to tak the
strums, an' ye dinna get a' thing yer ain wye. Mony
a time I had to fleech ye oot o' the dorts whan ye was
a callant. Div ye mind hoo ye was affronted because
I set ye doon to a cauld pigeon-pie, an' a tanker o'
tippenny, ae night to ye're fowerhoors, afore some
leddies—he, he, he! Weel a wat, yer wife maun hae
her ain adoos to manage ye, for ye're a cumstairy
chield, Archie."

Mr. Douglas still looked as if he was irresolute
whether to laugh or be angry.

"Come, come, sit ye doon there till I speak to this
bairn," said she, as she pulled Mary into an adjoining
bedchamber, which wore the same aspect of chilly
neatness as the one they had quitted. Then pulling
a huge bunch of keys from her pocket, she opened a
drawer, out of which she took a pair of diamond ear-
rings. "Hae, bairn," said she as she stuffed them
into Mary's hand; "they belanged to your faither's
grandmother. She was a gude woman, an' had four-
an'-twenty sons an' dochters, an' I wiss ye nae war
fortin than just to hae as mony. But mind ye," with
a shake of her bony finger, "they maun a' be Scots.
Gin I thought ye wad mairry ony pock-puddin', fient
haed wad ye hae gotten frae me. "Noo, had ye're
tongue, and dinna deive me wi' thanks," almost pushing her into the parlour again; "and sin ye're gaun

awa the morn, I'll see nae mair o' ye enoo—so fare ye weel. But, Archie, ye maun come an' tak your breakfast wi' me. I hae muckle to say to you; but ye manna be sae hard upon my baps as ye used to be," with a facetious grin to her mollified favourite, as they shook hands and parted.

"Well, how do you like Mrs. Macshake, Mary?" asked her uncle as they walked home.

"That is a cruel question, uncle," answered she, with a smile. "My gratitude and my taste are at such variance," displaying her splendid gift, "that I know not how to reconcile them."

"That is always the case with those whom Mrs. Macshake has obliged," returned Mr. Douglas. "She does many liberal things, but in so ungracious a manner that people are never sure whether they are obliged or insulted by her. But the way in which she receives kindness is still worse. Could anything equal her impertinence about my roebuck? Faith, I've a good mind never to enter her door again!"

Mary could scarcely preserve her gravity at her uncle's indignation, which seemed so disproportioned to the cause. But, to turn the current of his ideas, she remarked that he had certainly been at pains to select two admirable specimens of her countrywomen for her.

"I don't think I shall soon forget either Mrs. Gawffaw or Mrs Macshake," said she, laughing.

"I hope you won't carry away the impression that these two *lusus naturæ* are specimens of Scotchwomen," said her uncle. "The former, indeed, is rather a sort of weed that infests every soil; the latter, to be sure, is an indigenous plant. I question if she would have arrived at such perfection in a more cultivated field or genial clime. She was born at a time when Scotland was very different from what it is now. Female education was little attended to, even in families of the highest rank; consequently, the ladies of those days possess a *raciness* in their manners and ideas that we should vainly seek for in this age of cultivation and refinement. Had your time permitted, you could have seen much good society here; superior, perhaps, to what is to be found anywhere else, as far as mental cultivation is concerned. But you will have leisure for that when you return."

Mary acquiesced with a sigh. *Return* was to her still a melancholy-sounding word. It reminded her of all she had left—of the anguish of separation—the dreariness of absence; and all these painful feelings were renewed in their utmost bitterness when the time approached for her to bid adieu to her uncle. Lord Courtland's carriage and two respectable-looking servants awaited her; and the following morning she commenced her journey in all the agony of a heart that fondly clings to its native home.

END OF VOL. I.

Printed by R. & R. CLARK, *Edinburgh.*